ASCENSION:
THE WITCHES OF
PIONEER VALE
BOOK 1

DAVID COMBS

ALSO BY DAVID COMBS

Thieves' Honor

PRAISE FOR THIEVES' HONOR

"If a good story is your goal, this is the book to read." - B.E Sanderson, author of the "Once Upon A Djinn" series

"If you're looking for your next adventure, you've just found it! Stop reading the reviews and dive right in! - Douglas Pierce, author of The Hunted Maiden and The Seedling's Song

"This is a book that should be up there in the big leagues" - Bibliogyan.com

DEDICATION

To Emma and Libby,

And for the generations to follow

ANNE-MARIE CARMICHAEL CONCEPT ART
BY DAVID COMBS

ACKNOWLEDGMENTS

Cover art by oliviaprodesign

Alistair Carmichael

Anne-Marie Carmichael
b 1643

Jeremiah Carmichael
b 1640

The Firstborn

The Inheritors

Aiden Carmichael b. 1661

Thomas Carmichael b. 1668

Kenton Carmichael b. 1690

Abigail (Carmichael) Hunter

Phoebe Hunter b. 1711

Devlin Hunter b. 1712

Levi Hunter b. 1736

Barnaby Hunter b. 1747

Kelvin Hunter b. 1778

Grace (Hunter) Cooke
b. 1784

Kathryn Cooke b. 1811

Renee (Cooke) Wright
b. 1813

Brooke Wright b. 1845

Jacob Wright b. 1850

May Wright b. 1880

Faye (Wright) McCowen
b. 1885

Jennifer McCowen b. 1912

Michael McCowen b. 1918

Mitchell McCowen b. 1941

Gwendolyn (McCowen) Brighton
b. 1943

Christopher Brighton
b. 1961

William Brighton b. 1971

Angelica Brighton b. 2001

Jamie Brighton b. 2007

Carmichael Family Tree

CHAPTER 1
INTO THE WOODS - PRESENT DAY

Angelica Brighton shivered from something more than just the cold as she looked at the woods around her. Black and barren branches overhead grasped like gnarled fingers at what feeble bit of sunshine found its way through the thick trees. The icy winter wind slashed through her coat while a crow's echoing caw pierced the eerie stillness of the surrounding woodlands. This forest was ancient, even when her family had first come to Pioneer Vale nearly 400 years ago, and had settled the lands that had become known as the Carmichael Farms, one of the most prosperous pieces of farmland in the county. Dry leaves beneath a dusting of snow crunched beneath her boots with each step she took. A stream nearby bore a crust of ice that strangled the gurgling rush of water that normally flowed through here. This dismal place couldn't have been more unlike the pastoral home she had known all her life.

Angelica stared at her father's gray buzzed haircut marching along in front of her and wondered once again what had possessed her dad to drag her out here this morning. She suspected it had something to do with the fight that she had overheard from her parents' bedroom last night. The raised voices of her mother and father had made for an uneasy night as she had crawled into bed.

"Will, how can you even consider going through with this?" her mother had yelled. Her voice quivered, but with rage or fear, Angelica couldn't tell.

"Because I have to, Kim," her father had shouted back. "It's not like I have any other choice."

"Just because of an old ragged piece of paper your father gave you says so?"

"These instructions have been around for ages. I can't make you understand what I'm feeling right now. It's like a compulsion, and I'm telling you that I am more worried about what happens to us all if I refuse. I'm taking her in the morning."

The argument had ended with her mother's muffled crying, and the slam of the front door as her father had stormed out to the barn. It was her dad's place of refuge whenever he was upset and needed to be alone. In fact, the last time she could remember him doing so was the day that Grandpa Brighton had passed away four years ago.

The whole incident had unsettled Angelica for a different reason though. Her parents never fought, at least never in earshot of anyone else. The only other time in her 18 years that she could recall their voices raised to one another was on her tenth birthday. As the family had been cleaning up plates of cake crumbs and half-melted ice cream, there had been a knock at the door. Her father had answered, looked back and forth across their porch, and then bent down to retrieve something left on the mat. He carried in a mysterious letter, and Angelica would never forget the way her father's face had turned as pale as ash when he read it. That night she had heard the shouting between her parents that still haunted her. She had never found out what was so important about that letter, but Angelica couldn't help but wonder if the two arguments were somehow connected.

This morning had been strange from the moment she got out of bed. The usual lively breakfast conversation was absent. Her father, normally clean-shaven and well-groomed, had a face full of stubble as he silently ate breakfast and drank his coffee. She had tousled her 12-year-old brother, Jamie's, curly hair just like every morning, but he simply poked at his eggs rather than telling his silly jokes or regaling his parents about the latest video game craze. Her mother absently scrubbed a frying pan at the farmhouse sink. Her mom's long chestnut hair was hanging loose around her face, rather than pulled up in its customary braid. She glanced up at her daughter as she entered the kitchen just long enough for Angelica to see that her mom's eyes were red-rimmed with dark circles beneath them. Clearly, she had spent a sleepless night sobbing. Her own attempts at small talk were returned with distant grunts or nods and she soon gave up. When breakfast was over, Angelica had been all too relieved to grab her backpack and get out the door to wait for the Pioneer Vale High school bus, but her dad stopped her.

"Angie, honey, we've got a slight change of plans this morning. I need you to take a walk with me."

"But, Dad, I've got to get to school. Clarissa called me last night and told me that she found out that there's going to be a pop quiz in Chemistry today. We were going to grab a quick group study session before school. It'll be an easy A."

"Well, I don't know how Miss Brenner came to know about this quiz, but that's for your teachers to sort out. Something has come up that is more important than one exam. Go get your boots on and your good coat. We're going into the Pines."

"Dad, how could this be more imp-"

"Angelica," he said in the 'don't question my orders' voice of a former Marine, "get your boots and coat. We leave in five minutes." His tone

3

indicated that there was no further discussion on the matter. Angelica quickly changed into her sturdy work boots and grabbed her coat from the hook on the foyer wall. She took out her cell phone and shot a quick text to Clarissa.

"Can't make study sesh, Bumpkin," she typed using her personal nickname for her best friend.

"What do you mean, Hick," came the reply.

"Dad's being weird. Probably gonna be late."

"Gives me a chance to catch up with you, then." An emoji of a smiley face sticking its tongue out popped up.

"You never could catch me," she shot back, referring to the inside joke about their respective sports specialties. Clarissa was a varsity girls' basketball player while Angelica was the co-captain for the girls' cross country track team. The two had literally run miles upon miles together, but Angelica always set the pace between them.

"Let's go, Angie," her father called from the front door. Angelica hurried after him, but just before they walked out the door, her mother pulled her into a crushing hug while fresh tears ran down her face.

"Be extra careful today, honey," she said. "Never know what's around the corner." It was the same thing that her mother said to her every morning as she left for school, but there was something in her voice that gave it an added urgency today. She kissed her daughter's cheek and then turned and went back towards the bedrooms.

One hour later Angelica found herself following an old worn trail in a forest setting that she was sure she had seen before in some horror film.

Her dad pushed aside some branches, and the forest path opened up into a clearing. A large black stone rested in the middle, a giant monolith laying broken as if some giant hand has swatted it over. The splintered end rested upon the jagged base creating a sloped table-like top. Despite the age-old moss that covered the nearby trees and rocks, Angelica realized that this slab stood untouched by time, its glassy surface more like polished marble than some big old rock in the middle of the woods.

Her dad walked over to the stone and reached out to touch, but drew back before he made contact. His hand trembled as he lowered his head, closed his eyes, and sighed. Angelica saw beads of sweat on her father's brow, and that worried her even more. Her dad worked hard on the farm every day of his life. He had been a decorated marine in the Gulf War. Furthermore, the air was freezing here. If he was sweating, it could only mean one thing.

Will Brighton was afraid of something.

She looked into the polished stone and gasped when she realized that she could see her reflection looking back at her. Her black hair was neatly tied back in a long ponytail that she normally wore only for her track meets. Angelica wasn't just a runner, though. She had spent her life working alongside her father around the farm. Baling hay and tending fields had rewarded her with a lean athletic build. She had her mother's hazel eyes with long lashes. Even though she didn't date often, she knew that the boys at school thought of her as pretty, even if she didn't turn as many heads as the cheerleading squad.

"So, Dad," she said softly. "Are you going to tell me what's going on? Why are we out in the middle of nowhere freezing our butts off?" She gently reached out and put her hand on his forearm. Her father opened his eyes and gave her a sad smile.

"Angie, what do you know about the Witch of Pioneer Vale?"

Angelica stared at her father. "You mean other than that it's a stupid old ghost story? Dad, please tell me you didn't make me miss school for this." She threw her hands in the air and turned her back to her father and the strange rock. "I can't believe it! I'm getting a zero on a quiz and losing

5

a chance to run anchor on the relay team so my dad can drag me into the middle of a godforsaken forest to talk about urban legends!" She whirled back around to face him. "Dad, you need to work on your technique if you are trying to take mom's title as the family prankster."

Her father reached out and put his hand on the girl's shoulder. She again noticed how he trembled and she found his fear was growing contagious. Angelica saw his eyes dart nervously around the clearing. "Angie, you know I wouldn't have brought you here if this wasn't important. So let me ask you again. What do you know of the Witch?"

Her father's voice was firm and even. Angelica knew that whatever was on his mind was serious to him and not something he would settle for any of her jokes about. She closed her eyes and took a deep breath.

"I know what all the townies know. It's a local myth. Supposedly, some ancient, evil hag haunts these woods. Something about a woman who hung out with demons and got run out of town. Now whenever somebody goes missing, everyone says that the Witch snatched them away. It's a ghost story, Dad. Every Halloween, somebody throws a Witch party. Frat kids from the college send pledges out here into the Pines for hazing. Tommy Robillard told a bunch of us at lunch one time how his brother got sent out his freshman year to wander around the forest for the night. His fraternity brothers kept jumping out from behind trees and scared him so badly that he wet himself."

Her dad chuckled softly. "I remember hearing about that." The smile just as quickly faded though and he reached into his jacket pocket. He withdrew two folded pieces of paper, one weathered and heavily creased as if it had been read and reread dozens of times. The second piece was barely folded and appeared much newer. The paper was thick and fancy, like the vellum stationery that she had gotten for Christmas a few years ago, and each was adorned with a now broken wax seal. Her father held out the older piece of paper to her first.

"I've kept this letter in my desk at home, but I've probably looked at it twice a day since I first got it. It arrived at our house on your 10th birthday. No stamp or return address, just the letter addressed to me. Go ahead and open it."

Angelica took the letter hesitantly. The paper itself felt strangely warm to the touch as if some sort of energy pulsed through it. As she unfolded it, she saw the handwritten words penned in beautiful calligraphy. However, it was the ink with which the words were written that made her gasp. The script on the page shimmered as if the author had written the letter in quicksilver, and a rainbow of color danced across the page. Pushing aside her fascination with the letter itself, she began to read:

"William Brighton, 10th great-grandson of Alistair Carmichael, per the terms of the Covenant, you are hereby informed that the time of Ascension for your firstborn child, Angelica Louise, is at hand. Prepare your child as you see fit and deliver her to the Widow Stone when instructed to do so.—AMC"

She looked up at her father and shrugged. He then handed her the second letter. "This one arrived last night. It just appeared on the porch, while your mom and I were sitting outside. One moment there was nothing. We glanced away, looked back, and there it was." Angelica took the second letter and opened it. The same glittering script was on this page. It said simply:

"The time has come. Bring her tomorrow.—AMC"

7

"What does any of this mean? What's the 'Covenant'? What's my 'Ascension'? Who is 'AMC'? None of this makes any sense."

He leaned against a nearby tree and scratched his brow. "One question at a time, Angie. I don't have all of the answers, but I know a few. First, The Covenant." He sighed. "It's our dark family secret. We have a document that gets handed down to the second oldest child of each generation of our family. It's been around a long time, apparently drafted shortly after the first Carmichaels settled in the Vale. There is some sort of strange bond between our family bloodline and this valley. It's ancient and powerful and something else that I just don't understand. What I do know, however, is that the Covenant demands that, when the time comes, the oldest child of each generation must be brought here to the Widow Stone." He gestured to the large rock in the middle of the clearing.

"The second oldest is immediately designated as the heir to Carmichael Farms, and all the holdings that are in the family name until that child reaches legal age. If this isn't done, it is prophesied that the prosperity of the entire Vale will suffer. The Covenant promises that terrible things will come to pass if this pact ever gets broken."

"Wait a minute. You said this document is given to the second oldest of each generation. Wouldn't that be Aunt Maggie?"

Her father shook his head sadly. "I once had an older brother. I was only six years old when Christopher vanished. Dad told us that he had gotten caught in a flash flood and was washed away while they were rounding up some livestock that had gotten loose. Or at least, that's the story we were all told. It wasn't until I was older, until I learned of the Covenant, and inherited the farm that I found out the truth. Dad brought Chris out here like he was told to do. Just the same way as I have been instructed to bring you here." He looked straight into his daughter's eyes. "I never saw my brother again, Angie. I don't know what really happened to him, but I know it wasn't a flash flood." He cleared his throat and wiped away a tear that slipped down his cheek.

"As for this 'Ascension', I don't know anything about that. I guess it's something that you will learn more about once we meet whoever 'AMC' is. What I do know is that our family has no choice but to follow these instructions. I felt this strange call come over me last night when I found and read this second letter." He shrugged his shoulders and looked around helplessly. "I have hunted, hiked and camped these hills since I was a boy but I had no idea where this clearing was. Never been here before in my life. Something powerful showed me the way. I can't explain it."

"You brought me out here to die." Angelica felt her blood rush into her cheeks as rage blossomed inside of her. The nearby trees rustled as a breeze blew through the glade.

"No, of course not, Angie. I would never let anyone hurt you." Her father looked up as the clouds overhead darkened and rolled across the sun, throwing shadows over the forest.

"Am I going to get washed away in a flood? Or maybe get caught in a rockslide?" She stepped towards her dad, unaware that he was no longer listening to her. A tree limb from an ancient oak tree crashed to the ground near them and her dad wrapped her in his arms, spinning her away as branches scraped at the back of his coat. Angelica shoved him away, so lost in her anger that she didn't see the growing turmoil in the forest around her.

"Angie, we need to get out of here. It isn't safe." He tried to grab her hand but she snatched it away from him.

"Why don't you just go for total BS and tell everyone that the Witch took me like she's been taking people for the last 800 years?"

The wind roared through the clearing in a sudden gale that whipped leaves into her face. Angelica saw her father's look of terror as a smell like rotten eggs filled her nostrils. The air behind her crackled and a wash of heat rolled over her back. This time when her father's arms sheltered her, she didn't resist.

A swirling purple inferno the height of a man hung in the air between them and the polished stone. The maelstrom irised open into a portal from which stepped a beautiful, middle-aged woman who lightly glided rather than stepped onto the grassy ground. She held her arms out to her sides with her hands shrouded in lavender flame. A crown of the same encircled her head glinting off the faint streaks of silver that shot through her long wavy red hair that billowed around her. Her cool, green eyes sparkled with wisdom and power. She wore a long-sleeved dress of black velvet with gold and purple trimming. A leather bracer with gold filigree adorned her left forearm, and a dazzling amethyst pendant hung by a delicate silver chain around her neck.

"It's actually more like 350," she said as the fires around her flickered away and the doorway that she had emerged from snapped shut with a wispy trail of smoke. She stared intently at Angelica with a curious smile at the corner of her lips.

"Angie, run," yelled her dad as he jumped between his daughter and the woman. The former Marine advanced a step with his fists raised, tensed and ready to fight. The woman flicked a finger in his direction, as if she shooed away a gnat, without even bothering to look at him, and advanced towards Angelica. Her father was thrown across the clearing as if he had been kicked by a horse. As he pushed away from the ground, his eyes met his daughter's.

"Save yourself," he croaked as he gasped for breath. He clutched his chest and winced as he tried to draw in the wind that had been knocked out of him.

Angelica had other ideas, though. She retreated slowly, keeping her eyes locked on the approaching figure. She stumbled over a tree branch, and scooped it up, brandishing the crude weapon before her with a snarl on her lips. She saw a fleeting moment of approval in the woman's eyes before the redhead clenched her fist in the air then snapped it back open. A flash of purple fire leaped into the air from between her fingers. Angelica's branch burst into flame and crumbled to ash that drifted to the ground. A blazing cage erupted around her as the woman looked her up and down.

"How promising," the woman purred as she paced before the bars. Her voice had the lilt of an accent from the English countryside that had blended over time to sound more local. "Given fight or flight, you stood your ground. Maybe there's hope for us yet."

Angelica's eyes narrowed, and she reached out through the bars, but her grasp fell short of her captor. "You'll have to drag me off kicking and screaming, witch. You won't just make me disappear like the others you've taken." The woman grinned and shook her coppery mane.

"So fierce. I like that, but my dear Angelica, you will soon discover that each of those that have disappeared over the years have all come with me willingly. A strong sense of family duty is one of the hallmarks of the Carmichael line. We all bear a certain courageousness, or stubbornness if you prefer, that has created no small measure of trouble for us over the years."

"'We'? What are you saying?" asked Angelica.

The woman's smile widened as she saw the confusion on the girl's face. Her soft laughter carried like the tinkling of bells across the clearing. "My sweet child, like all of those who came before, you are the blood of my blood. My name is Anne-Marie Carmichael and I am your 10th-great-grandmother.

"And you are going to help me save the world."

11

CHAPTER 2
HOME AWAY FROM HOME - PRESENT DAY

"This can't be real," said Will. He had regained his feet and held one hand to his side, the other out towards Anne-Marie. He stepped towards the fiery cage that held his daughter and then put himself between Angelica and the witch. "Are you really her? The Witch, I mean? You've been a legend since forever, and now you're standing in front of me." He scratched the stubble on his jaw. "I thought I was out of my head to believe in all this family secret garbage. If this is some kind of trick to get to my daughter, I'm warning you that I won't be made a fool by some smoke and mirrors magic act."

The woman's smile darkened and one eyebrow rose up. "Then perhaps it would be best for you to quiet yourself now, William," said the woman. "Do your ribs suggest smoke and mirrors to you?" She stared at him until he shook his head. "I thought not. Now, to matters at hand. You have delivered your firstborn child to me as instructed by the Covenant. Your role in what we must prepare for is concluded. " She turned her stern gaze over to Angelica.

"Your role, my child, is just beginning." The fiery cage surrounding Angelica extinguished with a puff of smoke that smelled faintly of wildflowers.

"Now hold on a minute," Will said. He took a step back holding his hands out in front of him as Anne-Marie's glare turned back his way. "If you are who you claim to be, and I'm not doubting you," he added quickly, "then can't I at least get some answers before you so casually dismiss me? Can't you tell me what happened to my older brother, Chris?"

"There is justification enough that I am regarded as only a legend to this world, William. Your brother's fate is tied up in that myth for broader reasons than you can understand."

"So I'm too stupid to know the truth?" Will's face flushed and a vein across his forehead bulged. "Maybe what I ought to do is bring the law out here and let them start looking for missing persons. What do you say to that?" He took a threatening step towards Anne-Marie with his finger pointed at her. Before he could come any closer, she extended her hand towards the burly man. A ball of purple fire leaped from her outstretched palm and hammered him in the chest, sending him head over heels across the meadow once again. Angelica rushed to her dad's side, finding him in pain, but not too hurt.

"While I appreciate that you have found your spine once again, William, I beg you to spare me your idle threats. The power at my disposal is far greater than any smoke and mirror show you may have seen. You are dangerously close to learning that my patience is not without limits. Now, allow me to make a few things crystal clear to you," said Anne-Marie as she casually tucked a strand of hair behind her ear and crossed her arms over her bosom again. "First of all, you would never be able to find your way back to this grove. Such is the magic of this place. Secondly, the authorities would find no evidence of your brother or any of the other Firstborns of this family whose lives have been lost over the last 300 years."

"How has this been going on for that long?" said Will through clenched teeth. "You don't look a day over 35."

"Oh, William, if we weren't related, I might blush at such honeyed words." She mockingly batted her eyelashes at him, and then her gaze turned stern once again. "You still dare question me, despite seeing me step through a fiery rip in space, effortlessly tossing you around this grove, and hurling flame summoned to the palm of my hand?"

"Yeah, maybe I am too stupid after all, aren't I?" he growled.

"Enough of this," she snapped. Thunder rumbled in the sky, and Will grabbed his daughter tightly to him. "I am indeed Anne-Marie Carmichael, born in Britain in the year 1643. I married young and traveled to the new world with my husband and his family as part of a group tasked with settling a new colony. We established the holdings that you now tend and keep to this day, but our family has paid a terrible price for our prosperity. I have sought for years to find a way to remedy this."

"That's what you need me for," Angelica said. Anne-Marie looked back to her as if she had been forgotten. "This whole thing is about me since I am the first child of this generation, right? So why am I here? What is it that you need me to do?"

Anne-Marie's smile warmed and her gaze softened briefly as she regarded the young woman. "I see within you courage that will serve you well, my dear. It is a trait that you shall sorely need for the trials ahead. When the time is right, you must be ready to do everything in your ...power," she said with a smirk as the word passed her lips, "to fight for our very right to survive."

"I can't listen to another word of this. Magic and destiny? We are simple people. Farmers. My daughter is just a high school kid. Angie, honey, come on. Let's get you home. I'm sorry for all of this." As Will reached for his daughter's hand a circle of lavender fire sprang up around him. Angelica jumped backward but realized that she felt no heat from the flames.

"William, I will share with you the answers you seek, but I do suggest that you remember your manners." She stared at Will with a look of intense focus, her eyes dancing with violet fire, and the barrier around him vanished.

"What the hell are you?" Will asked. His voice trembled and he once more placed himself between his daughter and Anne-Marie.

"Why, I'm the Witch of Pioneer Vale, silly boy. Although, to be truthful," she said with a toss of her head and an eye roll, "our title is actually 'Guardian'. Witch is simply the name given to us by the everyday person who doesn't understand the truth of what we are or what we do. It's time for Angelica and I to be off, but I shall give to you what you have asked for, William. Your brother, Christopher, is sadly gone from this world, but let it comfort you to know that he gave his life bravely and heroically. Because of his sacrifice, just as too many before him, our world is a safer place for his loss. Now, I will give you a moment to say goodbye to one another." She turned and walked away towards the far end of the clearing.

"As in 'see you later' or 'it was nice knowing you'?" called Angelica.

Anne-Marie stopped and bowed her head as she looked back at the girl. "That, my dear, will depend entirely on you."

"Angie, I want you to make a run for it and get the hell away from this place," whispered Will harshly. "I'll buy you whatever time I can, although she will probably roast me before you get out of the clearing. I'm so sorry, baby. I should never have brought you out here." He kissed his daughter on the forehead.

Will looked at the mysterious woman who stood waiting patiently for his daughter. Anne-Marie absently played with the dazzling pendant around her neck as she stared back with a predatory smile.

"Dad, my legs feel like spaghetti noodles right, now," Angelica whispered, "but something about all of this feels right to me. I don't know why, but I believe her. Whatever she wants, it is far more important than track meets and good grades. I can't explain it, but I think I have to hear her out."

"Honey, she's some crazy woman who lives in the woods, and," he said as he glanced at Anne-Marie and absently rubbed the scorch mark on his chest where the purple fireball had struck him, "she may just be everything that the urban legends say. Angie, you can't expect me to just leave you here with her."

"You aren't leaving me, Dad. I am choosing to stay."

Will saw the familiar stubbornness that so often adorned his wife's face now in his daughter's eyes and tears welled up in his own. "What am I supposed to tell your mother, Angie?"

"Tell Mom and Jamie how much I love them." She folded herself into a hug in his brawny arms and then she stood on her tiptoes and kissed her father's cheek. "Tell her the Witch of Pioneer Vale stole me away from you."

* * *

Angelica watched her father leave the clearing. As he crossed back through the tree line, he paused a moment and turned his head back and forth. He looked around frantically, and she could see her name on his lips though no sound pierced the stillness of the glade. He dashed off deeper into the woods, shouting noiselessly. She started to run after him when a firm but gentle hand settled on her shoulder.

"Let him go, Angelica. He will search for a time, but eventually, the magic will settle over him, and new memories will be created to explain what happened to you. I always make each Firstborn's disappearance something that offers the hope of return should one of you succeed in our task at hand. It has never been my intention to keep any of my descendants from going home, but even the purest of motives may fail."

"OK, so no more fairy stories and half-told tales," Angelica said as she turned and looked Anne-Marie straight in the eye. "Why am I here? What makes me so important to you?" She paused a moment and scratched her head. "And what exactly am I supposed to call you? Our conversations will last for hours if I have to throw in ten 'greats' before each 'grandma.'"

"You shall address me as 'Dark Mistress of All I Survey'." Purple fire danced in her eyes as the silence drew out between them. When she could hold it no longer, Anne-Marie's stern visage broke and she doubled over with laughter at the shocked expression on Angelica's face. "I am only joking. You may call me by my name if you wish, or if you are feeling bold, you may skip all the 'greats' and stick with 'Grandmother'. Be warned, though, that jokes about my age might have dire consequences."

"You are the finest looking 350 something I have ever seen," said Angelica.

Anne-Marie arched an eyebrow. "That's exactly what I mean, dear. To answer your other question though you are here because of the power in the blood of the Firstborn. It is your fate to help me keep everything you know from descending into a living nightmare. There are many things that you will learn in the coming days, weeks, and hopefully months, but do not take anything I say lightly. If we fail then the world will fall to darkness. We Guardians protect this plane from Demonkin and other forces of such evil that want nothing less than to grind humanity to dust. It's an enormous burden to place upon you, Angelica, and , unfortunately, I have had to place it on so many others as well, but such is the duty that we have been charged with." Anne-Marie sighed and she tossed her coppery tresses back over her shoulder. She smiled and her stance became less stiff. "I know this whole morning has been unsettling for you, and perhaps we have gotten off on the wrong foot."

"Well, you sort of shook me up when you showed up by ripping a flaming hole in space. Not exactly how I envisioned my day starting."

"I find that throwing a little fire and brimstone into my entrance tends to grab one's attention, but perhaps not always in the best way possible. I have seen everything from abject panic to loss of bodily control."

"You actually scared the crap out of someone?"

"That was an awkward introduction, I assure you." She shook her head. "Let's start over again, shall we? Follow me, and we'll go to my home. It's where you'll stay as we begin your training and prepare to face the trials ahead. We can grab a bite to eat, and get to know one another a little better. I hope that you will see I'm not as truly terrible as you probably believe so far. We'll get you settled into your room, and then we can begin filling your head with all the details and history of what is at stake."

"Let me guess. Your house is made of gingerbread and gumdrops, isn't it?" Angelica said. Her grin was taunting and fearless.

Anne-Marie scowled and rolled her eyes. "Oh, you clever girl. To think that I haven't heard that one before in the 200 years since that silly children's story was written. I have no intention of popping you into an oven, but rest assured that your feet will be held to the fire. Metaphorically, of course. Come along, and please spare me any more of your scathing wit for now."

The older woman started down a neatly manicured grass trail that led out of the far end of the clearing. Angelica hurried along, feeling a strange tingling wash over her as she passed through the tree line. She glanced back wondering if she would lose the location of the grove the same way her father had, but she saw it clearly with the great polished slab of black stone proudly sitting in the middle of the glade. Puzzled, she looked ahead and gasped.

Blooming flowers and blossoming buds abounded before her. Birds sang in the lush green canopy above her head. The fragrance of wildflowers, honeysuckle, and lilacs filled the air. Drops of sweat rolled down her face as she realized that the heavy winter coat she wore was completely unnecessary on this side of the clearing. Anne-Marie flashed a telling and mischievous smile over her shoulder as she continued down the path ahead. Angelica pulled off her coat and jogged to catch up.

The trail soon led to a tiny cottage nestled in the woods. A well kept and freshly painted white picket fence encircled the house. There was a small herb garden to one side of the small yard and wood chopping block on the other. Flat river stone pavers led from the gate to the front door. Anne-Marie paused there with her hand on the doorknob.

"Angelica Brighton, I bid you welcome to Whisperwind." The older woman pushed open the door on silent hinges, and Angelica was once again left in awe at the scene before her.

The inside of the cottage was far larger than the outside could begin to suggest. The door opened onto a spacious sitting room where a lavish sofa of purple velvet faced a wide fireplace. Lavender fire danced merrily on logs that didn't show the least sign of being consumed. A similarly upholstered chaise stretched towards the hearth with an end table made of hand-carved oak between the two seats. Vines and flowers were intricately sculpted into the wood, and as Angelica watched she could see the vines writhing in a sinuous ballet. A great armoire sat in the corner with a velvet drape thrown over it.

Off of the sitting room was a formal dining room with a dark stained oak table flanked by chairs that looked so delicate that Angelica was afraid to sit on one. The table was set for two with the service made of fine china, silver, and crystal. An elaborate sideboard stood against one wall loaded with fresh fruit, steaming bread, a wheel of yellow cheese, and a juicy carved ham. Through an archway against the far wall, Angelica glimpsed a modest country-style eat-in kitchen that reminded her of her own home.

"I thought you might be hungry by the time we finally got here," said Anne-Marie. "I went ahead and made sure some of your favorites were on hand." She clasped her hands, wringing them together. Angelica smiled for she did the same thing whenever she felt unprepared for a presentation and didn't know what to do with them.

"Thank you," said Angelica. "I guess I shouldn't be surprised that you knew I liked a hot ham and cheese sandwich." Anne-Marie breathed a sigh of relief.

"I do know a great deal about you already, my dear, but I look forward to finding out who you are as we spend our time together over the coming stretch. I don't get many visitors, obviously, so I love to listen to each Firstborn tell me about their lives in their own words, beyond what I have seen from the shadows." She waved her hand towards the sideboard. "Please help yourself, and after lunch, I will show you to your room." Anne-Marie ushered Angelica over to the food and they each made a hearty sandwich. Angelica sat down on the delicate-looking chair but found it held her without any give.

"So, why do you live all the way out here away from everything?" she asked. She took her first bite. "Wow, this is really good, by the way."

Anne-Marie smiled. "Thank you. We only raised pigs for a short time when I lived at the farm. We had neighbors who were better at it than we were so we sold off our stock and focused on vegetables instead. Over the years though, I have learned a few tricks for seasoning food. As to your original question, though, I tried to live among those who knew me for a while. Once I realized that I wasn't aging as quickly as my neighbors, I decided to seclude myself. There were too many questions. Whispers as to the secret of my longevity. As soon as I heard the word 'Witch' in hushed whispers when I went about town, I removed myself from the world before something terrible happened. There were a dear few who knew that something was amiss, but they kept their own counsel. From time to time I still venture into the real world just to keep up with things, but I pose as a simple traveler, passing through town on my way to somewhere else."

"Why not stay at the farm? I mean it is still called Carmichael Farms. Were you afraid of your own family giving up your secret?"

"I moved out here once my own son took over the farm when he came of age. He was a young man on the cusp of starting his own family. I felt it was more respectful if he didn't have his mother still waiting in the wings as he tried to raise his children and start his own legacy. Of course, I was ready to offer any help that was within my power should they need it, but this place," she said as she waved at the home around her, "sort of came with the job. Whisperwind has been here for a very long time. It was lived in before me by my teacher and hers before that. I've ...re-decorated since then. Tried to make it feel more at home as the years roll on."

"It is beautiful here." Angelica washed down the last bite of her sandwich with a glass of milk. "If you are over 350 years old, how old would that make your teacher? Will I get to meet her sometime?"

"I'm afraid not. Although my friend and mentor lived to a ripe old age, she departed this world long ago."

"So the Guardians aren't immortal? The stories about the witch always sounded like you've been here forever." Angelica blushed. "No offense," she added.

"None taken. The legends have blurred together over time. Native lore tells that there has always been a Guardian of this valley protecting against evil spirits."

"Have the Guardians always been responsible for disappearing locals?"

21

"No, it wasn't until I came along with certain unique circumstances of my own that the element of people disappearing entered into the tale and the more sinister legend of the Witch was born. As to your other question, the Guardians aren't immortal, although I have known a few others of our craft who have lasted over a century. To my knowledge, there has never been another Guardian as long-lived as I have become. Perhaps that's because my own Ascension was somewhat unique."

"That term, Ascension," Angelica asked. "You mentioned that in the letter Dad was carrying. What is that? What does it mean?"

"The Ascension is the singular moment when the mantle of Guardian is fully granted by the Power that we serve. Lesser folk have been able to draw on the magic that we have, but a true Guardian is something far more powerful. When you have made your true commitment, and fully understand what this destiny asks, the universe itself will tremble before you. However, it is a responsibility that must be both earned and paid for." She dabbed her napkin at the corners of her mouth and stood up. She took their plates and carried them into the kitchen. Angelica followed her into the next room.

The kitchen felt more in tune with how the cottage looked from the outside. It was cozy and rustic, with rough wood cabinetry, and a great farmhouse style sink that Anne-Marie placed the dishes into. Instead of a faucet, a well pump was mounted to the sink deck. Anne-Marie brushed crumbs from her hands and turned back to her charge. The pump handle began to move up and down of its own accord and a dishcloth lifted by unseen hands began to wash the plates. Angelica gaped in awe as the dishes washed themselves, marveling at every new surprise this woman showed to her.

"Now then, would you like to see your bedroom?" She started towards the rear of the kitchen where, in a sparkling cascade of lavender cinders, a staircase slowly appeared. The older woman threw a wink at Angelica as she climbed the steps. She followed along, wondering just where Anne-Marie hid an entire second floor of the house when clearly none existed from the outside.

Anne-Marie waited for her at the top of the stairs, standing in the middle of a short hallway. To the left was a stout oak door banded with metal. To the right was a simpler door, not unlike the ones in the farmhouse where she had grown up. The Guardian opened this door and led Angelica inside. The younger woman again felt a strange tingling wash over her as she crossed the threshold, and then gasped as she looked around at the very same bedroom in which she had woken up that morning.

"This is my room! How did you bring it here?" Her banged up dresser, the marks on the door frame where her parents had measured her height each year, the dog-eared books on her bookshelf, and even her computer desk were all in place. "Am I at home, or is this some sort of trick?"

"This is not your room at the farmhouse. It is a perfect reflection of it, however. Your world has already been turned upside down enough for one day, my dear. I had hoped to provide you with something familiar upon your arrival here to ease you into an undeniably overwhelming situation. The dresser and closet have your clothes. Everything that you left behind this morning, you shall find here in perfect duplication."

"That's kind of creepy, you know?" said Angelica. "It's like you have been peeking in my window or something."

"My dear," Anne-Marie said with a flash of fire in her eyes, "soon enough I shall show you things that you will find far creepier. There are things you will face that will test the very limits of your bravery. I tell you this not to intimidate, but to prepare you. You have the flippancy of youth about you, and I would not dream of crushing that. However, the time approaches when you will see just how deadly serious our situation is." She let the silence hang between them, allowing her words to sink in.

"So when do we get started?" Angelica asked.

"I have a few preparations of my own to make this evening. Why don't you finish whatever you feel like doing in here to get yourself settled in? Afterward, you may feel free to explore the woods around the cottage if you wish. Don't fear getting lost. Should you feel unable to find your way, simply think of Whisperwind and it will draw you back here." Anne-Marie backed out into the hallway and gently closed the bedroom door.

Angelica shivered once her host left and she looked out the room's window at the surrounding forest. Her mind whirled with questions, and she fought back the welling tears as she thought of her family whom she feared she was never going to see again. She still had no idea what she was expected to do, and her shoulders sagged under the weight that now hung over her. With a sigh, she decided that the best thing she could do was what she always did to clear her head. She opened the bottom drawer of the dresser, and, as Anne-Marie had told her, found her running shorts and favorite t-shirt. She quickly changed clothes, and then found her running shoes in the closet. Feeling more comfortable already, she opened the bedroom door and made her way back to the cottage entrance.

Once her run was underway, she found the courage to smile again.

*   *   *

Freshly showered and wearing jeans and a hooded sweatshirt, Angelica flopped down on her bed. Even after years of farm work and track team participation, she couldn't remember ever being so exhausted. The run through the forest had been exhilarating. The freedom she had felt as she discovered long-unused forest trails that invited her to travel along them had cleared her mind of all the day's upheavals. The woods had been as vibrant as a spring day. Bees buzzed through the air, flowers blossomed all around, and she had even spooked a deer at one point during her jog. As her stomach growled, Angelica wondered if she could one day conjure up a sandwich or if she would actually have to walk down to the kitchen. With a groan, she pulled herself back to her feet and padded back down the hallway.

A few candles lit the kitchen up, and Angelica smiled as she saw a wooden plate with fresh bread, an apple, a slab of cheese, and a mug of hearty chicken soup. A crock of creamy butter stood next to it. A note was folded beside the spread. As she unfolded the paper she saw the same glittering script that had adorned the letters her father had shown to her that morning.

"Thought you could use this after your run today. I will be back shortly. --AMC"

She sipped the soup, delighting in the flavor as it warmed her up. She spread some butter on a hunk of bread and took a bite. If nothing else, her ancestor certainly appeared to be an amazing cook. As the moon rose through the window, Angelica caught a small flash of movement out by the tree line. She spied Anne-Marie slipping between the trees, the older woman glancing over her shoulder at the cottage just before she disappeared into the shadows of the forest.

"Now where are you off to at this hour?" said Angelica to herself. "I don't suppose there is a minimart hiding in the middle of the deep dark woods, is there?" She snatched the apple from the wooden plate and dashed out the front door of the cottage.

She easily found a well-worn path that led into the deeper growth of the forest. A trail of newly made footprints trekked off through the evening dew, marking the way that Anne-Marie had taken. As she walked along, Angelica noticed subtle changes in the forest. The air grew cooler and more mist like. Instead of honeysuckle and lilac, lavender and roses scented the woods now. From somewhere up ahead, the roar of rushing water steadily grew louder.

The path ended at the bank of a mountain lake with a beautiful waterfall cascading down the rocks at the far side. Flowers and fruit trees encircled the entire scene making it resemble the closest thing to Paradise that Angelica could have ever imagined. As she quietly stepped forward, the girl stumbled over a bundle on the ground and she came down hard on one knee. She bit her lip and leaned into the cover of nearby branches to avoid detection. As she rubbed the sore spot, she realized that what she had tripped over was the pile of Anne-Marie's clothing and boots.

A splash from the water brought her attention around. The moonlight rose over the cliff and lit up the lake like molten quicksilver. With long sinuous strokes, Anne-Marie swam across the lake until she reached the waterfall. Once there, she stood up in the waist-deep pool at the base of the deluge reveling in the silver rivulets that ran down her naked body. She leaned her head back into the shower, running her fingers through her thick coppery tresses.

Angelica looked away, sensing that she had intruded on something solemn and private, yet she couldn't bring herself to turn and run back down the trail. A sudden flash of violet fire from the corner of her eye drew her attention back.

A man-shaped figure made of Anne-Marie's signature flame now stood beside the waterfall on the far bank. The Guardian waded over and stepped out on to the shore. Steam rose from her bare skin as the lake water met the heat from the fiery figure. The shape offered her his hand and enfolded Anne-Marie into a passionate embrace, fiercely kissing the woman and she returning with equal ardor. A shroud of fire burst around the Guardian's body as she pulled herself tightly against her magical companion.

Angelica could feel the warmth rising in her cheeks. She finally found the determination to leave when the fiery couple fell to the ground behind some broad fern leaves in an amorous entanglement.

Chapter 3
Tools of the Trade – Present Day

Angelica's whole body ached. After yesterday's jog through the forest and subsequently stumbling through the dark on her way back to the cottage after the late-night trek to the waterfall, every muscle in her body complained this morning. She dragged herself out of bed, stumbling as she shuffled her way down to the cottage kitchen. The sideboard held a coffee service of fine china, a bowl with perfectly square sugar cubes, and a small pitcher of fresh cream. Angelica gratefully poured herself a cup and carried it into the sitting room.

Anne-Marie sat in her chaise near the fire, stretched out with her bare feet crossed at the ankles and sipping a cup of tea. She smiled warmly as Angelica entered the room. "Good morning, slug-a-bed. I was afraid I might have to come to your room with a bucket of cold water to douse you with."

"Dunking my head doesn't sound like a bad idea," she replied. She plopped down into the chair across from the older woman and stared at the subtle changes that she noticed. Angelica watched as the older woman stretched languorously, like a cat enjoying a beam of the warm summer sun. A gossamer robe did little to hide the purple silk nightdress that hugged tightly to her shapely curves. Gone were the faint gray streaks that had been in Anne-Marie's hair the day before, replaced now by vibrant fiery highlights. Her skin was smoother too, the lines around her eyes and lips much softer than before. Overall, she thought Anne-Marie looked ten years younger than she did yesterday.

"Would you care for some breakfast before we get started today?" asked the Guardian. She tossed an apple to Angelica which the younger woman deftly caught with one hand. "You dropped this down by the lake last night. Probably when you tripped over my clothes," she said with a wink.

"You knew I was there?" Angelica felt the blood rush to her cheeks.

"Very little escapes my notice within these woods, my dear, but the footprint you left on my skirt would have given you away just as well."

"I'm sorry. I never meant to intrude on your privacy."

Anne-Marie waved the apology away. "Of course, you didn't. I was a teen once myself, though those days are ages past. I am no stranger to girlish curiosity, though."

"What was that place? What happened there? You seem... different this morning."

Anne-Marie chuckled. "Worried that I will soon drink your blood to preserve my beauty? That's not why you are here, child. I must say, however, that I am truly astonished that you even managed to find the falls. I have glamours all around that spot to keep people from just wandering by accidentally. The fact that you saw through the illusion speaks highly of your potential."

"I just followed the trail. I never sensed any kind of magic trying to fool me."

"My point exactly. You already show an attunement to our power that allowed you to see beyond the veil that I wove around my little watering hole without even trying. Anyone else would have felt disoriented, thought themselves lost, and would have been inexplicably steered back towards the main road to town. As for what that place is, well, it is nothing more than a retreat that I created long ago. I needed a place that I could go to when I wanted to forget all about Guardians and demons and just remind myself of ... a simpler time."

"Forgive my saying so, but you look younger. You created a Fountain of Youth?"

"The magic there does rejuvenate me, but that is not the source of my long years in the Vale. That bargain was struck under unwitting circumstances by my own naiveté. However, just as modern women have their spa days, I take to my waterfall retreat. We are surrounded by a natural power that finds focus in peaceful locations such as that one and can soften the lines that time would write upon me."

Angelica bit her lip. "And did it come complete with that pool boy of fire?"

Anne-Marie's cheeks turned crimson this time and she laughed. "My dear, I may be about 375 years old, but physically I am still in my prime. A woman still has needs."

"I'm sorry. Forget I asked. That is none of my business."

"I assure you that the elemental you saw was not simply a plaything constructed for the occasional tryst. I captured the essence, the embodiment of someone who was once, and remains even now, cherished by me." An awkward silence fell between the two women. Angelica took a long sip from her coffee and then cleared her throat.

"So, what's on the schedule today then? When do I get to start throwing purple fireballs?"

Anne-Marie choked on her drink and set aside her teacup. She wiped her chin with the back of her robe sleeve. "We have a few things to teach you before we reach that stage, I'm afraid. Today, we will finish the tour of my home, and later, I need to introduce you to somebody."

"I thought you didn't like visitors?"

"This one is less a visitor, and something more of a permanent resident. Bring the apple along, if you wish. It's time to show you exactly what we are fighting against, and a few tools I've gathered over the years to prepare us for the battle ahead." The Guardian swung her legs off the chaise and rose from her seat. She took Angelica by the hand and pulled her from her chair to stand before the great fireplace. She moved to the stone hearth and traced her index finger along the stones in a swirling spiral. Wisps of lavender flame trailed behind her fingertip and burned a rune into the stonework. When she finished, a section of the wall slowly faded away into nothingness, and the fire in the hearth roared to life, reaching up to the ceiling in a ferocious crackling purple blaze.

"Now, are you ready for your first magic lesson? Stand close to me, and place your hand on my shoulder." Angelica jumped when a column of fire leaped up around the two women as they stood in the middle of the cottage sitting room. She looked around the room expecting to see the antique furniture bursting into flame, but the room remained as tranquil as before. The younger woman felt a thrum of energy flow through her body as though feathers lightly brushed over her skin. She looked up at Anne-Marie and grinned.

"This is incredible. I can feel the magic around me."

"Indeed, you can. As your affinity as a Firstborn grows, you will be able to sense whenever magic is used close to you. Right now, we are sharing the power of the shield that I have created around us. Now, step forward with me through the hearth's flame barrier. Just hold onto me, and concentrate on holding that flow of magic around you as if it were a blanket." She stepped through the flames of the hearth, gently pulling Angelica along behind her. The younger woman gritted her teeth as she followed behind.

Once again, a ticklish wave rushed over her skin as she passed the threshold to the other side of the magical doorway. For one brief moment, she saw a swirl of blue-white energy spin around her as if another force dwelt within her teacher's ward that enshrouded her and repelled the heat as they crossed over. With a flourish, Anne Marie dispelled the flaming shield around them and then leaned casually against a worked stone wall, watching her protégé like a hungry cat watching a wounded bird. A moment of dizziness assailed Angelica as the flames disappeared, but she shook her head and cleared it away.

"Does it do that every time?" Angelica asked. She steadied herself against an archway with darkness beyond as her eyes refocused.

"Using your powers will tax you physically, but you will grow more and more accustomed to just how hard you can push yourself. The stronger and more experienced you become, the greater feats of power you can create and the less you will feel the draining effects. Even I still feel a little addled from time to time whenever I have to bring my full power to bear."

"There was something else there. Inside your wall of flame. Did you see that bluish light? Was something attacking us?"

"I did," Anne-Marie said as she raised an eyebrow and touched the pendant at her throat. "So strange. There are things about you that no other Firstborn has experienced this early, which you shouldn't be able to do yet. I suspect that we will learn how that flash of light relates to you soon enough. To answer your other question though, no, we weren't attacked. What you felt was our passing through an extra-dimensional doorway."

"Like a secret tunnel?"

"Not exactly. There are more spaces to Whisperwind than just the cozy little cottage. No blueprint could ever capture my home's every nook and cranny. This place is tethered to my house, but it doesn't physically exist in Pioneer Vale. It exists somewhere between what you would consider the real world and a dream world."

"So this hallway isn't real?" Angelica rapped her knuckles on the stone. "Feels real enough to me, or do you mean that I'm dreaming all of this?"

Anne-Marie shook her head. "This is what is known as a pocket dimension. Imagine the universe as a sheet of paper folded over several times. Our world is the top side that you can see, but there are several other places that you could write on if you simply knew how to bring a pencil to that spot." She pointed to the roaring wall of fire in the hearth behind them. "We just found our way to another side of that page. Come along, now. We've a short walk ahead of us." She snapped her fingers in the air, and a series of candles lit up a short hallway that ended in a landing at the top of a spiral staircase made of worn stone leading down into the gloom below.

After a few twists and turns, Anne-Marie exited out on to a short landing that led off to a hallway ending in a beautiful wooden archway covered in decorative carvings of books, scrolls, flowers, and birds. As the Witch of Pioneer Vale walked into the room, candles burst aflame upon a massive chandelier. Angelica gasped as she crossed the threshold behind her.

A two-story bookshelf full of books climbed to the ceiling beside a fireplace with a reading desk nearby. A large stone table stood on the other side of the room covered with bubbling beakers. Angelica wasn't disappointed to see that the lab also had a large iron cauldron with colorful green smoke wisping over the rim. The shelves on this side of the room were packed with jars covered in faded yellow labels. She followed Anne-Marie over to the workspace as the Guardian took a jar from a shelf. The glittering script on the label said "Lizard Tongue" and Angelica's jaw dropped as Anne-Marie opened the lid and popped something into her mouth.

"Care for one?" the older woman asked, offering the jar, She chuckled at the horrified look on Angelica's face. "Relax, they are chocolate covered peanuts. A personal weakness of mine, I must admit. I learned a long time ago that the easiest way to not have my children devour all of my treats was to label it as something absolutely disgusting. I know, I am positively wicked, aren't I?"

"This room is amazing," Angelica commented as she took a piece of candy from the jar.

"This is my study. One of my uncles was a scribe and whenever he came to visit our home when I was a girl, he always brought me a written story of some kind. He would read it with me until I knew every word. I love books, and I have spent many hours down here over the years researching legends, studying herb lore, crafting new magics, and sometimes, just reading for fun. Please, have a look around."

Angelica began studying the labels to see what other nightmarish ingredients adorned the lab, but was relieved to see far more descriptions of things that she recognized from her mother's spice drawer than she would expect to add to the bubbling witch's brew in the cauldron. She turned and made her way over to the bookshelves where she noticed that all of the covers were blank. "How do you know which book is which? Do you just have all the titles memorized?" She pulled one from the shelf and opened it. The pages too were empty, but she noticed a faint vibration through her hands as she held the volume.

"Imagine any book in the world that you can think of," said Anne-Marie. "Then open the cover again."

Angelica closed her eyes and thought of the last book she had read for her English class. She opened the cover and the title page proudly proclaimed that she held Shakespeare's "Macbeth". She closed the cover and thought of another. This time the cover page said "A Tale of Two Cities". She tried over and over again.

The Catcher in the Rye.

Thieves' Honor.

The Joy of Cooking.

Each title she thought of was in her hands when she next opened the book's cover. "That is incredible," she exclaimed as she put the book back on the shelf. She scratched her head. "If any one book can change to whatever you want to read, then why do you need the whole shelf full?"

"I found that when I was doing research, it was far easier to have multiple magic books each open to whatever work I wanted, rather than have to keep flipping back and forth with a single volume. In addition to just specific titles, you can also focus on a particular subject, grab a stack of books and each one will offer up something different. That comes in particularly handy for our studies."

"What kinds of things do you research?"

"Everything under the stars at one time or another, I imagine. Languages, astronomy, chemistry. I can actually help you complete your high school graduation requirements here. Of course, what I study the most is magic. We Guardians don't work with chants and incantations. Our power is much more raw and unshaped. To put it bluntly, our magic is limited only by our imaginations. Whatever effects we can think of, we can fashion a way to create. Of course, you still must know your own physical limitations. Try to create a volcano on your first day on the job, and you will find it beyond your reach. Try to shatter the moon and the strain could kill you."

"That's why I got dizzy just walking through the fireplace."

Anne-Marie nodded as she grabbed the nearest book from the shelf, flipped it open, and handed it to her new student. Angelica read the title page.

Step by step: A graduated lesson guide for new Guardians.

"Have you sent this to an agent yet?" Angelica joked.

"For three centuries now, I have worked on this journal. I present it to each new apprentice so that they can direct their efforts as they grew more confident with the increase of their powers. I have read and compiled a list of magical effects taken from mythology, folklore, fiction, and as technology allowed, film and television. Through countless hours of practice and experimentation, I have written for us a spellbook of sorts. I can't tell you how dearly I wish I had owned something like this when I first started."

Angelica flipped open to a random page. "Long-distance eavesdropping." She turned the page. "Pacifying wild animals." She noticed as she riffled through the book that the handwriting on the pages changed from time to time.

"This work has passed down through each generation of the Firstborns," Anne-Marie said. "Each one has added their own observations, their own research notes, and more than a few new effects over the decades. You will find the easiest lessons at the beginning of the book, but the effects grow increasingly more demanding the deeper you read. This book is now yours, but please don't turn to the final pages first. Let's not spoil the ending." She took the book back from Angelica and slid it back into the shelf. "We'll spend plenty of time down here together, don't worry. Now, let's go to the next room I need to show to you." She turned and walked back through the archway into the hall. Angelica hurried along after her.

Anne-Marie led the way down the twisting staircase passing several landings before finally stepping off at one further down. The landing was cold, and Angelica could see her breath. Cobwebs hung from the corners while walnut-sized spiders waved hairy legs in warning at them. The Guardian ignored it all and led the way down another short corridor that ended in a heavy oak door. Black metal bands scintillated with a rainbow of energy that coursed through them.

"Is that some kind of enchanted metal?" asked Angelica. She was still trying to get a grasp on all the new and wondrous things that this woman continued to show her.

"No, the bands are simply forge worked iron and the wood is the same oak that all of the other doors in the cottage are made of. What makes this door shimmer is a ward of holding," said Anne-Marie with a glance over her shoulder. She closed her eyes, raised her hands to the door, and hit it with twin bolts of lavender flame. The door crackled as the fire intertwined with the ward, and then with a wash of heat that blew the women's hair out behind them both, the door swung open. Angelica could see a sickly yellow light pulsing from within.

"Angelica, meet our adversary," said Anne-Marie as she entered the room. A jagged yellow crystal floated above a pedestal in the center of the chamber. Sickly looking tendrils of energy reached out like some diseased octopus. A cage of lavender fire flared to life whenever one of those appendages reached forward from the gemstone. With each purple flash, the flailing little arms retreated back into the stone. The young woman looked from Anne-Marie to the crystal and back.

"He's feeling spry this morning. He must sense that you've arrived. He's testing the defenses for a weakness," said Anne-Marie.

"I don't understand. How do we fight a rock?"

"This rock is a prison for the monster that we will face together."

"You mean he's in there?"

"A fragment of him. There is enough of him trapped within this crystal to prevent him from manifesting in our world. His physical form is on yet another side of that folded sheet of paper."

"But if he's trapped, then why the need for the Firstborn of each generation? Why not just throw away the crystal or lock it away in some dark hole in the ground?"

"Because the magic that holds him fades and weakens as time passes. See how he batters away at his little prison? Given enough time, he would eventually breach my cage, shatter the crystal and then a gateway to the realm of darkness would open. If that were to happen, then we would be forced to fight a battle whose devastation would be tremendous. It is only through the strength of each new generation that the crystal prison's integrity is renewed. Although I have never allowed him to breach the barrier between our worlds, the cost to prevent him from doing so has been terribly high."

"This is what the Covenant is all about, isn't it?"

"Yes. It is our family's promise to keep the forces of evil on their side of the gateway so that they don't invade our world and enslave mankind."

"And the other Firstborns. Did they all die fighting this thing?"

Anne-Marie lowered her head. "Yes, child," she said, her voice choked and husky. "Though each fought valiantly, we have never achieved more than a stalemate. With their lives, they bought our world enough time to seek out a new champion, the next Guardian."

"And now it's up to me? Anne-Marie, how do you expect me to battle monsters from another world? I'm just an 18-year-old high school senior. I don't know the first thing about how to be a Guardian." She turned towards the crystal and looked into its pulsating depths. Tiny cracks sprinkled throughout the rough surface of the stone as if something hammered away from within the gem. She jumped back as a spit of yellow energy lashed out towards her, but was repelled back in a flash of purple flame. "How did you learn what to do?"

Anne-Marie placed her hand on the girl's shoulder and pulled her into a gentle embrace. "That my dear is quite a tale. It all began around 350 years ago."

CHAPTER 4
CHASING DESTINY - 1671

Anne-Marie straightened and stretched her aching back. Her hair and dress were soaked with sweat, but she could safely say that there wasn't a single weed remaining in the carrot patch. She sighed. Now she only had to go tend to the corn and potato fields.

The gleeful laughter of her two sons, Aiden and Thomas, drove away her fatigue as the boys burst out of the nearby cornrows. Aiden stood a head taller than his younger brother with his straight brown hair that she knew was overdue for a trim. His eyes were pale blue and took in the world with their insatiable curiosity. He was tall and skinny, and she knew that he would never be the workhorse of the two.

Thomas was his brother's foil. Sandy blond hair in tight curls framed his chubby face. His eyes were the color of doeskin, soft and brown, but they always gleamed with adoration for Aiden. He could already carry heavier loads than his brother, and he loved to help with the more physically demanding chores around the farm. It was in their dispositions, however, that they were most alike. Her boys were kind and loved each other, hardly ever squabbling as she had done with her brother and sister during her own childhood.

"I don't know why we even bother with it," said a deep voice from behind her. Muscled arms wrapped around her waist as Jeremiah, her beloved husband, squeezed her tightly. He laid his cheek against the side of her head, and she reveled in the scratch of his thick beard against her skin.

Anne-Marie closed her eyes and pictured his long chestnut mane, shot with just a sprinkling of silver around his temples. He smelled of dirt, leather, and the sweat from his own labors. She imagined him looking over their struggling fields with his soft brown eyes, always full of tenderness and compassion. She knew that despite the disappointment he undoubtedly felt from their meager crops, his lips still carried the same carefree smile that he always wore. She took great comfort in knowing that while Jeremiah Carmichael was every bit as tough as the land they tried so hard to tame, he remained one of the kindest and gentlest souls in Pioneer Vale.

"We bother with it because this is our home, love. We will find a way to make the crops yield. Surely we aren't the only ones struggling this year with a lean harvest? What have you heard out of the other farmsteads?" She turned herself around in his embrace and wrapped her arms around his neck, looking deep into his eyes. He was biting his lip, the telltale sign that he was concerned.

"That's just it, Annie. None of the other farms are doing as badly as we are. Every other holding around plans for a bountiful harvest. I have seen some fields so robust that they could be picked this very day. It's almost as if our land went sour right after we indebted ourselves to Preston Mathers."

"Please don't say that man's name around me," she said as she playfully smacked Jeremiah's chest. "That wretch is despicable at best and the Devil's right-hand man at worst. I cringe every time I think of how your father borrowed the money from him for this property."

"Well, like it or not, it was his land to sell, and my Da went to his grave wishing he had never made the bargain. I don't like it either, Annie, but we make do with what we have to work with."

A horse's whinny carried across the field from down the road to town. A plume of dust rose behind a horse-drawn wagon accompanied by three other riders. Anne-Marie's keen eyes saw the unmistakably portly landowner that her husband had just brought up at the reins of the wagon.

"Well, it seems as though when the Devil hears his name, along he comes to call," Anne-Marie said with a snarl.

"Annie, play nice, please. He afforded us the opportunity in this country when no one else would. It isn't his fault that the land suddenly stopped growing as it had before. I don't see him riding out all this way just to poison the ground." He gently massaged her shoulders as wagon and riders approached.

"I wouldn't put it past him. You do remember that the land defaults back to him if we can't make good with this harvest, Jeremiah?"

"I know it all too well, but does that make him the cause of our misfortunes? Take the boys into the barn and I will see what has brought Goodman Mathers this far away from his life of luxury." He gave her a playful swat on her behind as she walked towards the boys.

"Aiden! Thomas! To the barn with you both," she called to her two sons. The boys raced over to the building, pulling together to open the massive door at the front of it. Anne-Marie guided them inside where they jumped into a pile of hay. She looked over her shoulder as the boys played and watched her husband approach the slowing wagon.

Preston Mathers bulk took up the entire wagon seat. His round belly strained the buttons of his waistcoat as he leaned forward on the wagon bench. A thick ring of gray-white hair ran around the back of his head from jowl to jowl. Sweat beaded his forehead as the midday sun beat down on him. Circles of smoke from the clay pipe clenched between his teeth trailed behind him. It was the three horsemen that rode with him, though, that folks around the Vale were wary of. The menacing trio of rough mercenaries came to the new world running from past crimes in the old.

"Patch" Erickson was toned and well-muscled. The jagged scar that ran down his brow was only partially concealed by the cover that gave him his nickname. The man was quiet but stood close to Preston, and the rumors around the Vale suggested that Erickson was the result of a tryst from Mathers' younger days.

Landry Cross was brutish and slow-witted. He was Preston's muscle and made no suggestion that he was anything else. He had taken to dressing like the natives of the area, covered in fur and buckskin. His head was clean-shaven except for the long greasy braid that hung down his back.

Hollister Adams was a weasel, thin and cunning. His eyes darted around constantly and his lips were perpetually cracked and inflamed from running his tongue over them. He was a smooth talker and was regarded around town as the leader of the trio. Adams liked knife play, and could often be found throwing blades at targets. Anne-Marie always hoped that Jeremiah would remain the most vigilant around Hollister for he was the one most likely to make a cowardly stab to someone's back.

"Hallo, Preston Mathers," called Jeremiah in friendly greeting. "You've come a long ride on a hot day just to pay a visit to our humble home. How can I be of assistance?"

"Spare me your false courtesy, Carmichael," growled Preston. Mathers pointed his sausage-like finger at Jeremiah and scowled at him with his beady eyes. "You know damn well why I am here. Harvest Market is upon us in a fortnight and your accounts are due. If you haven't the coin to repay me, then the deed to this barren property defaults back to me. You and your family ought to be packing up your meager possessions instead of trying to save these blighted crops of yours!"

"Preston," Jeremiah said coolly, "our account doesn't come to term until the day after the Market. If you've come all this way simply to badger me about payments not yet due, then I might have grounds to file a complaint with the town magistrate." There was a flash of dark anger behind Mather's venomous stare, but it was the fiery red rush of Anne-Marie's hair from the corner of his eye fanning behind her as she charged forward that turned all the men's heads.

"Small good that will prove since he already keeps the Magistrate in his pocket!" Preston's men began to move to block her advance on Mathers, but she shoved past their mounts. "You may own most of the township, but you do not yet own this farm." She scooped a rock from the ground and drew back her arm to throw it. Mathers screeched and flailed his arms as he pitched backward from his seat into the bed of his vehicle. Before she could let loose though, Jeremiah's firm hand grabbed her by the wrist.

"Annie, stop," he shouted. "You'll only give him a reason to create more trouble for us."

"Your wife needs to be tethered and shown some manners, Carmichael. Put the wench on a leash before she gets you thrown into the stocks."

"You will address my wife with respect, Mathers," Jeremiah said as he took a step forward, his fist clenched so tightly that his knuckles turned white. Erickson moved his horse protectively between the bulky farmer and Preston's carriage, his hand resting on the carved bone hilt of the long knife on his hip. The two men glared at one another, silently daring the other to make a move.

Mathers clambered over the bench, regained his seat, and scooped up the reins. "Enough! I will take my leave, but you had better hope that you come up with my payment." A wicked smile crossed the man's round face. "I have no doubts as to how much Master Erickson and company would enjoy throwing you all out on your collective arses." He snapped the reins and turned his wagon back down the road to town. His men slowly followed behind, glancing warily back at Anne-Marie and Jeremiah. At last, they were lost in the trees at the edge of the farm.

"You should have let me throw that rock," said Anne-Marie.

"Oh, I'm sure that one day you will get your chance," said Jeremiah with a chuckle. "The man has a soul as black as night, but we don't need to sink to his level." He pulled her close against him and kissed the top of her head.

"To protect our family," she said as she stared down the road, "I will do whatever I am called upon to do."

*   *   *

"You know I don't like you going out into the woods by yourself, Annie," Jeremiah exclaimed. "That forest is dangerous. We have to start harvesting what crops we can tomorrow morning if we are going to make the Harvest Market."

"And you know as well as I do that those blighted crops from this accursed farm aren't going to bring us enough money to satisfy our debt to Mathers. We have to bring something more than what we can pull out of this poisoned farmland. Maybe I can find some truffles or wildflowers, or some hard to find herbs to add to our yield. I have to do something." Anne-Marie looked pleadingly at her husband, her hand on her hip.

"Then stay and help me get ready for tomorrow!" Jeremiah ran his hands through his thick hair and turned on his heel in frustration. "We've got baskets to mend. I have to set out and ready the tools, check on the wagon. I need you here with me, Annie." He turned back as she gently laid her hand on his forearm.

"Give me this one day, husband. Let me at least try. The boys can help you with those other chores. If I come back tonight empty-handed, then tomorrow I shall work my fingers to the bone for the good of us all.

Let's hope above all else that I can come back with something that will surprise us both." She stood on her toes and kissed him deeply on the lips.

"That's not fair, you know?" he murmured when the kiss ended. "Wait here a moment, then. I have something for you." Jeremiah turned and walked to the curtained off area that they called their bedroom. Anne-Marie heard the unmistakable sound of the old trunk at the foot of their bed creak open on its weathered hinges. The shuffling and clanging of the chest's contents getting rustled about echoed through their home. At last, Jeremiah walked back into the common room, his fist closed around something.

"Whatever you thought to get for my protection fits in the palm of your hand?" she asked with a smirk.

"This isn't for protection. It's far more than that." Jeremiah opened his hand. Anne-Marie gasped as a beautiful amethyst pendant fell to its full length on a gossamer silver chain.

"Jeremiah, wherever did you get this? It's breathtaking!"

"I've looked at this bauble so many times in the last few days, thinking that maybe I should just offer it to Preston and be done with our account once and for all. I can't do that, however. It's worth far more than that black-hearted bastard deserves." He stepped around behind her and fastened the thin chain around her neck. "Besides, this necklace is magical," he said with a chuckle.

Anne-Marie stiffened. "Magical? What do you mean?"

"Well, magical in the 'old family heirloom' sense, I suppose. When my mother gave this to me she told me that this little pendant would lead the one who wore it towards their destiny. She said her grandfather had it on him when he joined the Royal Navy and he ended up as a decorated officer and a war hero. Her mother began wearing it when she began learning herb lore and she became so skilled with healing the sick with her remedies that she saved an entire village from a fever that went around. She never told me what it did for her though, so maybe her destiny was just to make sure that it got to me."

Anne-Marie gave him a playful poke in his belly. "And when entrusted to your care, what great happenstance befell you? I surely hope that your destiny held something more than being the caretaker of this blasted farm. Did something bold and beautiful befall you the day you took ownership?" She hugged him tightly. "It is beautiful, and I will treasure it always, but I need to get going before I waste too much daylight." She went to the door and fetched the gathering basket that sat there. She blew Jeremiah a farewell kiss and left the farmhouse.

Jeremiah smiled and whispered to the empty room. "The day I received that pendant was the day I went to the county fair at Doncaster with my brother. We ate, drank, and had a grand time. I danced that night with this beautiful redhead whose family lived on the other side of the county. It was the night that I met you."

*   *   *

Anne-Marie threw her trowel into the dirt beside the hole she had dug and hurled her still empty basket into the trunk of a nearby tree. She had been searching for herbs and truffles all morning long and still had nothing to show for her time. Hot tears of frustration welled up in her eyes, but she refused to let them fall.

Determination and anger pushed aside her exasperation, and with a fierce scowl on her face she bent over to retrieve her tools. As she leaned forward the amethyst pendant fell out of the top of her blouse and sparkled with purple fire in the midmorning sun.

"And what of you?" she said aloud as she took the precious stone in her palm. "The only destiny you seem to be leading me towards is one of homelessness and starvation." The stone merely sparkled in her hand.

Anne-Marie stood still, then rolled her eyes. Had she expected the bauble to perform some feat? That the pendant would pull her in some unknown direction? That a ray of light would point her off towards what she was meant to do? She felt foolish, and yet she stared at the pendant a moment longer.

Still, the pendant did nothing.

She laughed at herself as she tucked the necklace back into her blouse. She fetched her basket and then looked around trying to decide in which direction she should resume her search. The forest trail led north to the neighboring Harmon family farm, and her own home lay to the south. To the east, the trail intersected the road that led to the town of Pioneer Vale. To the west, the forest grew thicker and darker and led into the as yet uncharted frontier. She knew that if she headed that way, Jeremiah would be furious with her for taking such a risk beyond the trail's edge. She also knew, however, that her chances of finding any sort of natural treasures that she sought were far greater in the untamed wilds.

Resolutely, she stepped into the brush, pushing forward as brambles caught at her skirt. Roots clutched at her feet, and branches slapped at her face. Anne-Marie felt as if the forest itself fought to hold her back. With a snarl on her lips, she drove forward through the tangle of leaves and vines.

The ground behind the green wall fell away steeply. Anne-Marie windmilled her arms, but couldn't slow her forward charge. She tumbled forward down the hill, bouncing off of rocks and tree trunks as she went. Something crunched as a bolt of fire shot through her left arm. She came abruptly to a stop with a splash in an icy stream at the bottom of the slope.

She screamed as she tried to push herself up on her left wrist. Her stomach twisted when she saw the unnatural bend in her forearm. She cradled her broken limb against her chest as she managed to drag herself out of the water and onto the bank with her good arm. She studied the cuts, scrapes, and bruises that now covered her bare legs and arms. Nothing too serious there, but she knew she would be worse than sore tomorrow morning.

Anne-Marie surveyed the slope that she had fallen down. Jagged spurs of moss-covered rock dotted the steep rise, and her body felt as though she had slammed against each and every one on the way down. Even if she had the use of both hands, though, going back up that way would be difficult. She looked upstream and down searching for a gentler incline that she could use instead.

Of course, she thought to herself. Nothing as far as the eye could see.

She knew the direction back to the farm though so she stood up and looked for her things. Her basket was a smashed ruin in the running water, and her trowel was nowhere to be found. She gritted her teeth against the pain and walked towards what she hoped was home.

"You damnable fool," she chided herself. "Not only do you have nothing to show for today, but what good will you be to Jeremiah tomorrow? How are you going to help pull in this miserable harvest?" As she walked, she felt the amethyst pendant bouncing lightly against her skin beneath her shirt. She yanked it out by the silver chain and watched the jewel spin. "And you," she said to the stone, "You'll go straight to Preston Mathers if I don't throw you over the next hill I cross first. If you've anything to show me, you had better stop wasting my time."

Anne-Marie stopped and looked around. The stream she had followed was gone. Lost in her thoughts, she had strayed away from its meandering path and was now even deeper into the woods.

"It can't be that far," she assured herself as she cut back in the direction she believed would keep her aimed at the farm and still allow her to intersect the stream again. After several more minutes, though, she stopped. She strained her ears listening for the gurgling sound of running water, but only the rustle of leaves in the wind filled the silence. A nearby rock formation gave her the eerie sensation that she had passed by it earlier, and hadn't she seen that same scar on another pine tree awhile ago?

Anne-Marie sat down and took a deep breath. Don't panic, she told herself. The day is still young, barely midday. I need to just pick a direction and be certain that I don't stray from it. Sooner or later I will cross over something familiar. She opened her eyes once again and looked to the sky. The sun struggled to peek through gathering storm clouds, further confusing her sense of direction. She sighed, selected a cluster of trees in the distance, and headed towards them.

The approach to the grove was surprisingly easy compared to the rest of the terrain she had traveled across today. The level ground was covered by soft grass that made the walk almost pleasant. As Anne-Marie drew closer to the copse before her, the pines ahead grew taller, clearly marking them as the elders of the forest. The air was fragrant with the smell of pine needles, honeysuckle, and lilacs. And yet, something about this place made her cautious and uneasy. As she crossed the tree line into the shelter of the grove, a cool breeze caressed her cheek and blew back her long red hair. Anne-Marie gasped as she looked into the clearing.

A massive slab of polished black stone filled the center of the glade. One end was propped up on a broken spur of the same stone, giving the impression that this was once a great standing monolith keeping silent watch over the ancient forest. Beautiful purple and blue wildflowers grew in clusters around the fallen rock. As she stepped closer she felt a strange energy begin to surround her. The hairs on her neck tingled and her coppery locks fluttered without a breeze. She slowly reached her hand out towards the glossy surface of the fallen monument.

"I'd mind a bit before ye touch, dearie," said a raspy voice from behind her. Anne-Marie spun around to see an ancient wrinkled woman leaning heavily on a walking stick. Wispy white hair spilled out of the threadbare hood of the brown cloak that draped her frail frame. Gnarled fingers curled around the smooth polished wood of her staff. A faded black dress with yellowed lace at the collar hung loosely down to the tops of cracked and worn leather shoes. The crone looked Anne-Marie up and down. "Seems ye've had a bit of a scrape, my dear. Even more reason for ye not to lay a hand on that rock." She chuckled as she studied Anne-Marie. The young woman couldn't help but feel she was being sized up for something.

"Who are you? What is this place?" asked Anne-Marie. "We've lived in the area here for some time now, and never had any idea that this grove existed. It's beautiful here."

"Aye, lass. This grove won't be found unless it wants to be, Anne-Marie Carmichael." Her wizened eyes narrowed. "Which makes ye being here something precious. Could it be that the time for Old Henna's vigil to be passed on is here at last?" A thoughtful expression softened her heavily lined face for a brief moment.

"I don't have a clue what you are talking about," said Anne-Marie. "What vigil? How do you know my name? All I know is that I fell down a hill, broke my arm, and got lost in these accursed woods. Somehow I found my way here."

"To a place of ancient power that only shows itself to a chosen few. Tell Old Henna, child, what does your heart hold most dear?"

"That's easy," said Anne-Marie with a laugh. "My family means everything to me. My love for them is exactly how I ended up here in the first place. Trying to save the miserable piece of dirt that we call home. Our harvest is suffering and won't raise enough money to release our debt. I had hoped to find something remotely valuable to help us out, but instead, I've nothing to show except my injuries. I won't even be able to help my husband bring in the few withered crops that we have."

"What is valuable changes from soul to soul. The power of this place can help ye out, but only if your heart is true and ye can bear the cost. What price would ye pay to save your family?"

"I would give my life for them, but I don't understand what that has to do with the woes of our farm. If you are trying to fleece me then you need to seek an easier mark, old one. Unless you have a magic cure for all of my family's troubles…"

The old woman threw out her open palm and a nimbus of green light encircled Old Henna like a halo. Anne-Marie found herself bathed in the soft warm glow as twinkling motes danced around her. She gasped as, before her very eyes, her cuts closed, her bruises faded, and the bend in her forearm snapped back into place with a crack that echoed through the grove. The throbbing pain gradually faded until it vanished altogether.

"Ye were saying, lass?"

Anne-Marie stumbled away from the old woman. "How did you do that? It's not possible!" She looked at the woman and scowled. "What manner of witchcraft is this?"

"Ah, I do so detest that word. I don't dabble in hexes or strange brews, however, it's not an uncommon mistake. Child, there are forces in the world, and in worlds beyond our own, who wage an eternal battle that the everyday man and woman know nothing about as they sit around their hearth fires, and tuck their babies in each night. The shadows, however, do indeed hide the horrors that we warn the wee ones of. The very fact that ye've discovered this place means that ye're offered the opportunity to take your place among the Guardians' ranks. To be a protector of this world from the fearsome legions that would tear it apart."

"If I am willing to pay a price, though? You've still not named the cost. I only want the ability to save our farm. Do you have the power for that?"

"The Guardian's might is not something for sale, child. It is an easy thing to save your lands, however, ye must accept the responsibility that comes with such strength." Henna leaned forward, her voice becoming a whisper as she pointed a bony finger at Anne-Marie. "Saving the very world, and everyone in it that ye love is far more difficult. If ye have the courage to accept such a charge, then lay your hand upon the stone slab. This place is a gateway between realms that the Guardians are sworn to protect. Through it you must go, however, to determine the price that will be asked of you."

"And that will give me the power to rescue my family?"

"That and so much more, if accepting the power is the destiny that lies before ye," Henna replied. Anne-Marie's hands reflexively shot to the amethyst pendant beneath her blouse at the old woman's words. She could have sworn that she felt the pendant surge with heat as Henna offered her bargain. Offered her a destiny.

With one hand clutching the jewel at her throat, Anne-Marie turned and faced the fallen slab of stone then placed her other hand upon it. A bolt of brilliant white energy shot up the length of her arm, and then everything went black.

CHAPTER 5
THE BETTER TO SEE YOU WITH - 1671

Anne-Marie's temples exploded and heat washed through her body as though fires raged beneath her skin. Spots danced behind her eyelids as she struggled to open them. The air reeked with the stench of sulfur and something worse. She recognized the miasma of something rotten and decaying. She finally opened her eyes to see a sunless gray sky overhead. Blood red streaks ran through sickly greenish gray clouds.

"Here I go again, picking myself up off of the ground, and aching all over," she muttered. Slowly, she rose to her feet but gasped as she looked down to dust herself off.

A ripple of purple fire rolled down from her shoulders. Her woolen blouse and long skirt burned to cinders but was replaced by a silky white off the shoulder top with a ruffle that ran across the bosom and wrapped around her arms as short sleeves. A shiny black corset with silver trim wrapped around her slim waist. Soft purple trousers hugged her legs and hips, tucking into the tops of boots made of the same leather and trim as the corset. A belt around her waist held a half skirt that was open at the front but flared out behind her like the hem of a cloak. The only thing that remained from the outfit she had worn when she left the farm this morning was the amethyst pendant around her neck.

"What pretty little plaything has been sent to me this time?" said a low growling voice. The swirling yellowish fog ahead thinned and the silhouette of a raised dais with a throne sitting upon it slowly emerged at the end of a broken cobblestone walkway. A cloaked figure sat upon the seat, with fingers covered in black fur that ended in wicked claws grasping armrests made of bone. "Come closer, my dear. I would have a better look at you." He beckoned her with a taloned finger, as he leaned closer.

"What is this place? Who are you? What happened to the grove?" Anne-Marie stood still and studied the figure as he rose from his chair. Black greasy hair covered the creature's body. Ragged trousers covered him from waist to knee, which were bent backward like those of an animal. Wide feet like those of a giant hound ended in black claws that dug furrows into the stone beneath them. As he leaned forward, she made out sickly yellow eyes that glared out at her above the rotting flesh of a wolf's muzzle. Long yellow teeth clicked together as his black lips pulled back in a snarling grin. A hole in his cheek revealed bloody bone, while maggots crawled through his fur.

The creature let loose a hissing chuckle. "So many questions. Old Henna must be slipping to have sent you to my world so unprepared. Oh, but I will happily fill in the details that she neglected to share with you.

"I am the Father of Nightmares and this is my realm, child. Every horror that haunts your world takes its first steps in this place under my nurturing care. Every foul deed that man brings to his fellow man is hatched by my whisper. Each monster under every child's bed calls me Sire. You, however, may call me Shade." He threw his head back and split the night with an ear-shattering howl.

"You are the force that Henna spoke of. You are the evil that she guards the world against." Anne-Marie backed up a step as Shade closed in, his prowling gait like a hunter stalking his prey.

"The witch and I have circled one another warily for some time now, but she grows old and tired. Henna knows that her time is fleeting, and very soon she will no longer be able to stand against me. Did you not realize that she sent you here in hopes that you would take her place?"

"I came here only to find a means to help my family from our troubles. I have no interest or stake in some ongoing war of witches and wolves."

"My sweet morsel, I am far bigger and badder than that," Shade said with a harsh and mocking laugh. "You make this all too easy. Say the word then, and I shall return you to the grove." He lunged forward suddenly, snapping his terrible jaws before her nose and forcing Anne-Marie to recoil and gag from the putrescent breath that washed over her. He caressed her cheek with the back of one filthy claw, and then grasped her chin. "But first, I shall show you why I am called Shade. Come see the shadows of the things that may come to pass. I will give you a true taste of the terrors I intend to inflict on you and savor the sweet taste of your fear."

The demon whirled his cloak in a wide circle around them both, concealing them in a whirlwind of foul-smelling smoke. Anne-Marie tried to scream but coughed and retched instead to clear the horrible fumes from her lungs. She shoved herself away from Shade, tripping on the edge of his swirling cloak. She fell back, not to the ground but into the soft cushion of a plush armchair.

She leaped immediately from the seat and looked around. To her surprise, they now stood in a lavishly decorated study, with a blazing fire in the nearby hearth. The craftsmanship of the room's furniture was nothing short of exquisite. The carpet along the floor was soft and colorful, clearly from some faraway land that Anne-Marie had only heard stories of. Shade sauntered over to the sideboard, selected a crystal decanter of fine brandy, and poured himself a glass.

"Where are we?" Anne-Marie asked.

"We are in the shadow of a possible future of your own making, my dear," said the demonic wolf. He threw back his drink in a single gulp. Anne-Marie turned her head as some of the liquor sloshed out the decaying hole in the side of his face. "Ah, he always does keep the good stuff," Shade purred.

"Whose home is this? One of your servants, or are you just playing games with my head?"

Shade leaned casually on the mantle and drank straight from the bottle he carried. He wiped his muzzle with the back of his hand. He tossed the decanter into the fireplace, shattering the crystal and causing the flames to leap up with a roar. "One day soon enough you shall have the answer to that question. What remains to be seen is if this shadow shall come to pass or if you have the means to forestall this path."

"What path, you fiend? Enough of your secrets," she yelled. Shade flashed a toothy grin and glanced over her shoulder. A floorboard creaked, and Anne-Marie whirled around just in time to see the flash of gunpowder, hear the thunder of a gunshot, and feel an explosion of pain in her stomach.

*   *   *

Foul smoke swirled around Anne-Marie once again as she opened her eyes. She lay upon the ground with pine needles poking into the bare skin of her neck and shoulders. Shade sat on a nearby log with his fingers clasped together. His decaying muzzle curled up as he fiendishly leered at her.

"That was a pistol shot," she said as she sat up with a start. Anne-Marie ran her hand over her stomach but found no indication of where the lead ball had blasted into her a moment before. There was no hole, no blood, and no pain.

"You aren't paying attention, my sweet," snarled Shade. "What you see has yet to happen. You are walking along in the paths of what may come to haunt you. I expect you to live in fear, looking over your shoulder, knowing that I am right there always ready to pounce. When the Guardians fall, then none shall bar the way for my conquest!" He sprang from his seat and grabbed her shoulders as he towered over her. "Ready for the next leg of our tour?" He threw back his head and barking laughter became an insidious howl.

Anne-Marie shoved him away. Her head was swimming and she felt heat rising within her again. She staggered aside and leaned against a giant oak tree trying to get her bearings.

Shouts echoed in the forest ahead of her. She cast a glance back at Shade who rose to his full height and extended his hand towards the trees before her. With a scowl, Anne-Marie plunged ahead into the dark forest. The sounds of battle joined the shouting around her.

Anne-Marie burst through the tree line into the now-familiar grove of the black stone slab. She gasped as she saw Jeremiah across the clearing, armed with his hatchet and locked in a struggle with another man whose features were lost in the shadows cast by the encroaching forest. Jeremiah took a punch across his jaw but countered with a mighty blow of his own. His opponent staggered back, and Jeremiah grabbed the man by the throat. He drew his hatchet back, ready to split the villain's skull.

Anne-Marie started forward, but Shade's taloned hand closed around her arm. A flash of movement to the side caught her attention. The second silhouette leveled a bow and arrow at her husband. Before Jeremiah's hatchet could fall, the twang of the bowstring sang its ominous whine in her ears. Time slowed to a crawl as Anne-Marie watched the arrow bear down on Jeremiah's chest.

Anne-Marie opened her mouth to warn her husband, but the world swirled once again with Shade's swirling acrid smoke.

*   *   *

"Ahh, it seems we are closing in on your deepest fears, dear girl," snarled Shade. Spittle dripped from his maw as he licked his muzzle. "You taste delightful," he said.

Anne-Marie felt feverish, her head buzzed with a dull whine and her skin was bathed in cold droplets of sweat. She staggered around in a circle looking frantically for Jeremiah, the archer, and the clearing she had just been in, but there was only an empty tree-lined road that stretched ahead into the dark night. Fear washed over her as she recognized that the road she stood upon led between her farm and the town of Pioneer Vale.

Shade pounced forward and shoved her, dropping her to her hands and knees. He slowly circled her, stalking her, toying with her as she tried to scramble away. His clawed hand shot out and grabbed her ankle. Anne-Marie lashed out with her free foot, her boot heel crunching into the demonic wolf's snout and spraying pus and a rotten tooth across the path. She scrambled to her feet as Shade fell back.

"Do not touch me again," she shouted. A wave of heat washed over her once more, and she fought to keep her knees from buckling. "What sickness have you put on me, you wretch?"

Shade threw back his head and howled at the moon above. "Oh, how you wrong me. I carry no plague with me. I seek only to feast on your terror." His voice dropped to a growl. "And here comes dessert."

A burst of fire erupted over the tree line in what Anne-Marie knew too well was the direction of the farm. She punched Shade in the jaw, driving him back a step, and then dashed down the road towards her home. As she ran, the pounding gallop of hoof beats grew louder ahead of her. A rider burst through the thickening cloud of smoke, barreling back down the road to town. Anne-Marie tried to leap aside, but a glancing blow from the animal's charge sent her sprawling into the mud. Her head exploded in pain as her brow struck a rock. Blood ran into her left eye and her world spun.

"Just let go, my plaything," purred Shade in her ear. "You've already lost. You cannot oppose me as you don't appreciate the threat that I truly bring." He once again grabbed her chin in his wicked claws and slowly licked the dripping blood from her forehead.

Anne-Marie slapped the carrion snout away from her and fought her way to her feet once again. A shrill scream of terror filled the night and jolted her into action. She ignored the snarling demon behind her and raced down the road and into the clearing of her family's farm.

A column of fire engulfed the barn. The fields too were ablaze, each burning row lighting up the night like thousands of torches. Another high pitched wail drowned out the surrounding blaze. Anne-Marie's heart dropped as she saw the faces of Aiden and Thomas peeking through a window in the barn.

"No," she screamed as she bolted for the door. She could see that an ax handle had been placed through the door pulls, preventing the boys from escaping on their own. Anne-Marie ran through embers and ash as she crossed the burning fields. She saw only the barn doors, shaking as her boys pounded on them from within. She reached her hand out, nearly within reach of the makeshift lock when Shade, bounding on all fours, hit her from behind before she could grab the handle.

They barreled past the doorway, rolling through the smoldering grass in a tangled heap with the demonic wolf snapping at her face. She threw him off with a knee to his stomach and tried to run back to the doors, but Shade's hand caught her left wrist. Anne-Marie screamed as the demon's icy touch seared into her flesh. The buzz in her head roared with the rage of a bonfire and a flash of violet light burst forth from beneath his fingers. Shade yelped in surprise and snatched his hand away as smoke rose from his blistered palm. She lashed out with a backhand slap that caught the side of his head in a burst of flame. The beast howled in pain, but he pounced on her again, bearing her to the ground with his jaws slavering inches from her face. He sat on her stomach, his hand tightly gripping her throat.

"Oh, no, my pet. You shall have no false hopes of coming to their rescue. First, you shall watch them die, and then so shall you!" He threw his head back and roared once again, but this time the bloodcurdling sound was more sinister as if the choirs of his nightmare realm joined in the chorus.

"I told you not to touch me again," she spat. Desperately, she struck at Shade in a futile attempt to free herself and get to her boys. Her strike was easily blocked, though, by the monstrous fiend who pinned her down and held her fast.

Collapsing timbers shot a pillar of sparks into the sky as the roof of the barn gave way. The piercing cries rose once more into the horrific cacophony and then were lost in the chaos all around.

"Ahhh, I haven't savored misery such as this in ages! You are truly a delicacy." Shade rolled off of Anne-Marie, his terrible laughter joining the fading echoes of her sons' screams. The demon danced around in triumph, his tongue lolling from the side of his maw.

As she watched the foul beast before her, her sorrow melted away and became rage. Anne-Marie felt blazing heat all around her. Her veins coursed with violet streaks beneath her skin. Her head reverberated with the growl of a mighty inferno. A surge of force wracked her body as a corona of lavender fire erupted around her. Anne-Marie basked in the unknown power that fed the flames that now enveloped her. She knew that the blistering fires were hers to command.

"Do you think that I have lost? That I won't oppose you, you hell-spawned fiend? I will not let any of your visions come to pass," she shouted. "You will not have my family!"

Shade stopped his prancing about and stared, his jaw dropping open. The broiling wash of fire set him reeling backward. He raised his arm as a feeble shield against the blinding radiance that Anne-Marie had become.

"So, the kitten has found her claws at last," he said. "Too little, too late, my child. If you take this stand, what you have faced tonight is but a sampling of what I shall inflict upon you as the price for your new-found courage." Shade tensed and sprang with inhuman speed, his teeth bared and talons grasping.

Anne-Marie moved faster though. A ball of purple fire filled her hand and she hurled it with all of her fury into the demon's face. Shade howled as the blast slammed him to the ground.

"Know this now and forever, demon. I will spend my life fighting you and your kind for the torments you have shown me this night. I will not rest until your threat is eliminated forever." A ring of energy pulsed out from her body as she finished her vow. Trees were torn from the ground and the remnants of the barn blasted across the burning fields in its wake. Shade was thrown across the scorched earth, and Anne-Marie saw a true look of terror on her adversary's face.

A wave of dizziness buckled her knees and blood ran from her nose. She shook her head to clear her vision, knowing that she couldn't take her eyes off of the demon. Sure enough, she saw Shade's own hands fill with a dark energy of their own. A smoky black portal suddenly opened beneath her, dropping her into the void below. As she felt herself blacking out, Shade's voice whispered in her ear one last time.

"And so your choice is made. I believe that you and I shall be at each other's throats for a very long time to come."

*　　*　　*

"Oh, girlie, what have ye done?" Anne-Marie opened her eyes to find Henna kneeling beside her. She was laying on the grass in the shade of the black stone slab. The old witch reached towards her, then snatched her hand back as if afraid to touch the younger woman.

"How could you know what happened to me in that nightmarish place?" Anne-Marie felt a powerful current charging through her body. The buzzing in her head that she had felt before remained but it was quieter now, subdued like a lurking shadow dancing at the edge of her awareness. Her forearm where Shade had grabbed her was still sore, and she gasped when she looked down at the red burns of the demon's fingers encircling her wrist. She rubbed it absently as the old woman trembled before her.

"Lass, ye've no idea the force of the oath you must have sworn in the demon's world. I felt your ripple of power here in the grove that could only have been from the moment of your own binding. We name it the moment of our Ascension."

"Ascended to what?"

"Ascended to the mantle of Guardian. You walk among us now. You have sworn your oath to the Elder that gives the Guardians their power. Ours is a natural force, an elemental power that we Guardians can draw from in exchange for our service. We each, in turn, make our vow, but it is usually done with ceremony and passed down from elder to younger. You, though, have made your pledge in a realm closer to the source. You opened yourself up and have made such a commitment that the call went out across this world and others."

"That damnable beast threatened my husband and children. I'll never forget the horrors that the monster showed to me. All of those terrible sights. I will not allow any of it to come to pass. I will swear a thousand such oaths to protect my family." She used Henna's staff to drag herself to her feet.

"I dare say that the one ye made already will suffice. Shade is a cunning trickster, lass. He seeks naught else but to find his way into our world and rip it to pieces. He would leave behind a wasteland to rule over. It is our role as Guardians to prevent his passing through the gate, and keep him bound to his world."

"Can we not destroy him? If we have access to this incredible power then why do the Guardians only seek to hold him back? Why not fight him? Destroy him and remove the threat of his very existence?"

Henna chuckled. "You and I against a force of darkness from the dawn of time? I in my twilight and you yet untrained in the arts that you've only now become attuned to? That, my dear Anne-Marie, would be a short battle, I fear."

"Then what do we do? Stand idly by looking over our shoulders and jumping at every bump in the night?" Anne-Marie stepped towards the other woman, her hands balled into fists. Henna raised her own hand, shimmering with a green twinkling light that shot forth and surrounded the younger woman. Anne-Marie found herself frozen in place, unable to move any closer.

The buzz in the back of her mind roared to life, and, in a flash of anger, a wave of energy pulsed through her body. Purple flames flared around her once again, and she tore apart Henna's binding magic like it was wet paper.

The old witch clapped her hands and laughed merrily. "Well done, my dear! And now you have the answer to your own question. What we do now is train ye to control that raw potential burning within your breast. Let Old Henna show you the way of the Guardians. Let us start with something far closer to your heart. Namely, how we can fix your struggling fields. Then we can move along to more trivial worries such as battling eons-old demons who want to rip out our hearts, hmmm?"

Anne-Marie looked at the wispy fires that danced around her hands. She suddenly felt ashamed for lashing out at the old woman. With a force of mental will, she extinguished the flames from her body. A moment of dizziness assailed her, and a drop of blood trickled from her nose. The disorientation proved fleeting, though, and she saw the old woman regarding her with concern in her eyes.

"Forgive me, Henna. If you will have me as your student, I wish to learn the ways of the Guardians. I want to keep not just my own family, but all of this world safe from the likes of Shade and his demon hordes. Will you teach me?"

"Indeed, I will," Henna replied solemnly. "Hear me well, child, for my time is waning. When I am gone from this world, you, Anne-Marie Carmichael, shall be the Witch of Pioneer Vale."

*   *   *

"The power of the Guardians isn't magic, exactly, although to the untrained it would appear as such," Henna said. The old woman kept a cozy cottage deep in the forest, but only a short walk from the grove of the black stone.

Anne-Marie was taken aback by the mix of Viking and Native American décor that adorned the Guardian's home. Above the fireplace hung a broad ax with runes inscribed into the handle crossed over by a beautiful bow adorned with feathers and beads. A dented iron helmet rested on the mantle with a dream-catcher leaning askew against it. Henna had kissed her fingertips and touched each relic lovingly when she had brought the younger woman into her home.

Henna poured tea for Anne-Marie into a simple clay mug. The room smelled of lavender and a fire blazed cheerily in the hearth. "As I told ye before, it is more akin to a force of nature. Ancient and elemental. It grows and thrives with nature's way of doing things, which is why we stand against the chaos that beings like Shade and his fellows would unleash upon our world."

"You make it sound as though we are servants of Mother Nature. Especially if the first thing I am going to do is save my fields," Anne-Marie said as she lifted the cup to her lips. She sipped the tea, tasting chamomile with a hint of honey.

"After a fashion, perhaps. I suppose our full title would be Guardians of the Natural Order. Growth, fertility, and the thriving of all living things are ours to protect and nurture."

"And Shade is the opposite of all of this?"

Henna sipped from her own mug. "Aye. His kind thrives on fear and death. He grows more powerful whenever the world weeps. He feasts on the suffering of mortal man. The Demonkin can influence our world from their own, but so long as a Guardian stands to oppose them, they cannot bring their full power to bear. Should the Guardians die out and any Demon Lord cross the threshold into our world...." She trailed off and shivered as she stared into the fire.

Anne-Marie leaned forward in her chair. "What would happen?"

Henna rubbed her gnarled hand across her eyes, and then looked over at the younger woman. "It would mean the end of days, child. There would be no one left to oppose him and he would become invincible. We have so much fear and suffering in the world already, that his powers would grow at an astonishing rate." She paused again. "And then the true devastation would begin." The fire popped suddenly, causing Anne-Marie to jump. Her tea sloshed over her hand, drawing a hiss of pain from her.

"Dammit," she said as she put her cup down, and looked at the slight burn. "How is it that when I wrap myself up in purple fire I don't feel a thing, but a cup of hot tea scalds me?"

"The purple flame is the signature of your power, just as my own is a twinkling green light," Henna replied. "It's a manifestation of who you are and your connection within the realm of the Guardians. I am but a quiet caretaker, tending to the forest and protecting the grove of the black stone." She took Anne-Marie's hand and gave it a firm squeeze.

Anne-Marie gasped, and reflexively channeled a rush of energy down her arm. Lavender flame flashed around her injury as the older Guardian quickly released her grip. Henna smiled and nodded her head towards Anne-Marie's hand. The burn was gone, her skin the same creamy color as before as if nothing had ever happened.

"You, my girl, are a warrior maiden. Your flame manifests as a reflection of the fiery tempest that burns within you. It's the signature of a true protector, capable of combat and healing in equal measure. Just as you promised Shade in his realm, you have come to do battle. He will find you far more of an obstacle than he has faced in many an age, I should guess."

"I won't be much of an obstacle if I don't learn how to control this power. Tell me, do you feel a constant buzzing in the back of your head? I have felt it ever since stepping into Shade's realm. It seems no more than an afterthought until I call upon my magic. Then my head hurts and I become weak and dizzy."

"Although I warrant that ye felt it more strongly than I do," Henna said with a nod, "that is the Whisper of the Elder and is what you will draw into yourself and shape to the intended effects you are striving for. Imagine it as the bucket you drop into the well. Ye must draw it up before ye can have a drink. As for the drain on you, yes, child. We are conduits for power beyond our world and our mortal bodies struggle to contain it.

However, the more ye use it, the more ye can withstand. Just like hard work will build up one's muscles, with time and controlled practice, ye'll be able to do astonishing things with a snap of your fingers." She demonstrated and a cloth floated through the air to mop up the spilled tea at Anne-Marie's feet.

"You do make it seem effortless," Anne-Marie said as she flexed her hand. She smiled. "But if you think drawing water from a well is easy work, then you need to come help out on our farm for a few days."

Henna threw back her head and laughed heartily, slapping her thigh. "Oh, my dear, when ye've been at this for as long as I have, it's more like falling into the well. For you, I suspect that one day it will seem as though you are diving into a lake."

"Why do I feel like I'm already drowning?"

"Let's start with something easy, shall we?" The old witch walked over to a nearby shelf and picked up the stub of an unlit candle, and set it on the low table between them. "Close your eyes. Tune out everything but that murmur in the back of your mind, and fancy a spark lighting up that wick."

Anne-Marie nodded, took a deep breath, and closed her eyes. The tingle in her mind intensified as she focused her will upon it, growing until it reminded her of a swarm of bees inside her head. She felt a rush of energy flow through her body and knew she was in contact with the Guardian's power. She furrowed her brow and pictured the candle, imagined the wick smoldering, an ember taking hold, and then finally bursting into flame. She gritted her teeth and gave a mental push towards the candle and from behind closed eyelids, she saw a flash of lavender light and felt the warm rush of air caressing her cheek.

"Oh, my," Henna said with a chuckle. Anne-Marie opened her eyes to see herself wrapped in purple flames once more. Though she felt no heat from the fire herself, the chair upon which she sat began to burn. Startled, she jumped up, knocking the seat over as Henna's hand flashed forward with twinkling green motes of light spilling from her palm. Her hand then snapped shut into a clenched fist, quickly extinguishing both her furniture and Anne-Marie.

"Well, that wasn't quite what I had in mind, but you had the right idea," quipped the old woman as she righted the chair and brushed off the soot and ash from it. She grinned at her student. "Let's try it a different way this time."

"Why do I get the feeling that this isn't going to end well?" asked Anne-Marie.

"Nothing more than first time jitters, lass. Surely the first time ye kissed your Jeremiah didn't go off as planned, did it? So ye set yourself on fire. One day remind me to tell you the story of how I mistakenly turned a goat inside out trying to find a shortcut to milking her. Now that was a true disaster."

"I imagine that the goat would probably agree with you."

Henna looked around her sitting area and pushed back her own chair. She picked up a vase of flowers and placed it on a shelf on the far side of the room.

"Just in case," she said with a sheepish smile. "Now rather than trying to light a fire from scratch, let's borrow the flame from an existing source." The old witch pointed to the hearth with one gnarled finger, and amidst a twinkling of green flecks of light, a tongue of flame reached forth from the fireplace and caressed the candlewick. She let the candle burn merrily for a few moments then made a pinching motion with her fingers. The fire snuffed out as though a breath of wind had passed by.

"OK, my turn now," said Anne-Marie. "I can do this." She reached her hand towards the fireplace and once again felt the rush of power flow through her body. She saw the dancing fires as if they were actually tangible. "I can feel it," she said with a start. "It's as though I can cradle it in my hand."

"Good," said Henna. "Now carry it over to the candle, gently though."

Anne-Marie flicked her wrist from the hearth towards the candle. Rather than a small licking tendril, a raging fireball tore through the living space between the two women and slammed against the far wall, setting it ablaze. Henna's magic flared in a flash of green light and extinguished the inferno before it could spread. Despite her quick reaction though, a scar of scorched wood crossed the floor from the fireball's path, and smoke wisped from tiny embers in the curtains that hung over the window. Anne-Marie threw her head back and screamed in frustration.

"Maybe we should have started with training ye to quench the fire first, lass," Henna quipped. The scorched tops of the wildflowers she had so carefully moved fell from the stem to the ground in a small puff of ash. "And while we're thinking of it, let's start having your lessons outdoors."

CHAPTER 6
SETTLING ACCOUNTS - 1671

Jeremiah leaned against the corner post on the front porch of the Carmichael farmhouse. He spared a glance away from the basket he was mending long enough to watch the black clouds rolling across the sky. A distant rumble of thunder sent a shiver down his spine.

"Storm's moving fast," he muttered to himself. "Annie, where the blazes are you?" There was something in the air tonight, and it unsettled him in a way little else ever had.

He was frightened.

Ever since that strange breeze had rushed across the valley earlier this afternoon, things had felt peculiar. The boys had been irritable, and Jeremiah had been forced to send them to bed after the last squabble ended up with Aiden bloodying Thomas' nose. The livestock had been restless too, and the normally soothing noises of the barnyard were agitated, and, if he didn't know better, fearful.

Jeremiah tried to shake off the unease, but the knot in his stomach led his mind to all kinds of tragedies that could have befallen his wife while she was away in the forest. He just wanted her home and in his arms, snuggled up in the blankets inside so that they could try to tackle tomorrow's chore of collecting their meager crops. Maybe a pounding rain would at least soften the ground up enough to make pulling the harvest out of this accursed dirt easier.

The thunder crashed again, closer this time, and Jeremiah stepped from the porch. Raindrops pelted his face as a flash of lightning brightened the evening sky. His keen eyes roamed across the distant tree line where the road to town was swallowed by the forest depths, but he saw no sign of his wayward wife. His watchful gaze followed along the natural border that surrounded the perimeter of their land. As the lightning creased the sky once more, Jeremiah saw a shadow of movement at the far end of the cornfield.

*   *   *

Anne-Marie walked with purpose and determination from the forest to the edge of the open field. Her senses blazed with a clarity that heard every chirp, saw every fluttering leaf, and caught every wildflower's unique fragrance. She was fully aware of nature's flow around her and she sensed that Jeremiah had caught sight of her.

She basked in the river of supernatural energy that flowed around and through her, waiting for her to bend it to her will. Her short time in Henna's tutelage had shown her that she was now an open conduit to a primeval force that was ancient even when the world was new.

"Ye've been accepted, chosen as a Guardian, lass," Henna had told her. "Power unlike anything ye've ever dreamed of is yours to command."

"You sound like I could use it to destroy the planet. What if I choose to become a conqueror instead of a protector?"

"Then ye'd never have located the grove in the first place. The Guardians are chosen because they are champions for the salvation of the world, and mindful to stand against the likes of Shade. There is an intelligence behind our power. As ye gain trust in yourself, so too will that force empower ye. Given time, ye'll find yourself capable of feats that will stagger your mind."

Anne-Marie pondered the old witch's teachings from today as she overlooked the withered fields. "Time for a miracle," she said to herself. She raised her arms, reached out with her senses, and soaked up the eddying waves of magic. The Whisper in her mind rose as the wind of the impending storm whipped around her. The energy she harnessed writhed as if she had taken a hold of the reins of a horse newly broken but not yet accustomed to the bridle. Powerful, but not quite tame. She knelt down to the ground, dug the fingers of one hand into the soil, and lifted her other palm upwards to the heavens above. As Henna had instructed her, she fully opened herself to the floodgates of the Guardian's might.

Her scream of agony tore through the night sky as a pillar of lavender fire blossomed around her.

*   *   *

His wife's shriek boomed in Jeremiah's ears, spurring him into a mad sprint down the row of his field. He saw the explosion of purple flame burst up around her and wondered for a moment if she had been struck by lightning.

The storm increased its fury as the blaze around his wife intensified. The wind and rain lashed out against him, making his footing uncertain and treacherous as the soil beneath his feet churned to mud and clutched at his boots. Jeremiah Carmichael, however, would not be deterred from reaching his beloved wife's side.

*   *   *

Anne-Marie's ears thudded with the heartbeat of the land itself. She could feel the rush of underground rivers coursing like blood through her veins. The fires of the Earth's core raged within her breast. She could see the roots of the crops burrowing through the soil, but something was wrong. Some impurity not meant to be there sapped the life from the field's natural growth. Something poisoned their farmland.

73

With a snarl on her lips, Anne-Marie dug her fingers deeper into the wet earth and unleashed a torrent of cleansing fire into the ground.

* * *

Jeremiah tripped and fell face-first into the mud. Something had grabbed his ankle as he dashed towards his wife. He looked down at his feet and saw the roots and stalks of the crops flailing about, surging with newfound vitality. Violet streaks of light raced up and down the veins of the plants. Before his very eyes, he watched the dry and stunted crops suddenly begin to swell and burst through the ground with new verdant life.

He turned his eyes back to his wife at the end of the row, barely visible beyond the screen of thrashing leaves. The glow of that violet fire still burned brightly in the night though. With a heave, Jeremiah tore himself loose from the tangling roots and resumed his charge towards Anne-Marie.

* * *

Pale gray tendrils of poison threaded through the earth, but Anne-Marie's magical flames purged the toxins out of the soil. The elemental force that she was now partnered with cleansed the fields and channeled new life into the crops. The damage caused by the unnatural venom in the ground was burned away.

Anne-Marie's body quivered as the power that raged through her began to push past the limits of her control. As she felt the last of the poison incinerate, her legs trembled, her arms fell limply to her sides, and blood sprayed from her nose and mouth. At the edge of her swimming consciousness, Anne-Marie sensed something otherworldly watching her, judging her, as she pushed herself onward. Setting aside all thoughts of everything else, she redoubled her focus and with teeth grinding, she slammed shut the open conduit. The sudden cutoff blasted her with a backlash of energy that knocked her senseless. Overcome by exhaustion, and her head pounding from her efforts, Anne-Marie pitched forward.

Strong arms caught her just before she hit the mud. She looked up, her fading vision locking on Jeremiah's soft brown eyes. Beyond him, the stars appeared once again as the storm clouds rolled away into the evening sky. She looked back to her husband, and for a fleeting moment, saw again the horrible flash of Shade's vision. She choked back a sob and hugged him as tightly as she was able.

"Oh, Jeremiah. Please forgive me," she said as she fought to keep her eyes open. He scooped her up into his arms and turned back towards their home.

"Let's get you dry and warm, Annie. Then we'll face whatever monsters you fear you've brought down on us."

*   *   *

Anne-Marie sat by the hearth with a cup of steaming tea in one hand, shivering beneath a worn blanket clutched around her body. A pool grew at her feet as her hair dripped rainwater from the tempest she had called down. She stared wordlessly into the crackling fire as Jeremiah, stripped to his breeches, hung their soaked clothes from a rope he had strung across the front room of the farmhouse.

"I don't even know what is real or if this is all some feverish dream," she said at last. "It's terrifying, but…exhilarating at the same time."

"Well, it's one hell of a tale, for sure," Jeremiah said softly as he plopped himself down on a stool beside her. His kind smile lit up his face, forcing one of her own. "Let's just start with what we do understand before we think any more about nightmare visions and monsters."

"What we understand? I understand that I have somehow made a bargain to spend my life fighting a demon who wants to lay waste to our world and feed on the misery and suffering he can cause. I understand that because I made this pledge in some supernatural realm that I have plunged myself into responsibilities far deeper than any other Guardian has been called to uphold. And I know that for my foolish rush into all of this, I must still pay some terrible price in exchange for this newfound sorcery!" She let go of the blanket and ran her hand through her long coppery tresses. Her lip quivered and a single tear ran down her cheek.

"What I know is this, Annie," Jeremiah said as he wiped the drop away with his finger, and squeezed her hand in his own. "Whatever bargain you made gave you the ability to save the farm. I've never seen crops as healthy as ours! You are treating this as a curse, but what if it isn't? What if instead, you have created a legacy? Maybe Carmichael Farms will now thrive in Pioneer Vale generations to come." He reached his fingers inside the blanket and drew forth the amethyst pendant that dangled around her neck. "Maybe all that befell you today was meant to happen. What if your destiny is to save us all?"

"So I should just accept all of this? Be grateful for what I have become? What happens when the townsfolk start muttering the word 'witch' as I pass by on the streets? How long before angry mobs show up to burn me at the stake?"

"Now, hold a moment. I never said that we should shout it from the mountaintops. Certainly, we need to keep this quiet. We'll let our friends and neighbors stay none the wiser, but I believe in my heart this happened for a reason." He let the pendant drop back against her neck. "Let's get past Market Day, Annie. Then we can get used to the idea of you hurling fireballs at me whenever I do something stupid."

His grin made her laugh despite the turmoil that raced through her thoughts. He raised their hands to his lips and kissed their intertwined fingers. She leaned into him, resting her cheek against his chest.

"You aren't afraid of this? Of me?"

"Of you? Never. Of angry mobs? Let them come. You know that I will go down fighting to my last breath to protect you and the boys." He stood up, kissed her gently on the top of her head and stepped away to throw another log onto the dwindling fire in the hearth.

"That's what worries me," she whispered.

*   *   *

Market Day in Pioneer Vale was a bustling event each year, and people from all the neighboring counties came to participate. Street vendors hawked everything from vegetables to woodwork to hand tools, bartering for the best deals on the things they needed at their own homesteads. The air was filled with the smells of freshly baked bread, smoked meats, and fragrant herbs. In truth, Market Day felt more like a county fair than a sales day.

Jeremiah jumped down from the seat of their wagon, landing lightly on the dew-covered grass. He watched Anne-Marie climb gracefully down the other side, noticing how she glanced at the tarp that covered their cargo. She chewed her bottom lip and played absently with the pendant at her throat. Jeremiah stepped up behind her and wrapped her in his strong arms.

"None the wiser," he whispered into her ear and kissed her quickly on the cheek. "Boys," he called to Aiden and Thomas who still wrestled around in the wagon's bed. "Untie those tarp cords and let's set up our shop!"

"Yessir," said Aiden as he and his younger brother began pulling at the knots. Anne-Marie threw back the corner of the cover to reveal baskets and sacks that overflowed with a harvest so bountiful that one passerby stopped and let out a low whistle.

"Mind you're whistling at those ears of corn, and not my wife, Goodman Wallace," said Jeremiah giving the old gent a good-natured handshake. Aiden and Thomas had each pulled a couple of baskets down from the wagon, allowing Jeremiah to jump up in the space they had come to town in. Standing tall over the crowd, Jeremiah shot his wife a quick wink and then went to work.

"Come one, come all and get yourselves some of the finest bounty in all of Pioneer Vale, courtesy of Carmichael Farms!" Jeremiah's deep voice boomed throughout the square turning heads from all corners of the market plaza. Curious bystanders stepped closer and upon seeing the quality of Jeremiah's wares, started reaching for their coins.

The crowd came and went throughout the day. Bushels and bags were bought up as the Market Day wore on. Whether the townsfolk purchased only a few ears of corn, a handful of carrots, or negotiated contracts for larger deliveries in the future, money continued falling into their hands and the coin pouches that Jeremiah and Anne-Marie wore around their waists. As he continued to draw the crowd in with his bellowing voice and easygoing salesmanship, Anne-Marie shrewdly finalized deals with local residents. Piles of coins were cheerfully given to the amicable husband and wife team.

As the selling day drew to a close, they sat in the back of the now nearly empty wagon and counted out their take for the day. They dropped a large number of coins into a single pouch, and with a smile and a quick kiss to his wife, Jeremiah drew the drawstring tight. Anne-Marie scooped the remaining pile into a separate bag as he jumped down from the wagon and scanned the dwindling crowd. His grin widened when he spotted his quarry.

"What fortunate timing, gentlemen," Jeremiah called loudly as he walked up to Preston Mathers. The moneylender stood in conversation with Jordan Lucas, the town magistrate. Jeremiah ignored the scowls of the two men he had interrupted. "It just so happens that I am in need of both of you at this very moment." He glanced around the square relieved that there were still several townsfolk standing nearby.

"As you both know, the term of the loan that my father had secured from Goodman Mathers nears its due date. I am overjoyed to announce, and in front of so many of our close friends," he said, waving a hand at the growing crowd of farmers to whom he was acquainted, "that I hereby settle all accounts with my proceeds from today's sales." Jeremiah placed the large bag of coins in Preston's hand. As he did so, all pretense of civility dropped suddenly from his face and was replaced by a rarely seen mask of cold hatred.

"Carmichael Farms now undeniably belongs to my family from this day forward," he said. Preston glared at Jeremiah, but as he opened his mouth to retort, Abel Harmon, one of the neighboring farmers who stood in the crowd spoke first.

"Here, here. I bear witness to the close of this deal. Make it so, Magistrate."

Lucas glanced nervously from Mathers to Jeremiah, and back. "Well, yes, of course. If all is in order. We'll need to verify the count, of course, and there are papers that will need written up...."

"There's no need to count it," said Jeremiah still locking his icy glare on Mathers. "You know damn well that every coin I owe is in that bag. The full sum of the account. I want the word here and now that our business is done."

Preston tried to return Jeremiah's malice in equal measure but found the younger man's will far stronger than his own. He took a half step back as he felt the weight of the stares from Harmon and the other gathered farmers bearing down on him.

"He's right, Jordan. Master Carmichael has never given anyone here reason to question his word." He cleared his throat and tucked the coin pouch into the inner pocket of his coat. "Our dealings are concluded. The terms satisfied. Make it so," he snapped to Lucas as he spun on his heel and stormed away.

Cheers erupted from the crowd. Jeremiah found himself bombarded by slaps to his back and firm handshakes from all sides. Anne-Marie pushed her way through the gathered crowd and threw her arms around his neck, and kissed him fiercely. Jeremiah lifted her in the air by the waist and spun her around in a circle, joining her in both laughter and tears of joy.

"We did it," she shouted, grinning from ear to ear.

"Did you ever doubt us?" He hugged her tightly and then reached out to ruffle the hair on Thomas and Aiden's heads as the boys elbowed their way to their parents' side. "Boys, tonight we celebrate!"

"Can we eat at the Huntsman?" said Aiden referring to the finest public house in town. "It's been a long time since we got one of Dorothea's meat pies, Da."

"Too long indeed, son, and I'll want a mug of Marcus' select stock ale to wash it down with," said Jeremiah. He gently shoved the boys towards their wagon where they secured it for the evening, and then the Carmichael Family headed up the street to the Hirsute Huntsman.

*   *   *

Marcus Brenner sported a wavy salt and pepper beard that hung down to his waist. Braids tied in intricate knots and dyed in various hues draped down his back and shoulders. His wife, Dorothea, by contrast, wore her hair shaved close to her scalp. She was but a slip of a woman standing beside her bear of a husband, but mighty Marcus yielded to her authority in the Huntsman.

"I bring in the game for the cooking pot, and pour the ale," Marcus was fond of saying, "but Dorothea runs the place."

The walls of the Huntsman were decorated with trophies from Marcus' greatest hunts. Deer, bear, and even a moose overlooked the ever festive common room. Marcus' prowess as a hunter had helped feed the town in its early days and supplemented many a family during the cold winter months. Musicians played a merry tune in the corner, while patrons whirled and danced, occasionally tossing a few coins into the basket at their feet. Raucous laughter filled the place as a jester capered, juggled, and made lewd suggestions towards Marcus' daughters who helped serve the guests.

The smell of food from the kitchen filled the air. Most notably was the smell of Dorothea's legendary spiced meat pies. She closely and jealously guarded her private recipe of seasonings that no one had ever been able to duplicate no matter how hard they studied the herbs that grew in her small garden behind the building. Regardless of the type of game Marcus brought home, Dorothea knew just how to bring out the very best flavors from the meat.

Jeremiah whirled Anne-Marie from the dance floor and spun his wife into her seat beside Aiden. He plopped down on the bench beside Thomas, ruffling the boy's hair as he sat down. Abel Harmon stumbled up to their table, swaying with obvious enjoyment of the evening's festivities.

"Pardon my interruption, folks, but I was wondering if you two would accept this humble sketch I did of your lovely family tonight while enjoying your company?" The old farmer handed Anne-Marie a thin sheet of paper that showed her, Jeremiah, Aiden, and Thomas sitting at their table, smiling and laughing over dinner. The artwork was as fine as the sketches of the old masters that she had seen in one of her uncle's books when she was a child.

"Abel, this is beautiful. I will treasure it always." She gave the old man a quick peck on the cheek. Abel smiled, blushed, and then tottered off to his own table. She looked at the smiling faces in the drawing and wondered if their lives would always seem this idyllic.

Jeremiah picked up his third mug of spiced ale and drained it at a gulp. He wiped foam from his beard, threw back his head and ripped loose a resounding belch that drew cheers and applause from some of the nearby patrons. Thomas let loose a far less resonant imitation of his father, but even that garnered a few huzzahs from the crowd.

"I have never understood that ceremony," said Anne-Marie with a rueful shake of her head. Her eyes sparkled, and her cheeks were flushed from dancing and the mug and a half that she had thrown back tonight with her husband. Aiden started to open his mouth, but shut it quickly and muffled himself when he saw his mother's reproachful glare.

"It's taken as a compliment to the house, Milady Carmichael." Marcus appeared at their table with a pitcher in hand and refilled their mugs. "A thunderous tribute to a fine meal!"

"It truly was," she replied raising her mug to the innkeeper. "I've already spoken to Dorothea about getting some of your stock to take home with us. I need to get you to add it to our bill for the evening."

"Tonight, my dear friends, your coins are no good here. However, should you find your way to leave behind half a bushel of those astonishing carrots and potatoes in my bin, I think we could call your bill for tonight well settled. I don't know how the two of you did it, but those were some of the finest crops I've seen brought to Market Day in many a year. Hell, make that ever!"

"Well, Marcus, my secret mirrors your own. I give full credit to my wife. She simply has a magic touch when it comes to gardening." Jeremiah drained his mug again and winked at Anne-Marie. His eyes were glassy and he swayed in his seat. Anne-Marie stiffened and dug her nails into Jeremiah's hand, but Marcus inadvertently stole away the crowd's attention.

"Next round is on the house," bellowed the big proprietor, "in honor of Carmichael Farm's welcome prosperity. May it last for generations to come!"

"To Carmichael Farms," roared the taproom's customers. Marcus, Dorothea, and their daughters all wended their way through the crowd, refilling mug after mug. The musicians tuned up and launched into a familiar melody, while the jester set his batons into motion in a dazzling display in the air. Everybody had a grand time.

In the dark corner farthest from the roaring fireplace, a solitary figure sat alone at a table, a cup of brandy untouched before him. Preston Mathers slowly raised his drink and drained it. "Magical touch, indeed," he chuckled to himself. He dropped a gold coin on the table and slipped un-noticed out the door and into the night.

CHAPTER 7
THROUGH THE WIDOW STONE – PRESENT DAY

"So what do I do?" asked Angelica. "Just touch the rock and then I become a witch? What if I get attacked as soon as I get over there? Don't suppose you have a magic wand I could take with me, or would that even cross over?"

Anne-Marie sighed. "The first lesson of the day, child, is knowing when to simply keep quiet and listen. The trip through the stone shows each new candidate something different. No other Firstborn has ever met with Shade as I did. All were instead greeted by one of the demon's minions who taunted and tempted them, trying to sway them to join Shade's cause. You will see horrific visions of possible futures. Do not take lightly anything that you are shown."

"Yeah, I got it. Scary movie stuff doesn't bother me anymore. If the big bad demon wolf hasn't been around for 300 years then how do you even know he's still a threat? Let's do this!" Angelica reached her hand towards the polished black stone slab. Anne-Marie's hand clamped around her wrist in a grip of iron before her fingers could brush the surface though.

"Angelica, hear me well. While the demon seeks only to frighten you, the nightmares you shall see are the phantoms of things that will come to pass if you fail to heed the warnings that you are given. Trust me when I tell you that these can become life-threatening to you or those you hold dear."

"Sheesh, Grandma. Melodrama much?" She yanked her arm from her ancestor's grip, but a blast of concussive force hurled across the clearing. She slammed to the ground and the breath exploded from her lungs as she skidded across the forest floor. A snarl crossed the young woman's face as she pushed herself away from the grass. "You bi-!" she started when her eyes fell upon her ancestor. For the first time, Angelica Brighton saw a true glimpse of Anne-Marie's full power.

The older woman stood bathed in lavender fire, like a miniature sun hovering in the glade. Waves of heat washed over the fallen girl as the radiance surrounding Anne-Marie grew blinding. Twin infernos raged in her eyes, as her long copper tresses whipped about in the swirling firestorm that surrounded the Guardian. Her face was a mask of pure fury, and at her throat, the amethyst pendant blazed in a conflagration of its own.

"The second lesson you are in dire need of, you foolish girl, is that I am not to be trifled with," said Anne-Marie, her voice crackling with explosive power. "You had better damn well respect and take seriously everything that we are trying to do here, or Shade will hang your ungrateful hide as a trophy in his hall!"

"What in the hell should I be grateful for?" Angelica screamed back. She struggled to her feet, shielding her eyes as she faced the witch. She stepped forward, undaunted by the ferocious display of unbridled magic that buffeted the clearing all around her. "You have stolen me away from everyone I have ever known or given a damn about and then tell me that I'm most likely going to die anyway at the hands of some boogeyman. I'm an eighteen-year-old high school student. I should be studying for math tests and reading dusty books written by people that you probably grew up with. I should be going to the mall with my friends to look at dresses for the winter formal, not stomping around the woods with my however many greats grandmother learning to fight demons!"

The blaze around Anne-Marie leaped higher, and her voice thundered across the clearing like a wildfire out of control. The branches of the trees nearby rattled and shook their leaves to the ground as if nature itself quaked with fear at the woman's might. The wash of heat staggered Angelica back one step, but she gritted her teeth, planted her back foot, and pushed two strides closer.

"Oh, you poor, stupid child. You are missing a school dance? I have lost more than I pray you shall ever have to endure! I must train you to stand against an eons-old evil entity so that you won't be forced to see everyone you've ever given a damn about ripped into bloody shreds! The only thing that has kept Shade from succeeding before now were the selfless sacrifices of this family time and time again. With each generation that has been born, I have dared to hope that this time I will have found the child that can actually defeat that cold-blooded animal rather than serving him yet another tragic loss."

The fires around Anne-Marie began to dim, and then flickered out altogether as the older woman's rage melted away. Angelica looked into her green eyes, watched as the steely glare softened and tears welled up. The older woman turned her back to the girl and faced the Widow Stone. Her hands hovered above the glassy surface, trembling as she studied the slab.

"I still hear their screams, Angelica. Every single night as I try to sleep, the tortured cries of every single child of my blood that I have lost in this damnable battle find me." She bowed her head and her shoulders began to quake. It took Angelica only a moment to realize that her mentor was sobbing.

"Grandmother," she said softly. She reached out and lightly touched Anne-Marie's elbow. When she turned Angelica saw not the fearsome Guardian of Pioneer Vale, but a simple woman wracked by sorrow over the loss of so many she loved.

"I don't want to lose you as I have lost all of the others, Angelica. I can't bear the thought of it." She took the girl's hands in her own and gently squeezed them. "I see so much of my younger self when I look at your face. Determined and resolute. You give me hope that maybe this time we have a real chance."

"I bet you say that to all the sacrificial lambs," said Angelica with a smile. "I am sorry. I never thought about how all these battles must have been for you watching so many descendants pass on. Even if you weren't around us as we grew up, I guess that still had to be painful for you."

Anne-Marie let go of her hands, rearranged her skirt and sat down on the grass. "What makes you think that I wasn't around? Angelica, dear, I have watched you from a distance for your entire life. You just didn't know I was there to look for me."

Angelica plopped down cross-legged beside her. The grass was dry and crunched beneath her. "What do you mean? Why wouldn't you introduce yourself if you knew we'd end up here together one day?" She gestured around the grove.

"Because I didn't want to influence the type of person you would grow into. Imagine if I had come to you when you were but a three-year-old toddler and placed such a terrible destiny into your upbringing. There's no way you could have developed into the young woman that you are now. You deserved the love and guidance of your parents, who are two incredible and remarkable people, by the way. Did you know that your father single-handedly defended an orphanage in the Gulf War? Or that your mother once saved a woman's life using CPR in a grocery store when she was perhaps a bit younger than you are now?"

"Really? I never knew that. Why didn't they ever tell me those stories?"

"Because that is who they are. Who you needed. Good folk both humble and generous. And, so you had to live your life on your own, develop your own personality and your own values through their examples before I could dare to step into your life and thrust such an overwhelming responsibility upon you."

"You could have pretended to just be some eccentric neighbor lady or something."

"Subtlety was rarely my strong suit. Or so Jeremiah used to tell me." A wistful smile crossed her face. "But I tell you truly, my child. I cheered from the stands when you won the state championship last year. I cried with you when your pet pig, Charlotte, died when you were ten years old, and it was I who made the tree fall between you and Old Man Danielson's pickup truck the day he nearly ran you over."

Angelica sat in a whirlwind of emotions as she recalled each instance. "We were always amazed by what an incredible coincidence that tree fall appeared to be."

"And she never jaywalked again." Anne-Marie laughed and wiped tears away from her cheeks. "There is no treasure of greater value to the Carmichaels than our own family. Nothing else matters"

Angelica nodded, and then rose up from the ground, brushing the dried bits of grass from her pants. "You're absolutely right." She offered her hand down to Anne-Marie and pulled the older woman to her own feet. "So how about we start this whole lesson over? Why don't you tell me again what to expect on the other side of this magic doorway, and let's figure out how we are going to go kick Shade's furry butt."

*   *   *

The foul stench of sulfur hit Angelica with her first breath in the Realm of Nightmares. She opened her eyes and gasped at the destruction that loomed all around her. Buildings were torn down to rubble. The air was full of greasy black smoke from cars that burned along the blasted streets. Carrion birds pecked at whatever bits remained on blackened bones that littered the road ahead. She coughed as swirling clouds of ash choked her. As she dusted the soot from her clothes she realized to her surprise, that unlike Anne-Marie's own experience, she was still dressed in the same faded blue jeans and hoodie that she had been wearing in the Widow Stone's grove.

"Guess I don't get the supernatural shopping trip," she muttered to herself.

Carefully, she stepped around a pile of bricks, giving a crow with bare patches where feathers should have been a wide berth. The diseased looking creature spread its wings and cawed at her with a gravelly squawk. Angelica whirled away as the animal plucked something gooey from the charred skull that it stood upon.

"This isn't real, this isn't real, this isn't real," she whispered. She walked down the road peering into the ruined buildings for any signs of life. There was an eerie familiarity to this place, but the devastation was so complete that she couldn't get her bearings. As Angelica turned the corner around a shattered brick building, a cry of anguish slipped from her as the dawn of recognition drove her to her knees.

The courtyard of Pioneer Vale High School stretched out like a battlefield before her. Sparking street lamps were torn from their concrete moorings along the lawn. A burning school bus was flipped on its roof in the horseshoe-shaped driveway. The charred corpses of the passengers who tried to escape through the windows screamed at her in eternal silence. The front wall of the old school that had once been a colonial fort was blown out and crumbling. The bronze statue of the Pioneer Valley Minuteman had been ripped from its pedestal and the face of the time-honored mascot had been melted and re-sculpted into the rictus grin of a skull.

"And along comes another would be Guardian," said a deep and echoing, yet bored, voice from behind her. Angelica spun around, startled by the sepulchral muttering.

A tall thin figure stood behind her dressed in a heavy black robe too large for the man's frame. His face was lost in the shadows of the robe's deep cowl. His hands, although gaunt, were perfectly human rather than the wolfish fur and claws that she had expected to see. He held them clasped together in front of his waist.

"Who are you?" she asked hesitantly. "You clearly aren't Shade." Angelica shivered as his resulting chuckle rose like the wind whistling through a tomb.

"Is that who she told you would be here to greet you, young one? Oh, rest assured, the old cur is about, but, no, I am not he."

Angelica drew herself to her full height, fists clenched at her sides. "OK, then I will ask you again. Who the hell are you? I know that none of this is real," she said, gesturing to the wasteland around them. She glared into the dark hood, seeing for the first time two dull red sparks where the eyes should be. "I'm not afraid of you."

The robed figure threw his head back and laughed again with that ominous hollow sound. "Of course you aren't. I'm hardly the one that you need to fear, girl. All of this," he said as he mimicked her gesture, "will come to pass because of the arrogance of your dear mentor."

"Anne-Marie? You expect me to believe that she would level the town? Not a chance."

"The town? Oh, don't be so small-minded, Guardian," he said with a sneer on the last word. "This is but the starting point of what will befall the entire world because of her audacity. The witch's thirst for power will ultimately lay waste to everything that you've ever known."

"This isn't her doing. Whatever you and the wolf try to throw at us, we'll stop you. Together, she and I will make sure that none of this ever happens. You, Shade, or any other scaly horror that tries to cross over to my world will be in for one hell of a fight."

"Such brave words coming from one who hasn't even managed so much as her first incantation." He walked towards her, idly kicking a rib cage like some macabre soccer ball, scattering the blackened bones in a cloud of ash. "I have heard your meaningless vow before, you know. Each champion of each generation that Anne-Marie Carmichael sends here tells me the same bold story, and with the same bravado." His voice dropped to a sinister hiss. He lifted his palm upwards and a skull floated from the ground to hover between them "And where are they now?" He snapped his fist closed and the skull crushed into powder, drifting back to the scorched asphalt.

Angelica swallowed hard but still met his red eyes without flinching. "Maybe the better question is where are you still? Seems to me that you and Team Fleabag still haven't found your way out through the portal yet. You seem pretty cozy trapped here in this little hellhole."

"And why do you think that is? Do you think we have been repeatedly struck down in one terrible battle after another?" The robed man waved his hand, creating a swirl of blue-black smoke that drifted across the scattered bones on the ground. He spun his fingers slowly into a twisting pattern, ending with a clenched fist. The bones drew together to fashion a grisly throne which he sat upon. "I assure you that we are not held at bay because of the overshadowing power of the Guardians, child."

"She and the Firstborns beat you. They kept you imprisoned here."

"Has she graced you yet with the boasts of 'the power in the blood of the Firsts'? We remain here because Anne-Marie Carmichael personally sacrificed those of her own bloodline to keep the gate sealed, and she will undoubtedly not hesitate to end you when the time comes." He grasped the knobby protrusions of bone on the armrests of his seat and leaned forward. "And it will come. When you return to your world, Angelica Brighton, ask the Witch of Pioneer Vale exactly how her past apprentices have met their respective ends. Let's see who among us is actually telling you the truth. Once your power is unlocked, Guardian," he said with mockery in his voice, "your blood will be infused with the magic necessary to restore the seals of the crystal prison, and she will end your life to preserve her own. She fears Shade and knows that only by giving up those from her own lineage can she stay free of his vengeance."

"Liar," Angelica shouted. In her rage, the young woman felt a rising surge of energy inside of her. The world around her blurred for a moment then refocused. She felt a shock run through her that reminded her of crossing through the gateway at the fireplace. "Anne-Marie would never do that. You are trying to make me doubt her. You hope to drive us apart and weaken us, but I'm here to tell you that it won't work! I swear, I will stand and fight at her side!" Tears streamed down her cheeks, and again a wave of pure force coursed through her frame, dropping her to one knee. She looked at her hand and saw arcs of blue-white lightning dancing between her fingertips. The tiny hairs on her forearms stood on end.

The robed figure lifted his arms once more, and a swirling black cloud formed around the man's hands. An icy wind howled through the courtyard, echoing with the low moans of suffering souls. To her left, the mangled, twisted limbs of a fallen body stirred. With creaks and pops, the decaying joints worked their way back into place, and the corpse slowly pushed itself up from the ground. Across the wasted lawn, the bodies of fallen classmates and teachers, townsfolk and friends all began to stir.

"Your time will come to choose a side, Angelica. The Guardians cannot hold back the Father of Nightmares forever. The barrier between our worlds is weakening. Join Shade and defeat Anne-Marie before she takes your life and you end up here!"

"I will never serve Shade," Angelica shouted over the rising moans of the dead. Lightning crackled along her forearms now, the storm in the skies overhead flashing with fierce intensity. She felt power sweeping through her body with every breath. "I won't let this happen," she said through gritted teeth.

"Ask her for the truth, and when next you and I shall meet, I think you will find your outlook vastly different." The undead shuffled closer and closer to her. Glazed eyes looked blankly into her own as cold fingers reached out for her.

Angelica threw back her head and screamed into the night as a bolt of lightning rained down upon her from the dark clouds above. For one brief moment, she felt a rush of agony, unlike any pain she had ever experienced before. Every nerve ignited with the blast, every cell of her body infused with an elemental fury that raced through her body. The bolt flowed out in a crackling ring of power around her, blasting the nightmare creatures back to oblivion. The robed man, however, sat on his throne and laughed at her.

Lightning struck her once more and with one final wracking scream that echoed in her very soul, Angelica plunged into darkness.

CHAPTER 8
FIRST LESSONS – PRESENT DAY

A cool rag dabbed her forehead as Angelica opened her eyes. Her head pounded and her skin felt prickly as if thousands of sparks danced back and forth along her entire body. Her eyelids weighed a ton and she struggled to open them. Even the soft glow of the lavender balls of light that floated nearby caused her head to throb. The soft leather of a fine chaise cushioned her back and the down of a fleece blanket tickled her legs. Firewood crackled in the hearth close by. The dark wood shelves of Whisperwind's lab swam into focus, as a horrible smell dragged her from the depths of unconsciousness.

Anne-Marie sat on a stool at her side, concern etched on her face as she dunked a pungent washcloth back into a water basin on the side table. When she saw Angelica's eyes open, she sighed, as though she had been holding her breath for some time. The corners of her mouth curled up in relief as the younger girl stirred.

"You're awake!" she exclaimed.

"Yeah, back to the land of the living," Angelica said. "Literally." She shivered with the memory of the shuffling corpses from her nightmare. She tried to push herself up on her elbows, but the room decided to go topsy turvy with her attempt, and she fell back onto the soft pillow. "Although my head might beg to differ. What the hell is in that bowl? Extract of cow manure?"

"No I skipped the manure for this one," Anne-Marie said with a grin. "There's a dab of this, a pinch of that. Things that all the best witches' brews contain. Honestly, you're probably better off not knowing until you get your strength back."

"I'm sorry I asked."

Anne-Marie tucked an errant lock of her hair behind her ear. "I was so worried. You gave me quite a fright at the grove. None of the other Firstborns have ever reacted to their passage like you did."

"What do you mean? What happened to me? Judging from the way my head feels, I think it must have exploded and you scooped my brains back in."

Anne-Marie's grin grew into a warm broad smile. "Well, nothing that vile, but you floated about three feet off the ground and then crackled with lightning from head to toe. I assume that isn't something you do often?"

"Not that I've ever noticed." Angelica shook her head to clear the cobwebs. She finally looked up at the older woman's face. "So does this mean I'm a witch now?"

Anne-Marie's smile faded as quickly as it had come. "It's Guardian, not witch. And, no, not yet. You have been accepted by the Power that we all channel, but you need training to use it properly. This is a very dangerous time for you now. You are a raw open conduit and without guidance, you could accidentally cause as much harm as Shade and his minions. I won't ask about your time in his realm. What you saw was meant for you alone. It is part of your coming destiny, and it falls on you to interpret how to prevent what you were shown from manifesting."

Angelica glanced away and bit her lip. "Someone did meet me there, but he never gave his name. It wasn't Shade though, or if it was him, then he was disguised and not at all how you described him. I saw a man in a black robe with a big hood. He kept his face hidden except for his two glowing red eyes. He had a deep and echo-ey voice like he was speaking from inside a tunnel. Or maybe from beyond the grave. Any idea who he was?"

Anne-Marie stood and gathered up the rag and water basin. She walked over to the great table with her head hung low, and set the bowl on the stone top. Angelica saw the Guardian's hands tremble. "Who he is shall be a lesson for another day. Let me just say that he is the demon's favored lieutenant and I know him far too well. He is crafty and very dangerous. His fate became entangled with our own long ago."

Angelica sat up on the side of the chaise. Her mind raced, but she knew she had to ask the question that burned inside of her. "He told me to ask you for the truth of what happened to all of the Firstborns. About how they all died."

Anne-Marie's proud bearing broke and the iron in her stance seemed to melt away. She leaned her elbows on the tabletop and dropped her head into her hands. She rubbed her face and temples before she looked back up, then launched the basin across the room with a blast of fire. "What would you like to hear? That I made some heroic choice to prevent Shade from entering this world?"

"Did you kill them yourself?"

Anne-Marie sighed. "Yes. For the sake of a world that doesn't even realize the danger it is in, I slammed the portal to Shade's world shut with the blood of my own family."

Silence hung between the two women as Angelica stared at her teacher. A log popped in the fireplace and broke the stillness.

"And do you plan the same thing for me?"

Anne-Marie looked at the girl, locking Angelica's stare with her own. Tears welled up in the older woman's eyes. "It was never planned for any of them. Shade's influence and power corrupted them. He fed them full of lies until they were swayed to his bidding. I wish it made it sound nobler to tell you that I acted in self-defense, but in the end, the simple truth is that I had to destroy my own family to keep our world safe."

"My vision was horrible. There was so much death."

Anne-Marie nodded. "This is how Shade manipulates those he preys upon. He will find what you fear the most, and use that to weaken your resolve."

"But I just told you that I didn't see Shade. He wasn't there."

"He was, after a fashion. The old wolf is never far from us. He always lurks close at hand. He's the shape just outside the corner of your eye that disappears when you look his way. Shade creates nightmares, and makes his moves through his servants."

"Is what I saw set in stone? Will the town be destroyed if we fail to stop him?"

"No, my dear." Angelica sighed with relief. "It will be far worse."

The young woman scowled. "You know that you aren't exactly boosting my confidence here, right? If I refuse to help, he breaks loose and destroys existence. If I help and we lose, he breaks loose and destroys existence."

"Then let me propose option three. You choose to help and we defeat him together."

"The odds sound pretty stacked against us. Or at least, stacked against me surviving this whole thing."

Anne-Marie walked back over and put her hand on Angelica's shoulder. "There is something different this time, and even I know not what to make of it. None of the others have ever displayed a signature like yours and mine before. I have seen sparkling lights, musical chimes, and once even a baby powder fragrance. You are the first and only student of mine to ever manifest an elemental force like my own."

"Meaning what?"

"Meaning that you possess a warrior's spirit. There is an untold strength in you, child. I have more confidence in your ability to stand against Shade than any other descendant of mine. It means that you just might have what it takes to become a true Guardian."

Angelica thought on Anne-Marie's words for a moment. "So what do I need to learn first? Will you teach me how to throw a lightning bolt?"

Anne-Marie smirked. "Let's start with how to quench a flame."

* * *

Thunder rolled across the sky as sheets of lightning cascaded all around Angelica. She reveled in the power that coursed through her body as she channeled the energy around her. Blue-white electricity erupted into the air as she grasped the snaking tendrils of magic that Anne-Marie had taught her to take hold of and draw into herself. The older woman stood close by, watching her student from the protection of her own shielding globe of purple flame, safe from harm as lightning bounced off the shell. The Guardian gave a nod to her protégé, and Angelica released the magical conduit.

"Well done," exclaimed Anne-Marie. "You have a natural inclination for harnessing our power. That is a very important first step. Now you must learn to shape those forces to do your bidding, or else you are nothing more than an open faucet spilling magical energy all over everything."

Angelica opened her mouth to reply when a wave of dizziness overtook her. She staggered and collapsed on the ground. Her head hammered and blood ran from her nose. "I tried too much. I wasn't ready for that lightning storm."

"Back on your feet, girl," said Anne-Marie. "Your lesson isn't finished yet."

"Give me a second to clear my head. Why does being a champion for the forces of good in the universe hurt so much? They need a better recruitment plan. In the meantime, how do I conjure up some aspirin? I think I'm going to throw up." She flopped back onto the grass when the hairs on her arms stood up. Her senses screamed as the air around her sizzled, and Angelica threw herself to one side just as a purple fireball slammed into the ground at her feet.

"No time to nap, child," said Anne-Marie. The elder woman lightly lobbed a second fireball from hand to hand and then pulled her arm back to throw.

"What are you doing? You could have barbequed me," shouted Angelica. She rolled to her feet and just barely dodged the second missile as it flew past her head.

"Do you believe that Shade will stand idly by waiting as you catch your breath? He will push you to your limits and you must always be ready to defend yourself." She brought her hand up swiftly and the ground upon which Angelica stood bucked and sent her sprawling. The girl kept her wits about her just enough to see Anne-Marie still in motion, winding up for yet another throw.

"I'm not ready, though," she screamed. "How do I protect myself?" She threw herself flat on the ground as flames washed across her back.

"Use the magic," Anne-Marie shouted back. "You can feel the energy around you. Draw it into you and shape it to your needs!" She brought her hands together then slowly drew them apart creating a sword of fire between her hands. She grabbed the fiery hilt and brought the blade down in an arc towards Angelica.

The younger girl's head thrummed as if a clarion call had gone off. As the sword of flame descended, energy rippled through Angelica's frame, and she crossed her arms in front of her face. A shield of pure lightning sprang into place and blocked the weapon's stroke just short of her forearms. Anne-Marie jumped back, dispelled her magic, and clapped her hands together.

"You did it! Just as I hoped you would. Oh, Angelica, your instincts called the Guardian's might to defend yourself. The only thing that you could have done better was to counter-attack after the block, but that too will come with practice."

Angelica dropped her shield, letting it dissipate in a shower of sparks. "Are you crazy? You could have killed me. What if I hadn't figured out how to make that shield? You would have cut me in half."

"But I didn't. Shade has centuries of tricks up his sleeve, and he will not allow you to strategize about your next move. Nor must you give him an equal chance to do so. You need to act and react on instinct. Plan your next weapon or shield before the previous one has even been brought to bear."

"Guess the attack before I even know it's there? So now I have to look into the future too? What other impossible feats do I need to master before the damn crystal shatters?"

"You think what we do is impossible? My dear Angelica, you just created a shield of electricity from the simple static in the air. Moments ago, you called forth sheets of lightning from the heavens that danced around you like children around a maypole. You have already done the impossible."

"You are supposed to teach me this stuff so I don't end up getting ripped apart."

"I first need to see what you can manage on your own. Angelica, don't be so upset. Feel proud for you have done remarkably well. You have the knack already. We can now shape that and turn you into a weapon that Shade will fear. Then together we can defeat him once and for all."

"I am not just a tool for you to wage a war with," Angelica shouted. A wellspring of energy flowed through her from the ground up to her arms and she leveled a two-handed blast of lightning at Anne-Marie. The older woman raised a wall of flames between them that absorbed the incoming blasts then she swept her arm to one side and disrupted the electrical assault.

Angelica acted out of blind rage. She sent a current into the earth and commanded the roots and vines to grapple Anne-Marie's legs. As the Guardian looked down, Angelica dragged another column of lightning from the sky and hammered it down upon the older woman. Blinding flashes of white and purple warred with one another in the space where the elder woman stood. So intense was the light that Angelica had to turn away. The lightning pillar vanished as she lost her focus and connection to the magic. When the smoke cleared, a charred circle was all that remained where Anne-Marie had been.

"Oh my God, what have I done?" breathed Angelica. The use of so powerful a blast dropped her to her knees and the wash of heat from the strike flattened her to the ground. Blood from her nose spattered the grass. "Anne-Marie," she cried out before she fell face-first into the dirt.

A ring of purple fire appeared in midair, and Anne-Marie tumbled out of the void beyond. Her face was rosy with faint burns, soot and soil covered her clothes, and her hair stood out in all directions. Wisps of smoke rose from her body. She dropped to the ground beside her granddaughter, gasping for breath. She gently brushed a strand of Angelica's hair from the girl's eyes, and with her thumb, she wiped a fresh trickle of blood from the younger woman's nose.

"Do you now believe in the impossible?" she asked. She fell back onto the grass and shook with weary laughter. Angelica watched for a moment and then joined in.

"I thought I had disintegrated you," she finally squeaked out.

"Oh, you nearly did. If I had fought against the pull of the ground instead of letting it drag me down into it, you might have found yourself without a teacher." Anne-Marie reached over and squeezed Angelica's hand. "You aren't after my job so soon are you?"

"Are you kidding? Your insurance plan sucks and there doesn't appear to be a retirement plan in the witch industry." She saw the flash of a frown on her mentor's face. "I'm sorry. This is just so frustrating."

"Don't apologize. You did exactly what I hoped you would do, although," she went on with a roll of her eyes, "I never anticipated that you would prove so efficient."

"I don't even know what I am doing. Everything is just a reaction."

"Study your guide book. Entire realms of magical tricks and effects have been discovered for you already. Knowing how to create such works in the heat of the battle could save your life. There won't always be time to plot out your next attack, so you better have something in mind that you can hurl at a moment's notice. Lightning and fire may not always be the right answer to winning a bout."

"My legs feel like rubber right now. If I get weaker the longer a fight goes on, am I better off trying to hit hard right away, or use more smaller strikes first?"

"There isn't a clear answer for that. Lashing out at full strength would work fine if your opponent is unprepared, but someone trained in magical combat might be able to block your first attack and then leave you with shaky defenses. Size up your opponent first. Just as you did with me, use a small distraction and then hit with the more powerful blow when they are unaware."

"Sucker punch them when I get the chance? Grandmother, I didn't know that you could fight so dirty."

The two women shared a heartfelt laugh. Aches and groans were felt by both women as they helped one another get up, and headed back down the trail towards Whisperwind.

"Angelica, dear? May I give you one final lesson for today?"

"Sure. What is it?"

"Don't ever try to disintegrate me again." Anne-Marie shot her a wry smile.

"I can't make any promises," said Angelica with a grin of her own.

CHAPTER 9
UNCAGED! – PRESENT DAY

Angelica woke with a start. The scant moonlight peeked into her bedroom through the curtained window throwing a thin blade of light across the bedroom carpet. She shivered despite how warm the room felt. She spotted her blanket on the floor where she must have kicked it off while she slept.

The hairs on the back of her neck stood on end, and the faint glow of electricity ran unbidden along her fingertips. A murmuring tickled the back of her mind as the Whisper of the Elder awoke within her. She grabbed her long gray sweater from the hook on the back of her bedroom door, slid her bare feet into her slippers, and padded down the hallway. She paused at Anne-Marie's chamber door, wondering if her ancestor even had to sleep anymore. *Probably just hangs upside down from the rafters,* she mused to herself. She raised her hand to knock, but after this afternoon's lesson, she decided that she didn't want to disturb her teacher unless she absolutely had to.

Angelica instead made her way down to the common room. The embers in the fireplace were the only light piercing the gloom and she banged her toe on the footstool at the end of Anne-Marie's chaise.

"We need to speak, child," said a whispery voice in her mind.

Angelica's senses roared at the magical intrusion. Her power blossomed, and a crackling shroud enveloped her. Ominous shadows danced around the room mocking her with phantom laughter. Her temples throbbed suddenly as she renewed her connection with the newfound power that coursed through her entire body, setting every nerve alight with unearthly energy. As a clawed hand of darkness stretched forward, Angelica made a pirouette, borne aloft from the magic coursing through her and released a sizzling bolt of lightning. The shadowy laughter turned to a howl of pain and faded away.

"Who are you?" she growled to the darkness. "And where are you?"

"We've met already, child. Beyond the Widow Stone. In the wasteland of the Realm of Nightmares. As to where I am, you know the answer to that question as well. Come to me, young one, and let me dispel more of the lies and misconceptions that the witch has deluded you with."

Angelica felt the unseen presence withdraw from her thoughts, and her mystically augmented senses pulled her attention toward the fireplace. She retraced Anne-Marie's gestures that had opened the secret gateway earlier and gasped as the runic spiral appeared on the stone glowing with her own telltale signature that now seemed to accompany her every action. The section of hearth once again disappeared, this time in a shower of sparks rather than the lavender fires of her teacher.

Is the barrier gone? Was the crystal already broken? Had Shade found a backdoor into their world? Angelica knew that Anne-Marie would be furious with her if she went into the Holding Chamber alone, but she feared that there was no time to waste. Plus, the robed figure from the nightmare world had told her the truth about Anne-Marie's willingness to sacrifice the previous Firstborns. What other secrets was the witch hiding?

Angelica checked her shield of lightning and wrapped it around herself like a blanket. Looking over her shoulder to make sure that Anne-Marie hadn't heard her, she stepped through the dimensional gateway.

*　　*　　*

Anne-Marie bolted upright in bed with a cry of terror on her lips. A chill ran through her that she hadn't felt in generations. The fleeting images of the town of Pioneer Vale in ruins slowly faded from her hazy brain.

It was happening already, she thought to herself. Shade was already on the prowl.

She threw off her covers and, on a cushion of fire, summoned her shawl to her hand from where it hung on the bedpost. She rushed to her bedroom door, but found it jammed, bound shut by a force that she hadn't sensed in decades.

Anne-Marie focused on the doorway and saw the tendrils of magic writhing around the frame. She knew this binding spell all too well though for it was virtually the same as the one that she had placed on the Holding Chamber. She raised a shield of flame around her, and then gently pushed at the swirling black energy. The magic triggered and released the wards in a backlash of teeth-rattling power. The shockwave of the explosion blew Anne-Marie's door from the hinges and staggered the Guardian even from behind the protection of her fiery barrier.

She stepped over the debris and spared a glance down the hallway. She shivered when she saw that Angelica's bedroom door already stood open.

Her blood ran colder still when sensed that the hidden gateway behind the fireplace stood open as well.

"Oh, no, dear Angelica," she whispered. "What are you doing?" The girl wasn't ready yet. Anne-Marie knew she had to stop her protégé before something terrible happened. She dashed down the stairs two at a time, racing towards the common room, praying all the while that she wasn't too late.

*   *   *

The wards on the door to the Holding Chamber fell before her. She had read that particular page in the journal of magic effects earlier and had learned the key to disrupting the energy flow. The door to the room swung open and the crystal's sickly gleam pulsed rapidly as if happy to see her as Angelica entered. A wave of nausea assaulted her but she fought back the urge to retch.

"I'm here," she said aloud. "Now what is it that you want from me? Is this so you can fill my head with more lies about Anne-Marie's motives?"

"I seek to open your eyes to the truth of her craftiness," said the whispery voice in her head. *"That witch has you fooled if you think for one moment that she strives to save the world. She needs you to maintain her immortality, child! She can only do so with the life-force of the Firstborns! She will destroy you, young one, just as she has done to so many who have walked this path before you."*

"So I should throw in with you and the wolf because you two have nothing but good intentions?" Sarcasm dripped from Angelica's voice. "Why should I believe a single thing you say? You are clearly just trying to make me distrust her. Divide and conquer, right?"

"Of the two of us, who has told you the truth thus far? Only when you confronted her as I asked you to at our last encounter did she confess to sacrificing your predecessors."

"The others gave their lives to keep you imprisoned. If they could have found a way to destroy you before now, then we wouldn't be having this conversation."

"You misunderstand her ambitions. Destruction is not what she seeks. She seeks to regain that which was lost to her so long ago. The others died so that she could continue her fruitless search. Her own obsession is the reason the others fell. She remains

unchecked in her power here! She stole the life force from their bodies only to continue her foolish quest."

"She did it to keep you from breaking into our world. To keep you from turning Pioneer Vale into what I saw in my vision. The Guardians may not have ended your threat completely, but she knew that she could at least keep you trapped away!"

"How can you so blindly believe that she is so full of kindness and altruism? Look at her! The woman is centuries old, but uses her power to maintain her youth and beauty! To satisfy her vanity! Oh, I can sense that you have stumbled upon her moonlight rejuvenations. Where do you think she finds the power to reverse the effects of time itself? It comes from the lives of her descendants, child, and when she has decided that she has no more use for you then your soul shall join with the others who have all perished in this same damnable cell!"

"Shut up," Angelica shouted. "You're trying to trick me." Crackles of lightning flashed between her fingers. Thunder boomed when she clenched her fists.

"I am trying to save you," came the whispery hiss. *"If you are too naive to believe me, then see for yourself what awaits you if you place such blind trust in her. Look upon the consequences of those who failed to heed my warning about your precious Witch of Pioneer Vale!"*

An apparition dressed in colonial garb materialized in front of her. He held out his hands, his stance clearly showing him in the midst of a magical battle. Twinkling motes of light spun around his head, but his expression was one of anger and hurt. Betrayal filled his eyes His mouth opened in a silent scream as a pillar of lavender flame engulfed him. Angelica screamed with him as his flesh melted away from his face. A blackened skull fell to the ground a moment later and vanished in a puff of greasy black smoke.

"One who arrived before you whose skills failed to impress your grandmother," came the harsh whisper in her head. *"Oh, but wait. We have more."*

"No, please," Angelica said as she choked back a sob. "Don't show me another one." Arcs of lightning raced up and down her forearms.

Despite her plea, the figure of a young woman in a Victorian Age dress stood before Angelica, crouched and determined to fight something unseen near her. Her hair whipped out behind her as an unseen gale-force wind assaulted her. The poor girl tried to push forward, but she staggered under the onslaught. Angelica reached out, but her hands passed through the spectral image as a phantom tornado laced with streaks of purple fire lifted the young woman from the floor. The girl was battered against the walls of the Holding Chamber, each brutal strike smashing teeth and bone. The tornado finally slammed her headfirst into the pillar with the crystal. Broken and bloody, the ghost fell to the floor, seeing through Angelica with lifeless eyes.

"Let's have a look at one last, shall we?" whispered her tormentor. *"This was one of my personal favorites. I'd wager that you have never had the misfortune to see someone literally turned inside out, have you?"* A dark chuckle filled Angelica's ears. She tried to close out the horrible laughter. The lightning she channeled now surrounded her in a globe of white-hot power.

"All of this is because of her lies. All of this suffering, all of these lost lives are because of her, and if you do not heed my warning then she will have you next!"

"Enough," screamed Angelica. She lunged towards the crystal and released a double-fisted blast of electrical devastation. She felt the roar of power blast through her, hammering at the gem that floated above the pillar. Little by little, the sickly pulsing stone blackened then went dark.

Angelica cut off her blast with a howl of rage. The crystal still floated but dripped as if it were candle wax from the barrage of raging energy that had poured over it. Without warning, a deafening crack echoed through the chamber and the crystal exploded into a thousand tiny shards.

She dropped to the floor as dozens of tiny stings peppered her skin from the slivers that hurtled through the air. The light in the chamber dimmed with the crystal's destruction and the few candles that remained lit cast long shapes across the walls and floor. As Angelica shielded her face away from the flying fragments, a monstrous shadow formed on the wall.

The dark fingers ended in wicked claws, and the joints of the shape's legs bent backward like that of an animal. The shape threw back its head, and an ear-splitting roar filled the tiny room. Angelica rolled away from where she had fallen but paused when she saw the source of the fearsome image.

Instead of anything from a lupine nightmare, she saw the now-familiar slim figure draped in his black robe rise out of the inky cloud of smoke. Thin human fingers reached up and pulled back the cowl, revealing to Angelica for the first time, the face of her foe from Shade's nightmare world.

His eyes were like blue ice, pale and cold, but tinged with a dull red glow around the lids. Long greasy auburn hair framed his pale and gaunt face, which seemed little more than skin stretched over bone. A cruel grin exposed yellow teeth behind thin lips enshrouded within a ragged beard.

"Oh, my! It feels so good to be out of that holding pen at last." He leaned back, bones cracking and popping with his sickening stretch. He sighed happily and then turned back to Angelica. "Before I go, however, maybe I've time for a little snack." His grin turned vicious, resembling the snarl of a wolf. The stench of rot and decay carried on his breath towards the young woman. As he stepped closer, swirls of black smoke followed in his wake and Angelica could feel the temperature in the room plunge as he reached his hand toward her.

"Get back," Angelica shouted as she threw another lightning bolt at the approaching figure. A greasy black cloud leaped up between them and sent the blast ricocheting into the stone wall.

"You'll have to do far better than that, young one. I offered you the chance to survive the coming darkness, but you threw your lot in with the witch. This will not end well for you." His laughter was savage and mocking.

Angelica tried to stand but fell back against the floor. She was too weak from practice earlier today and drained even further by the blasts she had just released. She watched in horror as her foe's fingers became hooked claws, and a black shadow began to pulse about his hand. As he approached, she knew that his touch would mean her death.

A blast of purple fire slammed into his chest just before his fingers could close on her arm, hurling him away from her. Angelica looked over her shoulder to see Anne-Marie standing in the doorway of the Holding Chamber wreathed in lavender flame.

"Don't you dare touch her," she commanded. She stepped forward, her bare feet heedless of the shattered crystal fragments that littered the stone floor and placed herself between Angelica and the intruder. The pale man scrambled backward across the floor where he had been thrown. There was fear in his eyes as Anne-Marie held her hands between them.

"Planning to keep her for yourself, witch?" he growled. His toothy grin was unsettling, leering even. "I'd love to stay and chat, but fear not," he said with a sneer. "We'll be seeing each other soon enough, *Mother.*" An icy wind howled through the room as a swirling black portal opened behind him. The vortex dragged him into its depths and then slammed shut before Anne-Marie could react.

Anne-Marie quenched the fire that raged around her and knelt beside the younger woman. "Are you ok? Did he hurt you?"

"No, but only because you showed up when you did." Hot tears welled up in Angelica's eyes. "Oh, God. What have I done? I was so stupid. He kept showing me these horrible scenes, and I lost control. I wanted to stop him somehow, but instead, I let loose the monster. Please forgive me."

"Hush with that now, my dear. What's done is done and will have to be dealt with." Anne-Marie pulled her close and held her tenderly, rocking her gently while Angelica sobbed. The girl was shocked when she realized that the Guardian's tears mingled with her own. She looked up into Anne-Marie's face and saw overwhelming compassion and love.

"He wanted me to doubt you. Tried to paint you as the real threat."

"That is his game. Deception and misdirection. What you faced was but a shell of what he will become. He is weak at the moment, but his power will grow." Anne-Marie stood up and pulled Angelica from the floor. "We must prepare ourselves to face him, and we now will need to move sooner than expected. Let's go back upstairs and get you cleaned up," said Anne -Marie as she ushered the girl towards the doorway. Angelica took one last look at the shattered crystal prison and shivered.

"He called you Mother," she said. "Are you telling me that was…?"

"The monster trapped in the crystal and whom you met in the nightmare realm was my son, Aiden. He was corrupted by Shade when he was but a young man, and my first student."

"I failed you," Angelica said. "I didn't listen and now we're in serious trouble, aren't we?"

"My child," Anne-Marie said, "you have no idea just how much danger we are all in now."

CHAPTER 10
DEEPER THREATS - 1671

Parson Corbin Reynolds silently stepped onto the darkened porch and closed the door behind him as softly as he could manage. He heard the bolt on the other side slide into place as he took his leave. He closed his eyes and placed his fingertips on the wood that separated him from the beauty on the other side. He quickly glanced up and down the town street, although he knew that anyone about at this late hour was the very sort he cautioned his congregation against.

As he straightened his cravat and stepped off the porch, his mind drifted to thoughts of auburn curls, rough kisses, and sweaty embraces. His heart pounded in his chest and he questioned not for the first time if the calling to which he practiced was not truly his place in this world. What if he were to renounce his station as the spiritual head of this town, make his feelings known to his paramour, and start over again? Where would he go, though, and what promise did he even have that she would come with him? Maybe he should just keep such flights of fancy in the back of his mind. He shook his head, dizzy with fatigue. After the exertion of tonight's 'tending the flock', he planned to sleep late on the morrow.

It had started so innocently. Young Madeline Pritchard had volunteered alongside so many other women of the town for various works of the church. She made food for community dinners, helped tend her sick neighbors, and minded the children of the town when called upon for help. She was liked and respected by all who knew her.

Madeline was unhappy though.

Corbin hadn't been terribly surprised when she showed up after church one day asking for a moment of his time. She had broken down in tears as she told him how disappointing her home life was. Horace Pritchard was kind and the man doted on his young bride, but at fifteen years her senior, they had no spark between them. There was little conversation when he was home, and too often she found herself alone while he was away on border patrols.

Reynolds had meant nothing more than to offer the sobbing woman some measure of comfort when he hugged her that day, but that small kindness had led to losing himself in her eyes. He had walked the streets of town for hours that first night before he had slipped through the shadows to her front door.

What had he hoped for? He was nothing special. He was tall and skinny with threadbare clothes that had once been of fine quality, but years of poverty had convinced his parishioners that he chose to live frugally. He kept his dirty blond hair tied back and he had been told that the steely blue of his eyes could make Old Scratch himself back away when Reynolds was in the pulpit.

When he had stood at her door and lightly rapped upon it, there had been no hesitation on her part, and she had let him inside without question. One kiss followed another and before he could stop himself he had lost himself to her charms, and she was swept away by his passion.

Corbin started whistling one of his favorite hymns as he turned towards the shadowy pathways that he used whenever he visited her. He took two steps when the orange flare of a pipe flashed in front of him.

"It would appear that the Lord's work knows no rest," said a voice from the shadowy side of the road. Reynolds jumped at the sound and stumbled against a nearby hitching post. The stocky form of Preston

Mathers, a wicked grin plastered to his face, took shape out of the darkness. "Pray tell what salvation you set upon Goody Pritchard at this late hour? Especially while her husband is away safeguarding the town for the next fortnight. Her soul must be in dire peril for our town minister to risk so scandalous a visit."

"Preston, I was…that is, she needed,…" Reynolds stammered.

"Parson, please. You've no need to explain yourself to me. I was a young man once and I too have enjoyed the pleasure of a clandestine tryst."

"Preston, I implore you," Corbin said as he looked up and down the street. "Please keep this transgression of mine in your confidence. I ask not for my own sake, but for the reputation of the Pritchard family. There is no need to sully their name because of my own weaknesses."

"Oh, Corbin. Of course, you can have my confidence. Have I not always been charitable to the growth and works of Pioneer Vale?" Preston draped his arm over the preacher's shoulder and drew him towards the darker side of the street.

Reynolds stiffened and slipped away from Preston's clutches. "You own most of the works of the town and are well paid in interest and rent. I don't know that there is much about you that would be mistaken for charity."

"You stand in my good graces, for now, sir. Let us simply say there is some charity in that."

"Until you have no further need to hold your tongue?"

"I deal in favors, Corbin. Usually centered around money lending, but certainly not to the exclusion of that. I, for the time being, shall do you the favor of keeping my knowledge of your dealings to myself. One day, however, I shall ask a favor in return. Then our slates will be cleared up."

"I suspect coercion, rather than favors, and certainly not in charity, Mathers."

"Call it what you will. Do we have an understanding, Parson, or shall I have an unwelcome announcement to bring before the elders at the next town council meeting?"

The minister clenched his fists and glared at Preston. He wanted nothing more than to strike the smug grin off of the man's pudgy face, but he knew that the moneylender had him cornered. How long would he last in town as the spiritual leader if he was discovered in a street brawl with one of the townsfolk, even one as mistrusted and disliked as Preston?

"Alright, Mathers. We have an understanding."

"Splendid choice, Corbin! Now, if I may give one last piece of advice, I suggest you head straight home and wash off the smell of this evening's festivities from your person. My confidence shall avail you nothing should anyone else catch wind of that particular scent of perfume that your Madeline always wears." Preston gave a curt nod of his head and walked off leaving Reynolds standing in the middle of the empty street, glaring at the back of the devil that walked away.

*   *   *

"What in the hell was that last night?" shouted Anne-Marie as she slammed a plate down on the table in front of her husband, bouncing his morning eggs into the air. "Jeremiah Carmichael, do you have any idea what so careless a comment could bring down on us? Magic touch? I can't even understand myself how I accomplished what happened that night!"

Jeremiah's head throbbed and his stomach was doing cartwheels. The plate before him seemed to mock the way he was feeling. Anne-Marie had driven the wagon home from town last night while he snored away in the back with Thomas. Aiden had beamed with the prospect of riding up on the bench with his mother, holding the lantern so that she could see their way home along the forest road. This morning, Jeremiah found that the repercussions of one too many toasts to his newfound prosperity was purely punishing him, but not nearly as painful as his wife's yelling.

"Annie, no one heard anything other than a drunken fool rambling on. Do you think that an angry mob bearing torches is already marching up the road to grab us? We live among friends. People who know us and our family. There wasn't a soul there who begrudged us our good fortune yesterday."

"Then you didn't see Preston Mathers sitting in the corner, did you?"

"Preston doesn't have a soul," he muttered. A slap to the back of his head made him jump from his seat with his finger pointed and a stern rebuke on his lips, but the flash of anger he felt cooled instantly when he saw a hint of purple fire flickering in his wife's normally green eyes. Anne-Marie's temper had been formidable long before she had gained these new abilities, and Jeremiah wasn't sure how he would fare in what could literally become a heated argument.

"You didn't just beat him at Market Day yesterday. You embarrassed him and did it so publicly that he had no recourse but to hand over the land." Her look softened and she took his hand. "Oh, love, you were masterful in the way you made the deal in front of so many friendly witnesses and I couldn't be more proud of you for it., but Mathers will hold a grudge against us. You robbed him from any means of weaseling his way out, and I fear that he will find some other way to strike against us. He wants this land for some reason, despite how horribly those fields were producing."

Jeremiah squeezed her hand but grabbed the table edge as the room swayed from side to side. He closed his eyes, took in a deep breath and cleared his head. "Annie, we paid what we owed in front of witnesses. Mathers has no further action he can bring against us without breaking the law. Preston's not a fool and he isn't about to throw away his own prosperity for petty revenge."

"What if he has something not so petty planned, Jeremiah? The villains I saw in Shade's realm weren't demons. They were men. Men who would shoot a man from the shadows or trap two children inside a burning barn."

"And these threats are already known to us so we are already prepared for anything Preston might throw at us." He hiccupped and chuckled. "Besides, should he prove so simple-minded as that in the end, then you can just turn him into a newt." He slapped his knee and threw his head back but his laughter faded as the purple flames and the scowl on the fiery redhead's face returned.

"I am glad that you find all of this so amusing," she said coldly. She flicked her hand at him, and Jeremiah was shoved backward by an unseen force. He tripped over the bench by the breakfast table and sprawled on the wood floor. Anne-Marie spun around on her boot heel and grabbed her shawl from the hook by the door. As she snatched up an herb basket from a nearby bench, she said, "Maybe once you've sobered up we can discuss the best way to protect this farm and our family now that we are finally getting back on our feet." She threw open the front door and stormed out onto the porch.

"Annie, wait," he called as he crawled back to his feet and stumbled along behind her. "Where are you off to now, woman?" She stopped at the end of the steps and whirled around with her fist clenched. A crown of purple fire flashed around her head and lavender flames raged in the depths of her eyes. The morning sun caught the amethyst pendant in a blaze of its own.

"I suppose that I'm off to learn how to turn someone into a newt."

*   *   *

"I don't know if I am angrier at Shade, Preston Mathers, or my thick-headed husband," Anne-Marie growled as she threw a fireball down the practice range that Henna had set up for her. The purple explosion sent a rain of ash and cinders across the already heavily scorched ground. "Which one should I turn my wrath on first?"

Henna chuckled from the tree stump that she sat upon. "Oh, dearie. I wouldn't fret too long about your man's foolish words. Even the best among them can be a little blind to good sense. So he got a little too deep in his cups last night. Anyone close enough to have heard him will take it as such. The other two ye mentioned, however, are the ones whom ye need to be ready for. I have an ill sense that they are not so far removed from one another as ye might believe."

Anne-Marie quenched the flames that surrounded her hands and turned to her teacher. She noticed as she did so that the usual dizziness was less intense. "What do you mean? Do you think Preston is doing Shade's work here? Is he the demon's version of a Guardian?"

"Not in so direct a way. I don't believe that Mathers has any idea what pulls his strings, but Shade's influence reaches into our world, no matter how we Guardians protect it. Any man who holds evil in his heart and head serves that beast. Unwittingly for most, but that is what makes Shade's game even harder to play. Few who serve him even know that the devil exists."

"How did the war between the Guardians and Demonkin start in the first place?"

"None of us know the true story any longer. Each Guardian 'round the world no doubt has their own fable about how their particular boogeyman arrived. The lore for Pioneer Vale that I choose to believe was that two titans battled across the cosmos when our world was still in its infancy. When the colossal battle arrived here, the champion whom we serve dealt a mighty blow to the dark power he faced. Fragments of that fiend were scattered across the world like drops of blood. Some of those drops became portals between realms while others spawned separate entities, powerful in its own right and lord over a particular domain of evil."

"Such as the Father of Nightmares?" Anne-Marie asked.

"Exactly. The wounded entity hid beyond the border of our realm but remained anchored here because of the drops of itself that were left behind. Those pieces were found by the first men who hid them away and worshipped the gathering evil that whispered to them from the shadows. The Elder Guardian sought his adversary but realized that he had fled beyond our plane. The portals needed protecting though so men and women of pure heart were chosen and given the power to fight against the dark powers to prevent the fragments from reuniting and ravaging our world anew."

"Those were the first Guardians, then? And the other portals are like the stone in our grove? There are more around the world?"

"Aye, lass. We spring from different backgrounds, but we all share a common purpose. Each Guardian passes on the responsibility to a newly Ascended to watch over the place that they dwell. To prevent the darkness from taking root wherever they abide."

"So does that mean we have an evil fragment of a dark god hiding somewhere nearby?"

"If we do then, it has been well hidden beyond the sight of Pioneer Vale's Guardians for ages past. My predecessor searched for decades to try and find a trace but came up empty. It is our place to simply stand watch, and keep the Vale safe. I suspect that the old wolf chafes that his influence here can't be greater."

"But what if you are wrong? What if Shade has someone here working to specifically further his plans?"

"Then that servant would be a threat to you and I both and his days would be spent trying to flush me out of hiding. Listen to me, lass. Shade cannot enter our world as long as Pioneer Vale has a Guardian. If I had passed in my sleep before discovering you, then the great brute would have knocked upon your door already. It matters not how skilled you are. You are an Ascended Guardian now. You have pledged yourself to stand against him with the power of the vow that you made in his own home. He needs both of us destroyed before he can ravage our world and ye're the only one who knows my whereabouts."

Anne-Marie let the old woman's words sink in. "Which means that I'll be the first one that Shade or his minions will come after. That's not very reassuring." She bit her lip and absently tossed a fireball into the sky. "So let's assume it is Preston and even if the bastard doesn't know that he is Shade's servant, why don't the Guardians take a more direct step to thwart him? Why not strike out against the likes of Preston Mathers before he has a chance to do more harm?"

"What would ye do, lass? Kick down the door of his home and roast him with your flames? We are Guardians, not Executioners. Let me make clear to you this point above all others. No matter what, we serve the world as defenders, not soldiers. We shield those who can't protect themselves. We are tasked with preserving life, not snuffing it out."

"Even if those we face have no such hesitations?"

"Would ye become the very monster we strive to defeat? Who would become more feared if we acted as such? The Guardian who openly walked down the street or the fiend that the majority of the world doesn't even know exists? We serve from the shadows, child. Quick to help those who need us."

"My first act of magic, my first real act, was to cleanse the poison from my farmland. There was no benevolence in what I did. It was for purely selfish reasons. So we could make enough money to keep our farm."

Henna slapped her knee and laughed until she broke into a coughing fit. Anne-Marie rushed over to help her, but the old woman waved her off with a gnarled hand. "My dear, ye still don't see the forest for the trees. You kept your farm from falling back to Preston Mathers, Shade's unwitting agent in Pioneer Vale. We may not have the wider reason as to why he wanted your lands so badly, but ye thwarted him, and by consequence, thwarted the old wolf as well." Her bony finger tapped the amethyst pendant at Anne-Marie's throat. "Ye're chasing a destiny, lass, that we know not where it shall lead you. I'll tell ye what I think though if ye've a mind to hear it."

"Of course, please tell me." She absently toyed with the dangling jewel around her neck.

"Preston Mather's role in this little drama shall play out far sooner than yer own, I think. Don't turn a blind eye to him while he's here, for he'll no doubt have it in for you and your family. But be ever mindful of the real and greater threat to us all. Beware of Shade." The sun fell behind the clouds as she spoke, casting long shadows all around. A chill breeze rattled the trees like old bones.

Anne-Marie shivered and hugged herself to ward off the chill. "I think I would still be happier if I could just dash off and roast Preston now," she said.

"What if I could meet ye halfway on that one then, hmmm?" Henna swirled her fingers and a stir of leaves blew up at the end of the range. As they settled, a twinkling green apparition, portly in stature, and bearing the heavy jowls of Preston Mathers stood smugly smiling back at Anne-Marie with hands folded across his chest. "Do as ye would like, lass," cackled Henna.

Anne-Marie's lips curved up in a wicked smile. With a snap of her wrists lavender flames once more engulfed her hands.

CHAPTER II
BUMP IN THE NIGHT - 1671

Anne-Marie bolted upright in bed, fighting back a cry of terror. The horrors of the dream stood out vividly in her mind, rather than fading away into the night. The screams of her children as the barn collapsed in flames around them echoed in her thoughts. The burn on her wrist where Shade had grabbed her throbbed with pain and heat. Weeks after her trip to the demon's realm, the blistered print looked as fresh as the day she had received it. She leaped from the bed as a hand touched her arm, and with her newly trained reflexes, Anne-Marie conjured a lavender fireball into her palm in the blink of an eye.

"Whoa, Annie," said Jeremiah from where he lay beside her. "It's just me. Are you ok?" He sat up reaching out to her. Anne-Marie flicked a spark to a nearby candle and then extinguished her own flame as the room lit up with a gentle light.

"It was the dream again. One of them, anyway. The one with the boys."

Jeremiah took her hand. "They are only dreams, love. The boys are safe. I am safe. Whatever you think you saw..."

"Think I saw?" Anne-Marie said as she snatched her hand away. "With everything that I have done now, everything that I can do, can you sit there and say there is nothing at all to fear? I am a witch! Magic exists and there is a demon out there who wants me dead so he can cross into our world. How can I dismiss even the possibility that what he showed to me might come to pass?"

"You have shown me unbelievable things, and I don't doubt a single word that comes from your lips of what you tell me you went through that day. Keep in mind though that the beast you met feeds on our fear and suffering. He told you that himself. What if everything Shade put you through was just an illusion because he knew what would hurt you the most?"

"And what if it is truly prophetic? He told me that as well, remember? Shadows of what may come to pass. You don't know how those words haunt me. I feel like I have to be on my guard all the time now in case something slips through to make those terrible dreams real. I will not let that monster hurt my family."

Jeremiah smiled and leaned over to her. He grabbed the front of her nightshirt and gently dragged her back onto the bed. His arm slipped around her waist and he pulled her down on top of him. "Which is precisely why I do not fear his threats. With you to watch over us, we couldn't be in safer hands." He drew her into a passionate kiss, his hands gently yet firmly roaming over her back and hips. She ran her fingers through his thick hair and pulled him tightly against her.

"Mama," called a sleepy voice from the doorway. Anne-Marie chuckled while Jeremiah groaned and collapsed back onto the bed. Aiden stood in the doorway holding Thomas' hand. "Thomas says he hears noises outside that are making him scared. He says it sounds like voices whispering. I told him it was just the wind blowing but he wants to sleep in here with you and Da for the night."

Jeremiah rolled his eyes and threw his hands into the air, which drew another laugh from his wife. "It'll be a bit crowded, but one night won't hurt, I suppose," he said. Thomas finally exhaled and jumped onto the bed. Aiden stood with his hands clasped in front of him. He looked at his parents with his eyebrows raised. His lips trembled slightly.

"Well, what are you waiting for, son?" said Jeremiah. "We can't have you going back to your room alone. You know how to comfort Thomas when he's frightened better than I or your mother, so you better crawl up in here too. Somewhere…," he muttered. Aiden's grin warmed the room as he practically tackled his younger brother, and the four of them tumbled together on the mattress. They all snuggled in, giggling and rough-housing as Anne-Marie doused the candle with a snap of her fingers.

Anne-Marie leaned over and gave Jeremiah a tender kiss on his bearded cheek. "Another time," she whispered, and Jeremiah wrapped his family into his thick arms.

"Alright, now, someone better scoot over and make me some room or the lot of you will go sleep in the barn," Jeremiah bellowed. "Now just what were these voices whispering about?"

"They were soft but snarly," said Thomas, "and they kept calling Mama's name." As if on cue, the distant howl of a wolf shattered the night. The boys cried out and each grabbed a parent, as Jeremiah's eyes locked with those of his wife.

"Stay here with the boys," she said as she got out of the bed.

"Like hell, I'll let you go out there by yourself," replied Jeremiah.

She placed a hand on his shoulder as he rose to follow her. "What do you think you can do if that howl belonged to Shade? If he's here, then I don't even know if I can do anything to stop him. He'll tear you apart, and then who will protect the boys?"

"Maybe it's just a normal wolf stalking close to the livestock. Let me grab my musket and come with you." He followed her out of the bedroom to the front door.

She placed her hand on his chest, and gently pushed him back towards the bedroom. "Grab your musket and keep it close, but stay here with the boys. They are terrified already and if it turns out to merely be something of this world snuffling around outside, then I am still better equipped than you to deal with it." She bit her lip as she saw the scowl cross his face. "I didn't mean it like that, but we haven't time to argue now. Please, Jeremiah. Stay with Aiden and Thomas." Her husband said nothing, but turned and went back to the boys.

"Nothing to fret about, lads. Your mama is just making sure that the door is fastened tight for us. Hey, Thomas. How did that song go that you overheard at the Huntsman on Market Day? That was a catchy tune."

Anne-Marie smiled as a cacophony of off-tune singing erupted from the bedroom. She unbolted the farmhouse door and paused a moment, steeling her resolve before she threw it open.

The cool breeze of the night air chilled her through the thin shift she wore. She padded barefoot out onto the wooden planks of the porch and summoned a fireball into her hands.

Crickets chirped in the tall grass and the full moon's light brightened the open farmland all the way to the encircling woods. It was there, however, that the shadows took control and dark shapes bustled beneath the spreading boughs of the trees. The wind blowing through the leaves turned what should have been soft reassuring whispers into threatening growls and snarls.

"If you're there," she called to the shadows, "then make yourself known." The night sounds of bugs and birds stopped abruptly as the darkness deepened in one point of the brush. Anne-Marie stepped into the grass and braced herself, ready to throw her fire into the woods. From the gathering shadows of the tree line, a dark shape loped forward on four legs. The black fur of the wolf blended the animal into the inky gloom behind it.

Pale yellow eyes stared at her, as the wolf's head swung between her and the low fenced-in chicken coop.

"Is that why you're here then?" she asked, sighing as she realized that the beast before her was far more of this world than of her adversary's. "Get yourself back to your den, you brazen cur," she called out. She threw her fireball, watching as it streaked towards the wolf and hoped that the burst of flame would spook the animal off in search of easier prey. Just before the fireball ended its path, the wolf rose up on its hind legs. A ragged and threadbare cloak fell down around its shoulders, while the flesh split and putrefied into the rotting muzzle of Shade. The demon caught the purple ball in his hands and spun it on the end of a wicked black claw.

"Having trouble sleeping tonight, morsel?" he called from across the field. "Perhaps I should just charge in and rip them all to shreds before you can muster the courage to fight back. Clearly, your little sparks aren't yet enough to incinerate the likes of me." The demon pranced forward hopping from one foot to the other as he juggled the fireball in the air, around his back, and between his legs before letting it dissipate into a puff of wispy smoke.

"I'm ready to fight whenever you are, you mongrel," Anne-Marie snarled back. She snapped her wrists and a shroud of fire rose around her, blazing so hot that the dew on the nearby grass steamed. "How are you even here? Henna said that you couldn't cross to our world as long as a Guardian protected the Vale. Despite your mockery, I am Ascended to the post. Shall we see just how hot things can get for you?"

Anne-Marie lunged forward, her entire body becoming a living embodiment of fire as a blast tore across the field at the demon. She saw Shade's eyes grow wide as he crossed his arms before him, deflecting the flames with a billowing cloud of sulfurous smoke. He chuckled as he dusted soot from his fur.

"So you have learned a few tricks, so far. Guardian you may be, sweetling, but only recently so. Perhaps I stand before you because I have found another way to cross between worlds, hmmm? You forget how ancient I truly am, and there are doorways between the realms that have been forgotten since ages past." He sauntered a few steps closer, a swagger to his stride as he closed the distance between them. "Perhaps this night I have already dined on the bones of the old witch, and have now come to make dessert of the new one."

"If such were the case, you wouldn't waste your time gloating. If I am the only one in this world that can pose a threat to you, then you would have struck without warning." She smiled as Shade's lips curled back in anger showing his decaying teeth. "If you have come only to frighten me, wolf, let me assure you that it won't work."

A deep rumble in Shade's throat shook off chunks of withered flesh from his muzzle. "One day, child, your family will find me truly on your doorstep. When that day comes, I shall savor every bite I tear from your mate and your pups." He leaned in close enough that she could feel the heat of his breath as he spoke. "Henna's wards weaken, and soon I will find her hiding place. Once you and that old crone are disposed of, your world will crumble to ash before me."

The demon turned his back in contempt as he stepped away, but with animalistic ferocity, his body twisted back around as he lunged towards Anne-Marie with claws and fangs bared. The Guardian crossed her arms in front of her and pushed a wall of flame forward as Shade leaped at her. The barrier knocked him flat on his back. The demon yelped as her fires washed over him. Embers smoldered in his fur as Shade snarled from his place in the grass. He patted them out with his paw and studied the woman before him.

"So, you're accursed magics possess a sting after all. I confess that I've not faced a foe like you in centuries, but it will take far worse than a flash of fire for you to defeat me now. I've stood too long in the shadows of your world." He jumped back to his feet, and drew his hands apart, a midnight black spear forming in the air before him. He grabbed it in his taloned hand and stabbed forward at her.

Anne-Marie deflected it with her flaming shield and then poured her energy into the ground at her feet. Roots and grass surged in a burst of growth, clutching and tangling at the demon wolf's legs. Shade slashed at them with his spear, though, and the plants withered beneath its touch.

The Guardian wasn't idle though, and too late Shade saw that the entanglement was but a distraction. The woman's eyes blazed with power as she released twin beams of lavender fire from her gaze. Shade raised the spear to block but only partially deflected the deadly barrage as his weapon crumbled to dust before him, blowing away in the evening breeze.

"You can't beat me here, wolf," Anne-Marie said. "You do not frighten me, and so long as I stand between you and those I love, then you have no power over me."

"Perhaps not tonight, witch, but you cannot remain vigilant always." The demon crouched and snarled menacingly, but Anne-Marie stood with her hands on her hips, her foot tapping as she awaited Shade's next move.

The wolf sprang without warning, but even his speed wasn't equal to Anne-Marie's reflexes. A burning wall erupted between them, but she realized too late that her shield, while formidable, was still only flame, and not impenetrable. With fur ablaze, Shade dove through the barrier, his decaying muzzle catching fire. His yellow teeth spread wide as he tackled her to the ground.

Anne-Marie drove her knee up into the wolf's belly as he snapped his blistering jaws in the air before her nose. His strength was monstrous and the woman could barely hold his massive paws away from her throat. Her eyes locked onto his, though, and all of her rage boiled over as she surged with the power of the Ascended.

"Get off of me," she screamed as she channeled another explosion of flame outward that blew the demon away from her. She struggled to one knee, just as Shade rose to his feet with his cloak and fur ablaze. Dizziness from the outpouring of magic washed over her, but she fought her way to her feet.

"I commend you, witch. You've provided us with a good bit of sport tonight. Savor your victory, though, morsel, for your time grows short." Shade swept his arm down and the lavender flames around him extinguished. The wolf gave a curt nod of his head as she squared off against him once again. The demon leaped once more, his black claws flashing down through the feeble shield that Anne-Marie tried to raise. His snarl filled her ears, and agony exploded across her abdomen as the points of his talons raked across her skin.

Anne-Marie bolted upright in bed, choking back a scream of terror. Aiden, Thomas, and Jeremiah all slept soundly beside her. The moonlight through the window lit the room up with a sickly yellow light. She looked at each of the peaceful faces in the bed and finally decided that any further sleep was beyond her tonight. Might as well go and put the kettle on, she thought as she swung her feet around to the floor. She got out of bed and looked down at the front of her nightdress. Although her skin was smooth and unmarred, the cloth of her shift bore four rips through it where Shade's claws had torn through the fabric.

CHAPTER 12
RAISING THE STAKES - 1671

Jeremiah wiped his brow and then put his straw hat back on his head. He had rounded up all but one of his escaped pigs, but the remaining sow was still nursing her little ones and he needed to bring her back. How the pen had broken open baffled him. The gate had been smashed by something in the middle of the night, but he hadn't heard anything. Maybe the boys' claims of something snuffling around in the dark last night hadn't been as farfetched as he had thought.

Anne-Marie had certainly seemed distracted and on edge this morning. Dark circles and a sleepy smile was enough to tell him that she must not have made it back to sleep after the boys had crawled into bed with them. Who knows, he thought to himself. He just wanted to find that last pig and get back to his house before it got dark.

He knew that Aiden and Thomas should have the fence mended by now, as they had rushed to get it started when Jeremiah had given them the job this morning. He loved how eager to help his boys were. He had no doubt that they would grow into fine young men in the growing community.

The bushes rustled up ahead, and he crouched down, holding his snare at the ready in case his missing charge barreled out of the brush at him. He crept forward slowly, and gently pushed aside some tree branches. His eyes grew wide and he threw himself aside just as an arrow thudded into the tree trunk behind him.

"Hold your shot," he called out. Jeremiah burst through the bushes to see Hollister Adams and Landry Cross standing over his quarry. Two arrows wavered into the air from the side of his dead animal at their feet. Cross had an arrow nocked and leveled at him, but Adams stepped forward and pushed the other man's bow to the ground.

"Beg your pardon, Master Carmichael," he said. "We thought you might be another pig. Lucky for you that Landry here isn't such a keen shot."

"I'll count my blessings tonight at vespers," Jeremiah said as he eyed the two ruffians. "That kill of yours happens to be my property. I don't appreciate running these hills all morning just to find her slaughtered. Had you bothered to look you would have seen our family mark on her. She had sucklings still that are now without milk."

"Pig running wild makes it hard to look for a brand, Carmichael," said Cross. "Why was she out in the first place? In the heat of the moment way out here, she was easy enough to mistake for a wild pig."

"So you shoot first and ask questions later?" asked Jeremiah. "Guess that explains why you nearly put one through me just now."

"Had to take the shot when I had it," growled Cross. "How was I to know she was yours?"

Jeremiah rolled the carcass over and pointed at his family's mark blatantly displayed on the sow's flank. "I can also easily enough prove that I have the younglings, and no mother to care for them. Do you want to try to play me for a fool?" Jeremiah locked stares with the brutish man and for a brief moment, the thug seemed like he might raise the bow and draw on him.

"Now, Jeremiah," said Adams. "We didn't mean any ill will towards you. This is a simple misunderstanding and one I'll be happy to make good for. Let me pay you a fair price for this here animal, same as if you'd sold her to me at market. She'll make many a fine meal for those of us who quarter under Preston Mathers' roof. A good bit of fresh ham and bacon will raise our spirits after working away for such an ill-tempered and stingy fellow, don't you agree, sir?" He walked over to his horse tethered nearby and rummaged around in his saddlebag. He came back with a small bag in hand and held it out to Jeremiah.

The farmer hesitated a moment then took the pouch and untied the drawstring. Several small gold nuggets spilled out into his palm. Jeremiah looked up at the two men skeptically.

"Preston is paying his men in raw gold these days? That seems far more generous than the man that I know him to be." He studied the two men before him. Adams stood with his thumbs tucked into his waistband rocking slowly on the balls of his feet while Cross still held the bowstring half pulled, glaring at Jeremiah with unmasked contempt.

"What you've given me here is far more than what one sow is worth. You said you'd pay fair market and I won't accept anything more than that." He took three nuggets from the pile in his hand and returned the rest to the pouch. With a gentle toss, he threw the bag back to Hollister. "I believe this squares us up."

"As you wish, Master Carmichael," said the weasel-faced man. "If we're all done here then, we'll get this sow carted up and back to town so we can get her butchered. I can taste that ham steak already, sir." Adams laughed and slapped his thigh. He gave Jeremiah a tip of his cap and then turned to Landry, swatting his associate on his thick arm. Together they started to drag the dead pig over to the cart that stood close by.

Jeremiah watched them drive off a short time later, rolling the gold nuggets in his palm with his thumb. This area of the woods outside of town was often hunted by the locals of Pioneer Vale, but something just didn't seem right about those two. He looked down at the ore in his hand and couldn't help but wonder.

If Preston was paying his men in gold, where was he getting it?

*   *   *

Jeremiah checked the fence posts around the newly repaired pigpen. Aiden and Thomas had done a fine job and he knew he needed to praise the boys for their work. He only needed to make a few last checks around the farm before he lost the last rays of sunlight, and then maybe he and Anne-Marie could spend the rest of a quiet evening reading to one another by the fire. He smiled at the memory of how she had patiently taught him letters after they had first met. He had struggled so badly at first and even now stumbled over some of the words, but she never made him feel foolish when she corrected him. He chuckled to himself. You would think that since they only owned three books anyway, he would have them committed to memory by now.

A wolf howled in the distance and set his senses on edge. He changed his direction from the barn back towards the hen house. Better make sure everything was secure there first. The farm was finally showing a decent living for them and he'd be damned if a rogue wolf or fox wiped out his livestock. As he neared the corner of the house ready to go around, he paused as he saw the flickering shadows of torchlight dancing across the ground. He pulled the hatchet from his belt, rounded the corner, and gasped at the sight before him.

A ring of townsfolk stood in the yard waving torches, pitchforks, and an uncomfortable number of muskets. It struck Jeremiah as odd that he hadn't heard the gathered crowd, even though they made no effort to be silent. Angry voices rose in a cacophony of shouts as he walked into view. Their words seemed strangely unintelligible to his ears though, and try as he might he couldn't distinguish what all of these men and women were yelling at him. The crowd broke as he approached, and he saw his most recent fear rising up into the night sky.

A stake with iron manacles attached to a hook at the top stood surrounded by logs that reeked with the smell of pitch. A man in black robes and a black hood held a torch, silently waiting to perform the duty to which he'd been assigned. The shrieks of the crowd finally became clear as Jeremiah fell to his knees.

"BURN THE WITCH," called the mob over and over again. Jeremiah heard the call in his head rather than in his ears, but the pure hatred and venom that filled the crowd was no less overwhelming. A boot from some unknown assailant kicked him in the back, yet spurred Jeremiah to action. He sprang up from the ground, and threw a punch at the nearest hulking figure, feeling his blow solidly strike the unknown man in the jaw and driving him back. The crowd pushed forward, reaching out to grab him, but Jeremiah would not be subdued so easily. He fought as if his life depended on it, for he was certain that if not his own, then certainly the life of Anne-Marie stood at risk tonight.

A heavy blow struck the back of his head, and Jeremiah went to the ground as the world around him swam in a dizzying display. Someone large pinned him down and wrenched his arms behind his back. Someone else tied his wrists together, grabbed his hair, and pulled him back up to his knees. Lights danced before his eyes as he tried to keep his wits about him. A movement to his side brought him sharply back into focus.

"Annie," he cried out as he saw his wife being roughly dragged towards the stake by Patch Erickson and Landry Cross.

"Jeremiah, help me," she screamed back. Erickson silenced her with a hard backhand slap that knocked her head hard to one side. Jeremiah strained against his bonds but the leather cords simply bit deeper into his wrists. The strong arms that held him tightened their grip as a brawny bicep wrapped around his throat forcing him to watch the spectacle before him.

Preston's mercenaries hauled Anne-Marie up to the stake and clasped the iron manacles tightly around her wrists. She tried to lift her head, but she was still dazed from the strike. A heavy iron chain was wrapped around her waist and shoulders binding her tightly to the post.

"Please don't do this to her," Jeremiah croaked despite the crushing grip on his throat. "You don't understand what you are doing!" Tears streamed down his cheeks as Preston's men left the platform. Anne-Marie slowly lifted her head and seemed for the first time to notice the chanting crowd around her.

"BURN THE WITCH! BURN THE WITCH! BURN THE WITCH!"

Her eyes found Jeremiah's at last and her fear softened into nothing but her love for him. The man in the black hood stepped forward, blocking her from Jeremiah's sight and tossed the torch on to the pyre. Jeremiah struggled to look past the executioner, but he could only see the flames mounting into the night sky. His own screams tore from his chest as those of his beloved wife's began, and they blended in a tragic harmony accompanied by the roar of the raging fire between them. Jeremiah shook and fought, but still, the arm around his neck held him tightly and prevented him from seeing her.

The executioner turned around slowly and pulled the black hood from his head. It came as no surprise to Jeremiah that the unveiled face belonged to Preston Mathers. A wicked grin creased the man's jowls and he waggled his fingers in a mocking wave at him. The arm around his throat suddenly rippled and sprouted thick greasy black fur, and rancid breath reeking of carrion blew hot against the side of his face.

"Do you not see, mortal? You may struggle until your final breath leaves your body, but I will bring your wife down, and this world shall become a living hell to those that resist me." Jeremiah saw the shadow on the ground of a wolf's head with a slavering maw rear back, open wide and then plunge downward towards his neck.

Jeremiah sat up with a gasp and fell out of bed onto the wooden floor of their bedroom. Anne-Marie rolled over, watching him with heavy-lidded eyes.

"Jeremiah? Are you ok?" she asked, her words thick and slurred.

He glanced around, searching the shadows as the terrors of his last few moments faded into the depths of his memories. He picked himself up off the floor and climbed back into bed. Jeremiah wrapped his arms around Anne-Marie's waist and buried his face into her hair. Tonight it smelled like the wildflowers she had picked in the south fields. She purred sleepily and pressed her body back against his, taking his hands and directing them to where she liked to be held.

"I'm fine, love," he replied as he gave her a gentle squeeze. "It was just a bad dream."

*   *   *

Preston Mathers crept down the dusty tunnel. The lantern light caught the roots that poked through the earthen walls and cast long grasping shadows that reached towards the man. He felt the familiar call as soon as he had crossed the threshold into this chamber. He glanced over his shoulder to make sure that no one had followed him down. This prize was for him alone.

Mathers made his way past the ancient barrows where skulls either leered or shrieked in silent agony at him with each step he took. He mused over which aspect his bones would assume when his time came to join them. The low light caught the dusty edge of the old sailcloth that he had thrown over the bundle at the end of the row just as he had left it the night before. He rubbed his chin, and wondered, not for the first time if he would be better off just collapsing the entire chamber, but he knew he couldn't bear the thought.

He knew that he wouldn't be allowed.

The whispery voice that directed him would see to that. Besides, someone else would simply find his treasure instead, and he was not of a mind to share with anyone. He reached for the edge of the cloth with a trembling hand, took a deep breath, and whipped the musty tarp away.

The chest stood untouched from his last visit. He caressed the smooth oak staves and black iron bands as tenderly as if it were the skin of his last mistress. He fumbled at the latch, sighing when the metal clip popped open. He raised the lid and felt exhilarated as the pale yellow light of the pulsing crystal washed over his face. As his fingers traced over the sickly glowing gem, his thoughts turned suddenly to those damnable Carmichaels and how they were making his plans so much more difficult. How in the world had they pulled off that harvest? The crystal's light throbbed like a pulse as if the heart of something rested under his hand.

"I have a task for you, Preston," called the gentle growl that always spoke to him. *"We have common enemies that you must dispose of for us."*

"Jeremiah Carmichael? I have thought of nothing else…"

"Not the farmer," the voice interrupted. *"His woman. She threatens all we hold precious. You must find a way to bring her here before me."*

Preston thought to himself as he stared into the stone's radiance. Vivid images of brutal scenes flashed through his mind, but they were crude and lacked the subtle anonymity such a deed would require. An idea took root and danced around the edge of his dastardly thoughts. His grin widened as he realized the perfect means to distance himself from what he had in mind. All he needed was someone who he could trust to carry out his instructions without argument.

He only needed somebody who couldn't refuse the twisted proposal he envisioned.

"Consider it done," he said with a bow to the pulsing stone.

Preston Mathers closed the chest back up and threw the cloth back over it. As he retreated to the tunnel entrance, he knew then that he already had the perfect accomplice to help him bring down Anne-Marie Carmichael and her family.

CHAPTER 13
DIRE WARNINGS – PRESENT DAY

"So how long will it take for him to get to his full power?" Angelica asked. "Does he have to get a feel for how magic works in our world?" She and Anne-Marie sat closely together at the dining table. The older woman had set a bowl of fruit out and was peeling an orange. Angelica took a small cluster of grapes and picked them from the stem.

"After a fashion, yes. Our adversary dwells in a world more closely attuned to the power we all draw upon. It reaches into our world, but it loses potency crossing the barrier between that plane and ours. We would find our own abilities enhanced, and maybe even beyond our control if we were to carry the fight into Shade's realm. As we are a step removed, it buys us a little time since Aiden needs to recharge his battery so to speak."

"The Guardians are chosen to wield the magic to fight Shade, right? Does Shade pull from the same source of power as we do?"

"Shade serves another darker presence. There are forces of good and evil of all degrees battling for dominance on a chessboard that we can't even begin to imagine. We are soldiers in a war that has been fought since time began. Each side has drawn its champions throughout the ages hoping to gain an advantage over the other side. We fight to hold our world safe from the intrusion of Shade's kind. The Elder Power that grants the Guardians our magic may not even be aligned with a battle going on three dimensions away. We are concerned only with a set group of enemies."

"How do we know if we are winning?"

"Because we are still alive, child. The world isn't set aflame and the streets littered with the dead."

"If humanity itself is threatened all the time, then why not come out of hiding? Let's spread the word about the truth of all of this. Maybe we could gain more than just a handful of Guardians scattered across the globe to help us fight."

"Because there are too many who side with the darkness. For centuries, Guardians and those who knew of and supported them have been persecuted by followers of Shade's kind. Many innocents have met untimely ends and allowed the Demonkin to gain ground in the battle here. The demon world strikes by influencing and corrupting mankind. All of the temptation, promises of hearts desires, wealth, and power are an easy coin for some to accept. They force those who would support our cause to be harshly dealt with. Furthermore, if we were to march down the streets proclaiming what we really are, how long do you think we would have before the torches and pitchforks come out? People fear what they don't understand or cannot control. For us, child, we would spend too much time defending ourselves from those we would save or else meet a fearsome end."

"You mean like burning at the stake? Like the witch hunts from your day?"

Anne-Marie nodded. "The witch hunts truly were little more than weak-minded men and women accusing their neighbors to cover and protect their own indiscretions. So many innocents suffered in those times. There were other scourges, though," she said as her voice grew soft and her eyes distant, "where the Guardians were flushed out of hiding and executed. Fierce battles were waged and so many lives were wasted." She shook her head. "We are getting off track. We can have history lessons once we have figured out how to find our former prisoner before he gains strength here."

"He already was powerful enough that his touch would have killed me if you hadn't shown up when you did. He popped open that portal out of the Holding Chamber without breaking a sweat. I don't want to see him get any stronger than that."

"Exactly." Anne-Marie reached across the table and took Angelica's hand. "All of the others, the Firstborns, I mean. They all failed because they were unable to resist Aiden's temptations. Every time we battled, he had convinced my student that I was the real threat. As his lies took root in the Firstborns' minds, he forced me to act before we were prepared. Every single time, my son forced me to sacrifice my family in order to chain him into his cage for just a little longer."

"Then maybe it's time to stop chaining him up. If we die, Shade crosses the barrier, and right now the only tool that bastard has is your son. Grandmother," Angelica said softly, "I think that it's time to admit that your son is gone. Aiden needs to die or he will continue snapping at our heels until there's no one left to stand against him and the furball."

"We just need to show him that Shade can't win in the end. Aiden was my most gifted student. If the demon's corruption can be driven from my boy, then…"

"Then what?" Angelica snapped. "He comes running back to mommy's arms? He has been looking for a way to kill you for over 300 years. That's not going to change. Before, he tried to corrupt the Firstborns to wipe you out, only now he is loose, and he doesn't need your currently unready apprentice. He is likely just waiting for his chance to do the job himself. We have to strike first!" She threw her grapes back into the fruit bowl.

"You are untrained, my dear girl, but remember what I told you before. You possess the spirit, the affinity of a warrior Guardian. Aiden has never stood against the likes of you before. As for Shade, well, not since the last time that he faced me. We may not have spent as many hours at lessons as I had with the others, but you have a raw power that may give us the chance to subdue my son and force the demon away. I will not give up the hope of saving Aiden so easily. I sincerely believe that when the time comes, you will discover the measure of your talents, and they will exceed your wildest expectations."

"How long did you train Aiden?" Angelica asked. Anne-Marie leaned back in her chair and folded her hands in her lap.

"He studied with me for about a decade before Shade attacked us again. He was brilliant, and such a quick learner. What I failed to see was that the reason he was so skilled was because Shade already had taken hold of his heart. I lost my son to a demon hiding right under my nose." She looked up into Angelica's eyes. Tears ran down her cheeks and she wiped them away. "I didn't understand that his magic was fueled directly by Shade and that he used me to learn as many effects and castings as he could over those years. I should have known better since Aiden never traveled through the Widow Stone to bind himself to the Elder Guardian. I was naïve and thought that because he was my son that I could teach him.

"I am the cause of all of this, Angelica. Once I realized what Shade had done, I could have stopped him, but that meant killing my own child. I couldn't do it. I stared my boy in the face even as he spat at me in hatred. I chose instead to imprison him in the crystal, hoping that I could one day find a way to rid him of Shade's corruption. I have instead been forced to give up my grandchildren and great-grandchildren on down the line to keep the monster at bay. Were their lives any less valuable to me, or have I just been too willing to pay such a high price for the foolish hope that I can still save my son?"

Angelica sat and stared at the floor. "I don't have an answer for that. It's a lot to think about. I do want you to know, though, that because I set him free I won't hesitate to put an end to him. I hope that when we get to that point, you find that you can stand beside me and fight. I can accept whatever needs to be done to clean this mess up even if the only way means sacrificing myself to blast his ass back into Shade's nightmare world." She watched an arcing flicker of static dance back and forth across her knuckles but sent it away when she looked up and saw Anne-Marie looking at her with heartbreak in her own eyes. "Don't get me wrong, though. I do hope we find a better way."

"No more of this talk today, child," said Anne-Marie. She stood and walked around the table, taking Angelica's hands again and pulling the girl to her feet. "That time may never come, and I sincerely pray that we never have to face such a choice. Aiden is weak now. We still have time to stop him before he becomes truly dangerous. I will try a few tricks I know of to see if I can get a sense of him, and then together we shall deal with our rat that has slipped his trap." She gave a light playful punch to her granddaughter's shoulder, and Angelica couldn't hold back a grin.

"OK, sounds like a plan. I should grab my journal and go clean myself up though before we start any new lessons." She shook her shirt and the tinkling of dozens of tiny crystal shards hitting the floor rose to their ears. Her face and arms were still dotted with tiny pinpoints of blood from where the needlelike barrage had peppered her skin. "I can hardly go demon hunting looking like this. I'd be the laughing stock of the entire Guardian community."

Anne-Marie laughed. "Then let's make you the belle of the ball. Come with me, dear. I may have something more suitable for you to wear for our little endeavor. Follow me." Anne-Marie walked back over to the fireplace and once again opened the hidden gateway.

"We're going back down there?" Angelica wrapped her arms around herself, shivering as she did so.

"We are, but deeper down the stairwell this time. Come along. I promise you that you are going to enjoy this." The two women passed through the extra-dimensional doorway and started down the staircase. Angelica shot a troubled glance as they passed the landing to the Holding Chamber, the door blown off its hinges and shattered crystal covering the floor. Anne-Marie continued past without a glance, and Angelica hurried along after her.

A few flights later, the Guardian stopped at a new landing, lit by a torch that merrily danced through every color of the rainbow, casting a delightful display on the solid oak door at the end of the short hallway. The door swung open on silent hinges at Anne-Marie's gentle push. As Angelica stepped across the threshold she laughed at the scene before her.

The chamber was covered in lace and tassels, leather and velvet, buttons and bows. It looked like someone had blown up the workshop of a madcap tailor. Dresses, shirts, pants, and boots littered the entire floor. Outfits of every era lay discarded across tables and thrown over chairs. Anne-Marie trampled across the clothing without regard to the damage her bare feet might cause some of the more delicate accoutrements. She pushed aside a huge pile of fabric to reveal a fine cedar chest banded in metal that shimmered with a light of its own making.

"What is this place?" Angelica breathed.

"Forgive the mess, but I haven't been down here to tidy up since…well, ever, I guess." She smiled and shrugged her shoulders. "I have come to call this the Fitting Room. You could call it a boutique for the Guardians, I suppose. If you are going to accept the mantle, my dear, then yoga pants and dirty sneakers simply won't do."

"I'm not getting rid of my hoodie, though," she said as she looked around the room. "So what do I do? Just dig through all this and pick out something I like? This could take a while, and how will I know how to find my size?"

Anne-Marie simply patted the lid of the cedar chest. "All you need to do is open this trunk. The perfect outfit befitting your role as a Guardian will be inside, customized to suit your personality. I shall wait outside and let you get dressed." She gave Angelica a quick kiss on the forehead. "It's time to suit up."

Anne-Marie took a step back and raised her hands over her head. Lavender fire danced around her fingertips, faintly lighting up the nightdress that Anne-Marie still wore. She brought her hands down with a snap of her wrists, the flames forming a circle above her and following her gesture towards the floor. The Guardian lifted away from the pile of clothes that she stood upon, her bare feet floating on the rising air currents as her fires began to enshroud her.

Her nightshirt vanished in a billowing plume of smoke that sinuously snaked around her body and obscured the older woman's curves. Sparks and embers shot from the cloud, cascading onto the floor and indiscriminately burning tiny holes in the articles that they fell upon. Angelica shielded her eyes when a final flash of purple fire blazed from her teacher's body. As the smoke dissipated, Anne-Marie stood before her dressed in the white sleeveless top, black corset, trousers, and boots that her grandmother had only spoken of until now. Anne-Marie shot the young woman a quick wink, spun on her boot heel, and walked out into the hallway.

Angelica looked around at the scattered clothing all around her. She carefully stepped past the piles of leather, lace, wool, cotton, and even denim to make her way to the shimmering chest at the far end of the room. She dropped to her knees and placed her hand on the smooth wood of the lid. A tingle ran up her arm with a gentle warmth. She felt a comforting glow about her as she opened the trunk. When she peeked inside she couldn't help but smile.

*   *   *

Anne-Marie sat upon the stone steps that led back up to the fireplace doorway. The multicolored torch raced through its spectrum, signaling to the seasoned veteran that her student was ready. The door to the Fitting Room remained closed but Anne-Marie's sharpened senses could hear the scuff of shoes approaching from the far side. She exhaled, realizing only then that she had been holding her breath in anticipation of Angelica's appearance. She tried to stay composed but jumped to her feet as the door finally swung open and her granddaughter's silhouette filled the doorway.

"How do I look?" Angelica asked as she finally stepped into the light. She held her arms out and did a little spin, then clasped her hands together in front of her as she waited for Anne-Marie's appraisal.

"I believe the expression of your generation is that you look like a complete badass." She stepped forward and hugged her granddaughter. When she let go, Anne-Marie held her at arm's length to get a better look at Angelica's new outfit.

Angelica's black hair was pulled back, held in place by a sapphire blue hair clip streaked with veins of white that resembled crisp bolts of lightning shooting through the night sky. She wore a high collared brown leather jacket that laced tightly across her chest but was cut high, ending halfway down her ribcage. A white tunic hung down to her hips with a thin brown belt cinching it around her waist. Soft leather pants with laces that tied at her hips were tucked into sturdy hiking boots.

"You know, it seems to me that the Elder Guardian has a thing for leather," Angelica quipped.

"We actually had a stretch where three in a row were swimming in lace. How intimidating must that have appeared to a demon bent on destroying the world? You, my dear, positively look the part."

"Thank you." Angelica's cheeks grew hot, but then she put her hands on her hips. "Now, how do we find our fugitive? I don't suppose that you know a spell for demon sensing that could lead us straight to him?"

"Unfortunately, no. However, Shade and his minions feed on misery, pain, and terror. Aiden won't waste any time waiting for something terrible to happen on its own. He will cause something as soon as he is able. We need to see if we can locate him before he causes some sort of disaster." She turned and started up the stairway, with Angelica close behind. Together they crossed the threshold back into the cottage's living room.

"Not to sound cliché or anything," asked Angelica, "but do you have a crystal ball or scrying bowl or magic tea leaves that we can look into?"

"In this day and age, child, we have something far more sinister to gather our current events with." Anne-Marie went to the large armoire sitting off to the side of the room and opened the doors. Inside the cabinet sat an old television, complete with crooked and bent rabbit ears sticking askew from the top. The old set looked so out of place in the cozy rustic cottage that Angelica burst out laughing.

"You are so desperately in need of an upgrade, grandma," she said. "Does that thing even work?"

Anne-Marie scowled over her shoulder then looked at the TV set and sighed. "If you are finished poking fun at my antiques, make yourself useful and give it a little charge. Electricity is your forte, correct? Just give it a little zap between the rabbit ears."

Angelica grabbed the ambient power in the room and flicked a tiny spark as Anne-Marie had directed. The current found its mark and grabbed hold of each part of the antenna like something out of a mad scientist's lab in one of the grainy old monster movies her father loved. Anne-Marie bent forward and turned the knob, bringing a black and white picture to the set. Anne-Marie snapped her fingers with a flash of sparks, and the picture turned to full color. The screen showed a man behind a news desk with the banner below him spelling out BREAKING NEWS in bold type. Anne-Marie turned the volume knob up so they could hear the report.

"...Please be advised that the footage we are about to show," the reporter said, "is intense and very disturbing. Children and sensitive members of our broadcast audience should change the station now." The camera cut away to another reporter at the scene of the story. Emergency vehicle lights flashed frantically behind the man.

The reporter's face was ghastly pale, his jaw hanging slack. Someone off-camera whispered, "Jack, we're rolling." Jack blinked twice, wiped his hand across his mouth, and stared blankly into the camera.

"We are live at the scene of a terrible murder. The...the victim has yet to be identified." Jack's voice trembled, and when he glanced over his shoulder he gagged and had to look away. "The only thing we know so far is that the victim is a young woman, only evident due to the bloody scraps of clothing present on the scene. In 12 years of reporting, I have never seen anything so...savage. At first glance, this would appear to be the attack of some ferocious wild animal, except that the culprit left a gruesome message on the nearby wall. We are going to show you what we may, but please," the shaken reporter said, "I am begging you to change the channel now."

"We're too late," Anne-Marie breathed. "He's already struck at someone. The fear he needs to grow his strength has already taken hold."

The camera panned around the crime scene. One of the police officers was pushing what could only be described as chunks of meat with a large scraper. Tattered and bloody rags were picked up by another officer with a pair of tongs and put into an evidence bag. Slowly, the cameraman took in the entire grisly scene and finally brought the camera around to the dripping red message splattered on the brick wall behind the officers.

Angelica's knees buckled and she dropped to the floor as she read the horrifying words on the screen. Anne-Marie buried her face in her hands and screamed in anguish.

The garish crimson letters spelled out, *"This is what inside out looks like, bitch!"*

CHAPTER 14
LIGHTING THE HOME FIRES – PRESENT DAY

"That girl is dead because of me," Angelica shouted. Lightning crackled around her clenched fists and she hurled a double blast into the fireplace, scattering logs and ashes throughout the living room. She threw her head back and screamed in fury as lightning erupted in a ring all around her. A wave of purple flame washed over her as Anne-Marie quenched the current before Angelica lost control of her rage, and destroyed the room.

"Her death is Aiden's to answer for, not yours. He needs to create panic to fuel his power, and it has ever been the Demonkin's ploy to create such atrocities to draw the Guardians out. This terrible murder is nothing more to him than a lure to bring us forth before we are ready to face him."

"You mean me. Before I am ready to face him. Why don't you just say that if we go out there now, that I will be the next bloody stain on the sidewalk?"

Anne-Marie stepped forward and put her hands on the girl's shoulders. "Fine. You aren't ready to face him, and I can't bear the thought of that black-hearted bastard killing you. If we rush into this, we will fail. We need to move as quickly as we can, but not without giving you whatever amount of training that we can in so short of a time."

"We can't just let him run free. You know as well as I do that he won't stop with just this. If we don't come out now, he will just hurt somebody else."

"And if you charge forward unprepared and he kills you, then this age-old battle is lost for good," Anne-Marie shot back. "There won't be another champion to step up in time to stop him. He knows where to find me, and we need to watch each other's backs more than ever now. The reason Shade must use Aiden as his agent is because of the shrouding magic of the grove. No one without magical training and ability can find Whisperwind, but he can. He spent years here. It makes this place unsafe for us if he reaches his full strength."

"So how many others do we let him kill? We need to be out there right now hunting him down."

"We aren't discussing this option, Angelica. That's exactly what he wants us to do. Rush headlong into an ambush. Too many members of our family have suffered because of what Shade has done to us. I will not give him another of my children."

Angelica studied her ancestor's face and the realization dawned on her. "Why didn't he strike the farm? He knows that place even better than this one. This was just an appetizer for what he has planned, isn't it? He'll go after my parents and brother at some point, won't he?"

"More than likely, yes," replied Anne-Marie. "All the more reason for you to be as well trained as we can get you before our showdown with him."

"If he touches my family, I won't spare him. Trained or not, I'll throw down against him with everything I've learned so far. Even if that doesn't make much of a difference."

A single tear rolled down Anne-Marie's cheek. "It would make all the difference in this world to me, child." The flash of a snarl crossed her face as she wiped away the errant drop. She flicked her hands at the television, turning off the set and slamming the cabinet doors shut. "Enough of this. We need to get you down to the practice field immediately. There are a few other tricks that I can show to you before we absolutely have to move. Let's hone your skills before the time to confront him reaches us. You have incredible power already, but it is wild and unfocused as the poor logs in the fireplace can attest to," she said with a wave to the smoking kindling in the hearth.

"So how much time do you think we have? I mean with what we saw tonight, how quickly will this sort of attack increase his strength?"

"It's hard to say. It depends on how far the story spreads. If this stays to the local news broadcasts then his growth will be gradual. Small. If it makes the national newscast, then it will feed his power far faster."

Angelica nodded slowly, and then her eyes grew wide. "Oh my God. We may already be too late."

"What do you mean?" said Anne-Marie.

"Oh, grandmother, you *really* need an upgrade. You are still used to a time where messages had to be carried on horseback from town to town. We're in a digital age, and if this news clip hits the internet, something like this could go viral in minutes. The entire world could potentially see this and Aiden's strength could ramp up before I could even spit a spark!"

Anne-Marie fell back into her armchair as her descendant's words struck home. A low moan escaped her as she gripped the arms of the chair. When she lifted her gaze back to Angelica, purple flame danced in her eyes. The younger woman started to reach forward, and hesitated, unsure what to do.

"I never even considered it," said Anne-Marie, her voice a low growl. "All these years and I never once considered how far his reach could spread. This changes everything."

As Angelica watched, Anne-Marie's fury melted away. She saw for the first time a wavering in the unshakeable confidence that marked her teacher. A shadow of fear passed briefly across the older woman's usually stoic face. The rock-solid determination that had grown so familiar to her was now tainted by uncertainty.

At that moment, something inside of Angelica awoke. Her back straightened and she tossed her ponytail from its place on her shoulder and knelt before Anne-Marie. She placed her closed hand over her heart.

"This is my storm. My responsibility. I have not taken your lessons as seriously as I should have all this time. That ends now. On my word, what you teach I will learn, and we will stop both Shade and Aiden together."

The young woman's clenched fist crackled with a wave of blue-white lightning that flared all around her. An audible pulse of magic radiated from her and Whisperwind shook in the ensuing press of power. A storm of energy streaked through the very walls and, for one brief moment, Angelica felt as though the ripple raced to the four corners of the globe. She sensed something from beyond their world watching her, smiling with approval as she made her vow to fight, and a rush of pure magic poured into her.

Every fiber of Angelica's body infused with a wildstorm of power. All of her senses went into overload. She realized that she could hear the whispers of a thousand conversations, smell wildflowers from the other side of the world, and even see every detail of every blade of grass in every meadow on the planet. All of the life-giving brilliance that the Guardians fought to protect was laid bare before her as she basked in raw magical might. A supernova erupted in a final nimbus of crackling electricity that wreathed her entire body and lifted her from the floor. With a thunderous clap that shook the walls of the cottage, the energy finally faded away.

"What the hell was that?" she asked when her knees touched lightly upon the floor of the cottage once more.

Anne-Marie watched the few remaining sparks fall in a tumbling cascade to the hardwood and smiled as she lifted herself out of her chair.

"Your vow is made, and your side is chosen. You now have much to learn and precious little time to do so.

"Arise, Guardian. Your Ascension is complete."

*   *   *

Angelica woke up and dragged herself from her bed. She dressed quickly, grabbing a Pioneer Vale High School sweatshirt from her closet, a pair of jogging shorts, and her running shoes. She knew that Anne-Marie wanted to put her through a rigorous training session today, but the new Guardian wanted to get in a quick run before the real workout began. She had spent the rest of the night pouring through the spell journal that Anne-Marie had given her looking for every advantage that might bring her growing powers to a level where she could contend with their adversary.

She threw open the curtains on her window, but rather than the cheery morning sun filtering through the leaves of the lush surrounding forest, a dull orange ball hung in the sky over a decimated landscape that she had known since she was a child.

The fields that she had helped tend her whole life were nothing more than blackened ash. Livestock lay slaughtered in their pens as clouds of black flies moved from carcass to carcass. The smoking rubble of the farmhouse she had lived in her whole life, though, sent her racing for the door.

Her bedroom opened up not into the hallway at Anne-Marie's cottage, but straight into the wasteland that she had seen through her window. She sprinted towards her ruined home across what had been the main cornfield. She charged through choking clouds of soot as she pushed herself towards the burned-out rubble. As she approached the charred porch at the front of the house, a familiar robed figure stepped out from the smoldering entryway.

"You're too late, dearie," said Aiden with a cruel grin across his face. "I've already paid my respects to the old homestead." He threw his head back and cackled with a thin high-pitched laugh.

"Where are my parents? My brother?" Angelica demanded. Aiden stopped and stared at her with an almost comically dazed look. He jerked his thumbs over his shoulder with agonizing slowness into the burning timbers of the demolished home behind him. His grin returned and then became a snarl.

"What I did to that girl, was nothing compared to what I did in there before I burned the place to the ground. Oh, how they squealed for me as I pulled the flesh from their bones!" He jumped lightly off the step and watched with an almost childlike fascination at the puffs of ash that his feet stirred up, much as a toddler jumping into a puddle would watch the splashes around her rain boots. He snapped his gaze back over to her. "I felt it was time for me to come for a visit after we felt that little ripple across the world as you made your Ascension. You'll forgive me if I don't congratulate you, but you have picked the wrong side, cousin, and now those you love most have paid for your mistakes." He sneered at her and raised his hands as black fire swirled around him. He fell into a fighting crouch and raised an eyebrow at her in challenge.

Angelica felt her knees wobble, thoughts of her family facing horrors that she had created turning her stomach in knots. One look at the anticipation in Aiden's eyes, however, told her that he waited for her to fall so that he could pounce. She wasn't about to give him the satisfaction.

She reached out for her magic, ready to raise her defenses and counter with a surprise of her own, but she felt nothing. There was no inflow of energy, no wispy tendrils of magic for her to grasp. That hadn't happened since before she had met Anne-Marie. It was as if the world's primordial power had never even existed.

Something was wrong here.

"This isn't real," she said. Aiden who had been leaning forward on the balls of his feet, flexing his fingers in nervous expectation, suddenly rocked back. "No matter what you and Shade threaten me with you can't cut off an Ascended Guardian from her magic. Is this just one more feeble attempt at making me afraid of you, cousin?" she said mocking his own sneer on the last word.

Aiden started to lunge forward when a low menacing growl came from the shadows beyond the corner of the broken porch. A massive black wolf loped out of the inky darkness and stood next to him. The beast's thick and powerful muscles rippled beneath his pelt as he regarded Angelica with cold yellow eyes.

Angelica smiled and with a sudden snap of her wrists, her lightning ignited, and the Whisper of the Elder sang within her once more. Aiden jumped at the blue-white flash and took a step away from her.

"I was wondering when I would get the chance to finally meet you, Shade," the young woman said. "Although I guess this is just one more of your nightmares. Too bad for you I stopped being afraid of the boogeyman years ago." The great wolf's lips curled back from its wicked fangs and he snarled at her. Murder gleamed in the wolf's stare as the girl's electricity glinted in his eyes. Angelica's declaration of bravery wasn't false bravado though. She felt no fear here. She boldly took a step forward, raising a shield of lightning around her that shredded the encroaching shadows.

The wolf reared back on its hind legs and began to writhe with the sounds of snapping bones and grinding tendons. The forelegs grew longer and thickened into fur-covered arms, huge paws popped and crunched until they changed into long fingers ending in wicked claws. As the wolf rose to his full height, Angelica got her first look at the Father of Nightmares. Aiden fell to one knee and bowed his head.

"You have the smell of my old foe upon you," he growled at her. "So disgusting."

Angelica raised one eyebrow. "Are you saying that *I* smell bad? You're the one with rotten hamburger for a face."

"I come to offer you one final chance, whelp. If you abandon the witch and serve me then I can promise you that this need never come to pass," he said with a wave at the destroyed farmhouse. He leaned forward, his decaying muzzle dripping ichor that sizzled as it fell upon the shield she kept between them. "Or choose instead to fight against me, and this shall be but a taste of the torment I shall put you through."

"Do you make this same offer to every Firstborn, or are you only here because you are afraid of us? You must be some kind of stupid to think I would actually make a deal with you," Angelica shot back.

Shade moved with blinding speed, his claws swiping down at Angelica's face. The newly appointed Guardian, moved faster, raising her shield with one hand to deflect the demon's strike, and firing a bolt of white-hot lightning into the creature's stomach with the other. Shade was thrown back across the yard, but skittered to his feet, smoke rising from his singed pelt.

"You may be safe for now, little witch, but the time draws closer. My servant is loose in your world and your reckoning comes due. Through him, I shall enjoy ripping the flesh from your bones while your mentor watches. And upon her death, there shall be no one left to keep me from feasting on your world." Shade nodded his head as a smoky black swirl of smoke appeared behind him. He stepped backwards into the yawning portal, turned and padded off into the darkness. Aiden stood dumbfounded as the doorway slammed shut, and he looked helplessly back and forth between Angelica and where his master had stood a moment before.

"Hear me well, Aiden," Angelica said. "Your time here is short-lived. I am coming for you. Your mother and I are going to do what no other Firstborn has been able to do. You and that rotting furball are finished." She balled lightning into her hands, gritting her teeth as the energy surged within her, but Aiden dashed off into the night before she could throw her magic at him.

*   *   *

Angelica woke from the vision and saw that she was back in her room. She jumped out of bed and threw open her curtains, relieved this time to see the sleepy forest, slowly waking up with the coming dawn. Despite her victory in the dream world, she knew that facing Aiden wouldn't be so easy. Anne-Marie's son was free and his strength increased. It was the only explanation for how he could have reached her while she slept.

She heard Anne-Marie's door shut from down the hallway, and heard the creak of the stairs as her teacher went about her morning preparations. Angelica bit her lip. This was her fault. Her fight. The very thought of Aiden striking out at her family frightened her far worse than facing Shade had done. She reached for her hooded sweatshirt but spied her new clothes folded neatly on the dresser. She decided instead to put on her Guardian outfit. She pulled the white tunic over her head and decided that Shade had been right about one thing for certain.

There was a battle coming soon.

CHAPTER 15
WORTH FIGHTING FOR – PRESENT DAY

The farmhouse stood quiet in the early evening light, with only the chirps of a few solitary birds breaking the stillness. Angelica stepped quietly from the tree line and stared wistfully at the home she had known her whole life. The grass was wet with dew, and she knew that it would frost over by morning. Each breath she took came out in little wisps as they greeted the chilly wintery air.

Angelica wanted nothing more than to run to the front door, throw it open, and rush inside. She ached to see her family, throw her arms around them all, and assure them that she was alright. She knew she couldn't do that, though. They had to continue believing that she was lost to them.

She studied the empty field, thinking back on fond memories of working with her dad, chasing her brother up and down cornrows, and sitting on the porch steps while her mother sang and played her guitar. She looked at the chicken coop and smiled as she listened to the soft clucking of the hens inside. All of this had been turned upside down because of a destiny that had been forced upon her centuries before she had even been born.

Angelica reached out with heightened senses, searching for any indication that Aiden might be lurking about, but the magical currents remained undisturbed. With a sigh, she wrapped herself in a wall that buzzed with no more energy than a static electricity charge. She had learned today from her spell journal that she could obscure herself from prying eyes, bending the light around her to cloak her presence. She made her way over to the horse pen, where her favorite mare, Bonnie, raised her ears and sniffed the air.

"You know it's me, don't you, girl?" Angelica said softly. "Any way that you can let them know I'm still around?" She reached out to pet the horse, but a spark from her shield zapped the mare's nose. Bonnie snorted and trotted away to the other side of the corral. Angelica leaned against the fence and watched their horses plod and graze around the pen. She let her fingers trace along the fence as she made her way over to the hen house, and past the old barn.

Angelica knew that the barn dated back to colonial times, and had stood like a monument on the Carmichael lands for as long as anyone could remember. She vaguely remembered hearing her grandpa tell the story when she was just a little girl about how the barn had burned down ages ago. The townsfolk had all come together and helped that generation of her family rebuild it into the structure that stood here now. Strong and proud, with "Carmichael Farms" chiseled into the stone lintel over the doorway. It had weathered the years almost as if something magical held it in high regard and protected it from the ravages of time. Angelica smiled to herself and made a mental note to ask Anne-Marie about that someday.

If there ever was another 'someday'.

She meandered around the fields, now lying fallow waiting for the ground to thaw and the next planting season to arrive. Angelica reached the side of the farmhouse and paused beneath the triple window that opened into her parents' room. She laid her fingertips against the glass and her senses were immediately bombarded with waves of sorrow and loss. The young woman snatched her hand away, wiped away the tears that came unbidden to her own eyes, and slowly made her way back to the edge of the field and the tree line where she had started from. The newest Guardian cast her eyes back to her home. She was determined to get back to Whisperwind before she was missed by Anne-Marie, but she needed one last look.

A familiar beat-up green pickup truck turned off of the main road and pulled into the gravel driveway. Angelica knelt down, covering her mouth as she watched Clarissa Brenner hop down from the cab. The two girls had been best friends since they were toddlers, inseparable at school, and sharing playdates and sleepovers without count over the years. Tall and lean, Clarissa had her dirty blonde hair in two braids today that hung down past her shoulders. She was wearing faded blue jeans, the garish red running shoes that Angelica always teased her about, and her 'lucky' school jacket that she had gotten after lettering for the girls' basketball team. Clarissa had something in her hands that Angelica couldn't make out from here, but she bent the wind currents with a twist of her hand and a crackle of light so that she could hear what was going on at the house.

The front door opened, and her mother, Kimberly, walked out onto the porch. Angelica took a step back towards the trees, ready to lose herself in the foliage should her mother turn her way, not entirely trusting her static shield to keep her hidden much longer.

"Hello, Clarissa," Kimberly said. "What are you doing here? I imagined that you were headed to the school by now? Isn't tonight the State Championship game?"

"Hi, Mrs. Brighton. Yeah, I am on my way into town now. The bus won't leave for another 45 minutes though so I have some time." The girl's normally bouncy personality was noticeably subdued. She cast her eyes to the parcel in her hand and squeezed it. "I was getting ready this evening, and while I was digging through my closet, I found something that I thought you might want to have back." She shook out a balled-up denim jacket that was covered in pins and buttons.

Kimberly smiled sadly. "Angie's silly game day jacket. You two always wore these when you went to each other's games."

Clarissa laughed. "Yeah, she must have left it at my house after the semi-finals. She always managed to collect way more pins and buttons than I ever could, though."

"You never could catch me, Bumpkin," Angelica whispered to herself from the tree line.

"Anyway," Clarissa continued, "I just thought that maybe you would want to hang on to it." Kimberly took the coat and hugged it to her chest.

"Thank you, so much, Clarissa. You have no idea how much it means to us how you have led the school in searching for signs of her."

"You don't need to thank me, Mrs. Brighton. Angie is like a sister to me. I'm not going to stop looking for her until we know something for certain. One way or another." She blushed when she realized Kimberly was smiling proudly at her. "She's out there. Somewhere. I don't know why she can't reach out to us, but I'm sure that she has a good reason."

"I feel the same way, Clarissa," said Kimberly. "I can't shake this feeling that there is something brewing that Angelica is all mixed up in the heart of. I just hope that whatever it is she manages to come back safe and sound to us." The two women stood in silence, Clarissa kicking at the wooden porch post while Kimberly absently stroked the fabric of Angelica's jacket.

"It's not going to feel right tonight, being there without her," said Clarissa. "Angie always stirs the crowd up more than the cheerleaders do. I heard that the coach plans to dedicate the game to her if we win tonight. Well, I should probably get going. I really wish I were here picking her up to go with me, though. That's all."

"So do I. We can't give up hope. I have to keep believing that I am going to hear the screen door open one morning and I'll hear her voice in the kitchen shouting for pancakes." They laughed and Kimberly pulled Clarissa into her arms, hugging her tightly. "Thank you again, dear. Run along now, and go have fun tonight." The younger woman wiped her eyes, and stepped back off the front porch, giving Kimberly a shy wave as she stepped into the grass.

"And please tell your mother 'thank you' for that wonderful pot pie she dropped off the other night. I thought Will and Jamie were going to fight over the last of it."

Clarissa looked back over her shoulder as she walked back to her truck. "I'll tell her. She says that maybe as a graduation present she will finally let me in on some of our old family recipes. Goodnight, Mrs. Brighton." With that, she hauled herself back into the cab of her truck, fired up the engine, and backed down the driveway to the main road. She then drove off in a cloud of dust towards town.

Kimberly leaned against the porch post, studying the denim coat she held, and then gazed out to the highway. It dawned on Angelica at that moment that her mother always stood in that same place and the same position every single day waiting for Angelica to step off the school bus. The first thing she saw each day whenever she arrived home from school was her mother waiting for her on the porch.

And that too would never happen again.

A gentle whuff like a gas burner igniting behind her made Angelica look over her shoulder. Anne-Marie stepped from one of her fiery portals and touched down on the ground. The older woman walked over, surveyed the farmscape before her, and stood beside her student.

"He's not here. Aiden wouldn't risk attacking the farm as weak as he still is. He knows that we are keeping watch over this place," the elder woman said in a hushed voice.

"I'm going to kill him. He and Shade have threatened me directly. Threatened them," Angelica said as she pointed to the house.

"We are not murderers, my dear. We will stop him and the old wolf, but we protect, not execute."

"Well, you can bet your ass that I'm not going to wait around and have to avenge, either." Anne-Marie placed her hand on her granddaughter's shoulder and gave it a gentle squeeze, and then she turned her attention back to the dormant fields.

"The farm is so different now from how it was when I lived here," said Anne-Marie. "We kept the chicken coop closer to the front door in the event that we needed to rush out and scare off a fox or a bobcat in a hurry. It was always so nice to serve my boys fresh eggs whenever they wanted them. I do so love the color of the house now that it has siding on it. All we had to look at were the rough sawn timbers that Jeremiah and his father, Alistair, had cut down. They cleared the land and built this farm from nothing when we first came to this country.

"We owned a lot less of the surrounding land, though. That all came later once the farm became truly prosperous and many acres were given to us by our neighbors as dowries. Everybody wanted to marry into the Carmichael family. Did you know that your dear friend, Clarissa, is actually a not so distant cousin of yours?" Anne-Marie sighed wistfully. "We had good friends back then. People who stood beside us in those early days and we repaid their kindness however we could."

Anne-Marie stepped forward to the edge of the closest field. Her eyes fell upon a single spot on the ground and she dropped to her knees. The grass in that place, about the size of a handprint, even this time of year was lush and green, unlike the surrounding dull brown of the wintery landscape.

"This is where it all began," she whispered.

"I used to call it The Fairy Lawn," replied Angelica. "I always imagined as a kid that this end of the field must have hidden the entrance to a world of magic. I pretended that pixies had tea parties here and that if I could catch one, they would carry me off to a castle beyond our world." She snorted. "If only I had known then what the future held in store for me, right?"

"This is the place I came to when I cleansed the fields that first night. How much differently might things have played out if that harvest hadn't saved the farm? I have asked myself many times over the decades how our family would have fared if we had simply left and let Preston take back the land? We could have just started over somewhere new. Our friends and neighbors who knew us best would surely have helped us through the roughest times." She played with some of the dry dirt, letting it crumble between her fingers. "How widespread might our family be today if I had allowed the Firstborns their own chances to raise children?"

"How do you know that they would have even gotten that chance, though? Without you, who would have been there to hold Shade back? You and your descendants held the crystal together. You kept the doorway shut. There might not be a world worth living in if you hadn't made your choice. We're all here because you chose to fight for a better life for your family."

Anne-Marie stood and dusted off her hands. She flashed a knowing smile at Angelica. "Then why are you here, convinced that you won't see them ever again? Have you already resigned yourself to the idea that your life is now over, and you have come for one last fleeting glimpse of those you leave behind?"

"I'm scared," Angelica whispered. "What if I'm not enough? What if I face Aiden and my magic can't stop his? If I fall, I don't just let you down, or even just them. You have put the survival of the entire world on my shoulders."

"It is a terrible burden and one that I wish I did not have to place on anyone, ever. When I made my oath in Shade's dark realm all those years ago that I would oppose him until I died, I didn't realize then the immensity of that promise. I never expected to be here 300 years longer than I have any right to be." She lifted Angelica's chin and looked into her eyes. "But here I am, and with a responsibility no less important now than it was at the time of my own Ascension. Through no fault of your own, you share that responsibility, as unfair as that may seem. However, as you said yourself, I chose to fight so that our family could have a future.

"What choice will you make?" Anne-Marie asked as she raised an eyebrow. She looked one last time back at the farmhouse. "Don't stay too late, child. We need to begin our hunt for Aiden as soon as possible before he strikes again, and I would feel better if we spent even a small time more in training tonight." Anne-Marie walked behind a mighty oak tree. Angelica saw a flash of purple fire from behind it and knew that her tenth great grand-mother was gone.

She returned her attention to the farmhouse. Her dad was on the porch now. He wrapped his arms around her mom, and Angelica saw her shoulders quake as she rested her head on her father's chest. From the corner of her eye, she saw her brother, Jamie, riding his bike up the dirt road, probably coming back from his friend, Billy Harmon's house. He coasted to a stop upon seeing his parents, set down his bicycle in the grass, and slowly climbed up the porch steps. He paused for a moment then threw his arms around them both. The family stood together as one, strong because of the love they shared for each other, and for the one that was no longer beside them.

Angelica swallowed the lump in her throat. She clenched her fist and felt her lightning sizzle from her fingertips to her elbow and back down again.

"What other choice is there?" she said as she spun on her heel and began the trip back to Whisperwind.

CHAPTER 16
TENSIONS RISING - 1671

"Mama," cried Thomas, "may I please have this tin soldier? It's been so long since I've had a new toy of my own!" Anne-Marie's youngest son held the brightly painted metal man up for her inspection.

"Did something happen to your old one? The one that Aiden gave you?"

"I have him still, mama, but he's all alone and is painted blue. This fine fellow is red and could give Captain Halloran someone to finally square off against instead of simply pretending he has an enemy."

"It's hardly wise to look for someone to square off against, son." She looked at the few remaining coins in the palm of her hand. Her trip to town with Thomas had been intended solely for some cloth, a new washtub, and some nails that Jeremiah needed to mend a section of the barn wall.

Micah Robillard, the town smith, appeared from the back room of his shop carrying the large washtub with the bag of nails inside it. "Here you go, Mrs. Carmichael," the young man said as he set the items on the counter. "Please let your husband know that if he needs any help with those repairs, I would be happy to lend a hand if he can hold off but another day."

"I'll pass it along, Micah, but it's only a few loose boards on the back barn wall that our plow horse, Blaze, kicked out during that thunderstorm the other night. Besides, Aiden jumps at every chance he gets to work on a project with his father."

"I know the feeling, ma'am," Micah said.

"I'm so sorry, Micah. That was thoughtless of me. Tell me, how is your mother these days? I am sure it must be difficult for you both so soon after your Da's passing."

The young man smiled sadly and nodded. "No offense taken, Mrs. Carmichael. Ma's a strong woman, thank ye for asking. Some nights I can hear her crying from her sleeping loft, and I know she misses him terribly. He did well by teaching me his trade, though, and the forge is doing well. There's plenty of work these days so that I am able to provide for us."

"You are a good and devoted son to her. I have no doubt she is proud to see you take up your father's hammer. I am so relieved to hear that your forge is thriving."

"Aye. Why just yesterday I delivered up a rather large order of picks and shovels over to Preston Mathers' home. The account was paid in full by coin."

"Picks and shovels? I have a hard time imagining that man doing any sort of labor that requires tools such as those."

Micah laughed. "I can't argue with you on that one, ma'am. That burly brute who's never far from Mathers' side was the one who accepted the order from me. I'd say it's more likely that he'll be the one doing the hard work. He or one of the other ruffians that are always about that house."

"Mama," Thomas said as he tugged gently on Anne-Marie's sleeve. "Could we ask about the tin soldier, please?"

"Yes, yes, Thomas." She ran her fingers through his hair with a playful shake. "Micah, how much more would the tin soldier my son is so enamored with add to our bill? I believe I still have enough that I can quiet this little scamp."

Micah grinned and squatted down so he was face to face with Thomas. "I'll tell you what, my good lad. If you promise me that you'll not make your dear mother tote this heavy tub to your wagon by herself, then you may have the honorable Corporal Benson as payment for services rendered. How say you, sir?"

"Oh, Micah, I can't let you do that," Anne-Marie said. "The cost of the metal and paint, not to mention the detail you put into the carving. Your time for such lovely work alone is…"

"Is well covered by your Jeremiah and his father's regular business to my Da for all these years past, and if that didn't square the account, then you are covered several times over by the business I had with Mathers yesterday. Please, Mrs. Carmichael, as a small token for all the kindness you and yours have passed along to me and my mum."

"Thank you, sir," said Thomas without another word as he dragged the washtub from the counter into his arms. The boy stumbled under the heavy load, but he held it steady. Anne-Marie thanked the young smith again, paid for her purchases, and led Thomas out the door to their wagon.

As her son hoisted their goods into the cart, Anne-Marie spied two of Preston's mercenaries loading a wagon of their own with crates, tools, lanterns, and food down the street at Mathers' home. Hollister Adams climbed up into the driver seat while Landry Cross settled himself into the cargo bed. Preston Mathers waddled out from the doorway of his house with his shadow, Patch Erickson, standing close behind. A wisp of fire danced unbidden between her fingers as the portly man approached his men. She took advantage of the errant flame and brought their conversation to her ears, glancing about to make sure that no one else saw the subtle twist of her hand.

"Take the supplies to the site, and unload quickly. I need you both back in town this evening. If you can crate up some of what's lying around loose then fine, but otherwise, leave it for later. I've a larger plan to set in motion over the next few days."

"Yes, sir," said Hollister. He gave his employer a chance to step away then with a crack of a whip to the horses, turned the wagon up the road headed out of town. Hollister tipped his cap to Anne-Marie as the wagon rolled by, while Landry gave her an exaggerated wink and let out a lewd whistle. They left her in a trail of dust as they headed in the same general direction as her farm.

Anne-Marie turned and saw Mathers staring at her from his front steps. He raised his hand to his brow in a mocking salute and then turned to go back into his home. Erickson leaned against the porch post, his arms crossed over his chest as stared at her and her son. She met his gaze without flinching, but she snuffed the pale fire that still burned in her palm lest he catch sight of it.

She turned and lifted Thomas into their wagon, settling him in beside their parcels. The boy addressed his new recruit about the struggles and trials that lay before him as a member of Thomas Carmichael's elite legion.

"...but most importantly, Corporal," the boy said in a deep commanding voice, "is that you must know when to prepare yourself for war."

It was an ominous sentiment, but one that, at that moment, sent a shiver racing down Anne-Marie's spine.

*　　*　　*

Jeremiah and Anne-Marie waved to the Brenners as they left the Huntsman for the evening. Jeremiah had ridden to town with Aiden on horseback and caught up with his wife and Thomas before they had started back to the farm. Convincing his family to enjoy a fine meal among close friends had been an easy thing. The burly farmer wrangled his two boys into the bed of the wagon while Anne-Marie held the reins to their mare, Sadie.

"...And then I'll stop by the lake along the road home and launch you two ruffians into it," he playfully growled as the two boys wrestled within his thick arms. Anne-Marie laughed as she watched the antics of her boys, and was grateful that Jeremiah was such a devoted and loving husband and father. He wasn't one to overindulge in drink, and he had never in all the years they had been together ever raised a hand to any of them. She knew that Jeremiah would never back down from a fight should the need arise, though, and she had no doubt that the man knew how to take care of himself should words come to blows.

The scuff of a boot behind her prompted her to glance over her shoulder. Hollister Adams and Landry Cross stood nearby watching Jeremiah and her sons. The smell of spirits wafted from the two men, and Cross, in particular, seemed as though he swayed like a sapling in a gentle breeze. Adams watched them and snorted. The scrawny man twirled a knife in dazzling circles around his fingers and then whispered something to his fellow. The bigger man brayed derisively and slapped his friend on the shoulder.

Anne-Marie's temper flared. "It's a fine evening full of good humor, gentlemen. Pray share the joke that we might all enjoy it."

"Good evening, to you as well, Goody Carmichael," said Hollister with a tip of his hat. His words carried a slight slur as his eyes lewdly looked her up and down. "I was just having a jest with my friend here. Didn't mean any harm by it, but I fear too that it might not be well received in proper company, so I beg your pardon."

"A jest not suitable for sharing sounds more akin to an insult," she fired back. She made no effort to keep her voice in check, and her words carried up and down the length of the street. A rumble of thunder filled the night as her fist clenched at her side, and the heat within her began to rise.

*   *   *

Jeremiah looked up from his sons and saw his wife squaring up against Preston's men. He had seen the look on his wife's face aimed in his direction too many times and knew it would only lead to trouble. He tried quickly to free himself from the clutches of his two sons, but they wrapped him up like vines on a tree. The burly farmer finally freed himself from his boys' clutches and hurried to his wife's side.

"Annie, pay him no mind. Clearly, these boys have been enjoying themselves tonight, and are just poking fun at our expense."

"That's right, 'Annie'," said Cross. "Mind the Pig Chaser, and the Scourge of Young Lads." He burst into laughter, snorting like a hog. Adams roared and slapped his knee as tears ran down his face. A small crowd had gathered in the street to see what was going on, and some joined in with uneasy chuckling of their own as the two mercenaries clowned about.

Anne-Marie's lips pulled back in a snarl, and Jeremiah saw for one terrifying moment the flicker of purple roll across his wife's irises. His nightmare vision flashed through his mind and he knew that if he couldn't diffuse matters right away, her temper would reveal her secret to the growing crowd of bystanders.

"Ahh, so I'm the real target for your ill-suited remarks, is it?" he said as he stepped in front of his wife. "Perhaps one or both of you would like to try your mettle against me then rather than so rudely play the bully to my wife? Or would you rather I wait here a minute so that you can go fetch your bows that you might take another shot at me the way you did in the woods the other day?" The crowd's laughter turned to gasps and murmurs. Preston's men eyed each other nervously as Jeremiah stepped closer.

"Ye know good and well that shot was an accident, sir," stammered Adams.

"I know no such thing," Jeremiah growled. "You had just killed one of my pigs, and, for all I know, you could have been hoping to make sure that there was no witness to your theft."

"You wouldn't be standing here now if I wanted you dead, Carmichael," said Landry. The dim-witted thug raised his fist and stepped towards Jeremiah, but the farmer was ready. Cross was powerful but as slow with his fist as he was with his mind. Jeremiah ducked the clumsy swing and threw a hard right of his own. His punch caught Landry squarely in the jaw rocking him backward. The farmer fell into an easy fighting crouch that revealed to the onlookers that this was not his first scrap. Cross regained his footing and spat a bloody tooth into the road. He snatched the wicked knife from his partner's hand and drew back to throw.

Hollister jumped in between the two men and elbowed his friend as hard as he could in the ribs, fouling the brutish man's aim and driving him back a step. "Put that away, you fool," he shouted. He turned and opened his other hand to Jeremiah, stopping the big farmer before he moved forward to meet Cross' attack. Marcus jumped in front of Jeremiah as well and placed his brawny hands on his friend's shoulders.

"Turn your man loose, Adams," growled Jeremiah. "Let's see where that knife ends up." He glanced as quickly as he dared at his wife, hoping that she had enough sense to stay out of the fight. He could see the lavender fires burning in her eyes, but at least for now, she held her power in check.

"I think that we are all just off on the wrong footing tonight," said Adams. "Master Carmichael, can we not just chalk all of this up to a terrible misunderstanding and all of us go about our business? I would remind you that you were paid in gold for the loss of your animal that we mistakenly killed. We'll head back to our bunks, while you and your family head on away to your home. As you said, sir, we've all had a few drinks tonight, and we've let it reach our tempers. I trust when tomorrow dawns we can all forget any hard feelings when next we cross paths." He bowed and backed up pulling at Landry's arm as he did so. The crowd began to melt away although the hushed whispers continued in the night. Marcus stood with Jeremiah until the tensions had vanished and then left for his inn after giving a clap to the farmer's back.

Jeremiah turned back to his family. Aiden and Thomas hugged each other in the wagon bed, staring wide-eyed at their father. "No harm done, lads," he called out to his boys.

.Anne-Marie redirected her scowl from Preston's retreating men to him. "Don't ever stand in my way like that again," she said. "I could have ended the fight far more easily than you could have."

"And what then?" he shot back. He kept his voice soft and level for her. "Let everyone in town know what you are capable of? You know of my own vision concerning your nemesis, Annie. Don't do anything that will make it come to pass." He jerked a thumb back at the duo. "They were drunk and Cross might as well have told me where he planned to punch me. I liked my odds in this one."

"And what of my dream? How can I let you take unnecessary risks knowing that the worst thing imaginable could happen to you?" She took his hands, and her scowl finally faded.

"A street brawl was not the way I fell in your vision, so even if Shade has his way with me one day, that time was not now." He pulled her close and kissed her forehead. "I'll make you a deal. Next fight we get into with them, I'll take the weasel and leave the big one for you."

She laughed and looked up into his warm smile. "Next time, you'll have to race me to get to either one of them before I finish them off." She paused a moment and then stepped away from his embrace. "Adams said that they paid for the pig in gold. I don't think you shared that detail with me the other day."

"Didn't I? Must have slipped my mind. I know that I told you they paid for the old girl, though."

"Yes, but those gold nuggets. I saw those buffoons leave Mathers' home earlier today with a wagon full of picks, shovels, and other mining equipment. Mathers has found something," she said.

"He'll find my boot in his hindquarters if his men take any more of our livestock," Jeremiah said as he looked down the street. The two thugs had already disappeared into the barracks in Mathers' courtyard.

"Whatever he has found, I suspect that it has something to do with why he likes to harass us so frequently," Anne-Marie said.

"And I intend to find out what it is," she added under her breath.

Chapter 17
Tortured Soul - 1671

Parson Corbin Reynolds closed his Bible and set it on the end table beside his chair. The heavy pounding on his front door hammered through his sparse cottage again. Whoever was on the other side clearly wasn't in the greatest mood.

"Open the door, you scoundrel," roared an angry voice from outside. "Come answer for what you've done with my wife, you charlatan!"

Corbin scrambled from his chair and crouched down behind it. He could see through the tiny front window the hulking shadow of Horace Pritchard on his front stoop. Behind the man stood a crowd of people in the street, several of whom carried bags with feathers falling out and floating slowly to the dusty cobbles while others carried pots sticky with black tar.

This is it, he thought to himself. I have to run before they catch me. Corbin snatched up his Bible and dashed into the adjoining bedroom. He grabbed a small pouch that had a few meager coins he had scraped together. A loud boom at the front door sounded suspiciously as though someone with very broad shoulders had thrown themselves against the frame. A second boom rattled the window beside him, and the distinct crack of splitting wood assured him that his time was short.

Reynolds looked frantically around the room and realized that his escape was far more important than anything he owned. He quickly decided that he could just squeeze through the narrow window beside his bed. He glanced out the pane and sighed in relief as he saw no signs of anyone standing watch to see if he should come out that way. Just as his feet hit the ground, the unmistakable crash of someone splintering his front door followed behind him. Without a second thought, Corbin Reynolds raced down the street towards the edge of town.

"There he goes," shouted someone standing at his porch. Corbin didn't look to see who had spied him. He simply ran as fast as he could. He raced past the curious faces of bystanders who were not a part of the lynch mob, and who had no inkling of why the town minister ran as though the devil himself was close at hand.

Reynolds dashed out of the town limits into the dark woods that surrounded the town of Pioneer Vale. He could still hear the shouts and calls of people who had been part of his congregation, who now sought to deliver the preacher his reckoning. Horses whinnied, pistol shots cracked into the night, but none of it sounded as loud to him as the sound of his heart hammering in his chest. He looked down the pitch-black road as it stretched into the forest and shivered. He had no choice though. It was either into the untamed wilds or back to face his due for his crimes. He chuckled nervously as he thought that the wild creatures of the forest would probably maul him far more gently than Goodman Pritchard intended to. He gripped his Bible a little more tightly and plunged into the darkness.

The sound of hoofbeats thundered closer and closer, and he knew that the search party was closing in on him. The road he followed was faster traveling for him, but they would ride him down in short order if he stayed upon it. As much as it terrified him, he knew that he had to get himself into the brush or risk being overtaken.

Brambles and thorns tore his hands as he pushed his way into the underbrush to the side of the road. His pursuers' shouts echoed deafeningly in the night around him, echoing from all around. He spun about thinking that someone had already gotten behind him, and blindly he charged into the thick bushes. Galloping horses raced by on the road, the clatter of their iron shoes sounding as if they were right alongside him, thought the road lay some distance away from where he hunkered down. Corbin trembled with his back against the trunk of a large oak tree and listened to his pursuers slowly fade away. The sudden cry of a howling wolf split the night and a soaking warmth spread through his trousers as his fear overtook him.

"They'll be back as soon as they realize that they must have passed you by," said a voice from the shadows. The hood of a lantern opened nearby, blinding Reynolds with the harsh light. Preston Mathers leaned into the beam, catching a flame with a twig from the flickering wick and lighting his long clay pipe. "You just keep running into me at the most opportune moments, Corbin, although I regret that I haven't any dry knickers to offer you." The portly man's belly shook as he laughed mockingly at the minister.

"Preston, what are you doing out here?" A thought suddenly crossed the preacher's mind and he found his backbone. He rose up straight and tall and pointed an accusing finger at Mathers. "Did you betray my confidence? Is this all your doing?"

Preston blew a smoke ring into the air, "Corbin, I am still owed a favor for holding my tongue. Why would I throw away such a valuable bargaining chip as that? No, my friend, have you not heard the good news that Goody Pritchard has recently learned that she is expecting an addition to their family. The only complication is that her husband was not home to tend his own hearth fires at the time the little bundle of joy would have been conceived. She didn't require much convincing before giving away the name of the unexpected father."

"Where is she? Did he hurt her?"

"Of course not, Corbin. Horace loves his wife, although she did betray his trust. He would never lay a hand to that woman." The sounds of returning horses drifted closer. Angry shouts filled the night, and Preston's mouth curled into a wicked grin. "I don't think you shall fare as fortunately though. But I come to you once again as a friend, Parson. Come along with me. I know of a place where you can safely hide out until we can find a way to spirit you away from Pioneer Vale and the dangers it now holds for you." Preston held out his hand, waiting for the clergyman to shake it and seal their bond.

Corbin's hand trembled as he started to reach forward. He looked at the overly eager look on the moneylender's face and was suddenly disgusted. He yanked his hand back and wiped it on his shirt.

"I think not, Preston. I'd prefer to take my chances rather than seal myself any deeper with you." The baying of hunting dogs made Reynolds jump. Preston laughed, a deep chuckle at first but growing into a raucous bellow. He slammed shut the hood of the lantern, once again casting Corbin into the gloomy night. The preacher turned and ran opposite the direction of the oncoming pursuit.

Branches slapped his face as he raced through the forest. He tripped over a tree root and sprawled into the dry leaves on the ground. His Bible flew from his hand, lost in the dark underbrush. He shook his head and looked around at the clearing he had stumbled into. The silver moonlight shimmered off of a polished stone slab that lay in the grass before him. A strange sense of peace washed over him, driving away the terror instilled by his pursuers. He reached his hand towards the stone when the snap of a branch cracked behind him.

The preacher whirled around and studied the tree line. A strange smell filled the air, carrying with it the stench of foul decay, and Corbin gagged as he tried to regain his feet. The calm feeling he had felt but a moment before changed into a cold wash of fear that clutched his heart unlike any horror that the skittish man had ever known.

Pale yellow eyes burned into him from the bushes ahead, and Reynolds scrambled back on all fours as the monstrous shape of an enormous wolf rose upright on its hind legs, hugging the shadows around the grove. The beast circled slowly, and the low chuckle that rumbled from the wolf's maw chilled Corbin's very soul.

"You should be more careful whose side you choose, Parson," growled the creature before him. A flash of fire to the side revealed his Bible, consumed in seconds by a sickly yellow flame. Just before the fire went out, Corbin saw the snarling creature crouch, then leap at him with razor-sharp fangs bared.

*   *   *

It was true.

Corbin had woken in his chair at home drenched in sweat and had felt as if the very walls were closing in around him. As the horrible nightmare pecked away at the back of his mind, he had raced to the Pritchard household and bounded up the steps to the porch.

Madeline had opened the door before he could even knock. The smell of her hair weakened his knees as she took his hands and drew him inside. Without a care of who might see from the streets, he followed her, but pushed past her, pacing in the entryway and wringing his hands. She looked at him with her eyes alight and pulled him into her arms when he turned to face her. Her lips were soft, but she kissed him aggressively and pressed tightly against him.

"I didn't expect to see you until later," she said in a breathless hush as she began to unbutton his jacket. He gently pushed her back and held her at arm's length.

"I didn't know that I would be here at all," he said. "I have had a horrible vision and it compelled me to come see you at once." He closed his eyes and took a deep breath. He gently placed his hand on her belly. "Are we discovered? Or rather, are we soon to be?"

Her mouth dropped open and she stared at him in shock. "How did you know, Corbin? I only just discovered it myself yesterday. Isn't it wonderful?"

"Wonderful? My love, your reputation will be in tatters and it is my fault. At best your husband will only throw you out into the streets. At the worst,..." his words slipped away as he didn't dare think of what he was about to say.

"Hush, my love," Madeline said. "I have already figured how we can keep our secret to ourselves. My husband returns from his patrols in another week, and whenever he is away for so long, the first thing the oaf ever wants to do is drag me to the marriage bed. It will be a simple thing to hide our tryst. I can simply say that the child is his, and upon the day of its birth, that it came into the world early. We need never be discovered."

Corbin chewed his bottom lip and plopped down onto the wooden bench near the fireplace of the Pritchard home. "That might work," he murmured. "Oh, Madeline, you might have just saved us all."

The young wife untied the ribbon holding back her hair and shook her curls loose. She then stepped forward with a playful swagger in her step, unlacing her bodice as she moved, and straddled the clergyman. She took hold of his shirt and pulled it over his head. Her lips found his and after a few passionate seconds, she leaned in close and whispered breathlessly in his ear.

"Have no fear. I will take care of everything."

*   *   *

Corbin closed the door of the chapel and rested his forehead against the rough wood. After he had left Madeline, nowhere else felt safe to him. He feared going home in case the angry mob from his vision became as much of a reality as their unborn child. The hollow emptiness of the vacant church mirrored what he felt in his soul.

He swallowed the bile that had risen in his throat as he had walked through the dusty streets. Every set of eyes seemed to carry glares of hypocrisy and scorn as he passed, although truly his congregation merely went about their evening business. In fact, every townsperson he met had greeted him with warmth and gratitude for being their guide towards salvation.

Corbin sneered at himself. The only man in this town that was more despicable than he was Preston Mathers. Reynolds stood in the pulpit each Sunday and looked over those expectant faces, wanting nothing more than to shout for them to see him for the fraud that he truly was. What would they do if he could confess his own sins to them? More than once he wondered if he should pack his meager belongings and just disappear. Let the town prosper or fail without him.

Yet he couldn't bring himself to do it. Despite the loathing he felt for himself, he knew he couldn't leave these people without a spiritual leader. So where did his hypocrisy end? He walked down the aisle of the chapel, his hands caressing the straight wooden back of each pew as he made his way to the front of the church. He climbed the short stair to his pulpit and opened up the Bible that rested there.

The book fell open to a delicate handkerchief laying flat between the pages. It was a token he couldn't bear to part with though it would surely damn him if ever it were discovered. He brought the hidden treasures to his face, closed his eyes, and breathed in the sweet scent that still clung ever so faintly in the fabric. His mind wandered to the day that Madeline had given this to him. The sound of her laughter, the crinkling of her nose as she laughed, and the taste of her lips on his own always burned within his mind.

He sadly understood that what he felt was more than just a physical longing, and it was so much more than an infatuation. Regardless of everything he was supposed to stand for, he had fallen in love with a married woman. None of his choices were promising. He could never have her for his own.

He gently placed the handkerchief back in its hiding place and closed the cover. He had no business here. He didn't deserve the respect and admiration that the town had for him. He was a wretch. He was a fraud. Worse still, he was a coward. Too afraid to accept the responsibility of what he had done, and now he was indebted to the devil himself.

He expected every day that Mathers would call in the favor for his silence. He was such a fool. Why did he trust that Preston would even hold his tongue? Surely everybody in league with the man knew the truth already. He had seen the sneers from Preston's hired guards whenever he passed them on the street. Had Magistrate Lucas ever gazed upon him without contempt in his eyes?

Corbin went into the tiny study off of the main hall where he wrote his sermons. He sat down behind the desk and pulled a leather folio from the drawer. The parson drew out two sheets of paper covered in his handwriting, placing them on the desktop and gently smoothing them flat. He dipped a fresh quill into the inkwell and then read the lines on the front of the first sheet.

Herein are the written confessions of a failed clergyman. I, Corbin Reynolds, do set the record straight for all of the marks against my eternal soul....

He skimmed through the listing of every sin he could ever remember committing, large and small. He saw where he had stolen his brother's

Yuletide treats when they were boys. Here was his account of cheating at the card game that had won him passage to the New World to escape the debts that he had inherited when his father had died. His brother had suffered for that cowardice as well. Corbin took a deep breath and read past several others until he got to the most recent entry:

I have engaged in an adulterous affair using my position as the Spiritual leader of Pioneer Vale to gain unfair influence over the young woman whose virtue I have compromised. I shall not name her so that I might spare her and her family the indignity of my own transgression, but I have not, however, escaped unnoticed. The Devil of Pioneer Vale, Preston Mathers, was witness to my late-night egress from the lady's home and uses his knowledge to leverage me into assisting him with some as yet unknown plot of his own devices.

With a sigh, Corbin put his quill to work, adding the new details of the child he had fathered and the plot to deceive everyone of the baby's true parentage. He reread the entry when he was finished, satisfied with the confession he had put forth. Although he was certain that his lover's name would be dragged to light should anyone ever find this document, Reynolds held to the glimmer of hope that she might escape with her dignity unblemished. He would own up to his role in the affair but swore to spare her family however he could.

He sprinkled some sand over the paper to dry the ink and blew away the excess. The pages before him stared back with a damning solemnity. There was more than enough in these words to get him run out of town. He gathered the sheets and thought of the real possibility of life on the run. Where could he go that his deeds wouldn't find him? Into the wilderness where he could be attacked by wild animals or the savages that hunted the outskirts of the colony? He would be as good as dead. If he wanted to get himself killed he might as well meet Horace Pritchard when he returned and tell him to his face about his time with Madeline.

He crumpled the pages into a ball in his hand and knelt before the small fireplace. The ashes were cold so he threw in a few pieces of kindling from the bucket at his side. He placed the sheets in the center as he built a small stack of twigs and small branches into the hearth. A loud knock on the study door startled him, and he nearly dropped the candle he had picked up from the desk.

Corbin fell back on his rear as the door swung open and a hulking shadow crossed over him. As he looked up, Reynolds realized that his time of reckoning had come sooner than expected. Patch Erickson leaned against the door frame and spit a stream from between his teeth onto the floor of the chapel.

"Evenin', Parson," the gruff man said. He glanced into the fireplace. "Awfully fine paper to be using for fire starters. Something important you're trying to be rid of?" The man's wicked grin showed stained teeth. Corbin noticed that the one in front had a chip taken out of it.

"Just a draft of a sermon that hadn't moved me as I had hoped. If it doesn't fire my own passions, how can I hope to lift up and inspire my congregation? Is there something I can do for you this evening, my son? I have so many things I need to attend to, so I do hope we can be brief."

"Pretty sure we both know why I'm here, Parson. Preston Mathers would like to have a word with you."

CHAPTER 18
DOWN IN A HOLE - 1671

It had taken three days before Anne-Marie found a chance to break away from the farm again, but at least discovering the wagon ruts left behind by Preston's' thugs had been easy enough. The tracks had turned off the main road at the smaller trail that snaked up the side of Alistair's Climb, a mountain overlook named after Jeremiah's father who had discovered a coveted fishing spot in a lake at the top. Over the years, the people who lived in and around Pioneer Vale had carved a veritable road, blazing a back and forth trail of switchbacks to make the ascent easier to reach. Timbers cut from the cleared trees lined the path clearly showing the way. Although the trail seemed narrow for a full size wagon, Mathers' men had managed the tight turns all the same.

Jeremiah had left for town early that morning with the boys in tow. He had deliveries to make to the Huntsman as well as satisfying a few other contracts with some of their neighbors. She knew that it would be well into the evening before he returned to their farmhouse. His departure left her free to discover just exactly what Preston's business was up in the hills so close to their land. She had set out on foot after giving her husband ample time to drive away, making certain that he hadn't needed to double back for anything.

Anne-Marie stuck to the side of the winding trail, allowing herself the opportunity to hide in the underbrush should she meet any of Preston's mercenaries along the path. She was just making the turn for the third switchback when she noticed that the wagon ruts vanished from the road. It was as if the wagon had stopped and been plucked from the ground by some unseen hand.

"Well, where did you go?" she muttered. "You didn't take to the skies, did you?" Anne-Marie backed down the road and stood between the wagon ruts. She extended her hand and let the flow of power roar through her body. The trail suddenly streaked out ahead of her in twin lines of lavender flame, and she smiled as she saw the path lead off the road entirely and into the dense bushes nearby.

She walked forward again and studied the grass. Now that she knew what she was looking for, the telltale signs of the mercenaries' attempts to camouflage the wagon's course became obvious. Someone had stirred up the grass to conceal where the wagon had gone straight into the tree line instead of making the turn to go higher up the Climb. As she stepped closer, she saw a screen of bushes and branches held up by a camouflaged rope and pulley system that masked the newly created avenue that led to the low side of the mountain, and back down towards the valley floor.

Anne-Marie checked both ahead and behind her. Satisfied that she was still the only person on the trail, she stepped behind the makeshift barrier and proceeded down the concealed pathway. Beyond the screen, she quickly found the wagon ruts once again and knew she had found what she was looking for.

As she crept forward, Anne-Marie opened herself up to the river of magic that surrounded her, ready to call upon its power should the need suddenly arise. She brought forth a small ball of lavender fire into the cup of her hand both to illuminate the shadowy path before her, and to have ready to throw in the event of an ambush. The sunlight punched through the foliage ahead of her as the trail opened up into a clearing. Using the cover of the encroaching trees, Anne-Marie made her stealthy approach.

The clearing ahead was stacked with tools and lumber. Picks and shovels peeked out from beneath oilskin tarps. Dozens of empty crates were piled near the wagon that Mathers' men had driven to the worksite. At the base of the hill, a smelter and empty molds shaped like ingots stood next to a cave entrance that plunged into the side of the mountain.

The echo of voices floated up the tunnel, and Anne-Marie crouched into the nearby bushes as Hollister Adams and Landry Cross emerged from the cave mouth. With a swirl of the fire that capered across her fingers, the Guardian bent the air current to carry their conversation to her ears.

"This sure would be a lot simpler if we didn't have to do all this skulking around to bring the gold to Preston," said Cross.

"Well, he blames us for the Carmichael's crops doing so well. He swears it was us that screwed up such a simple plan to poison their farmland. I still don't know how they pulled off such a bumper crop like they did, though." Hollister took off his hat and scratched his greasy head. "Hell, you saw the farm yerself. The soil was dying, and those crops shouldn't have been enough to feed their family, let alone half the damn Vale."

Cross nodded. "Yeah, and now we're stuck digging in this blasted hole, sneaking back and forth to town each day. I swear, we ought to just go down to that farm and burn the whole place to the ground. Show that family what happens when they cross the likes of us. I'd still like to stick a knife into that son of a bitch. You shouldn't have stopped me the other night."

"Too many people around the Vale like those folks. If something bad like that happened, then someone in town would start asking questions. Figure out the whole story. They'd run Preston out of town the moment that he tried to reclaim that land." The skinny man picked something out of the stubble of his beard and flicked it away. "No, Preston's a smart man, even if he is a heartless bastard. He always has some scheme brewing and I bet even now he has some trick up his sleeve. Probably something to do with that one tunnel he always visits when he comes out here. You ever go down inside of it?"

"Hell, no!" Landry made a sign to ward off evil spirits that the local natives used. "Preston said he'd skin alive anyone who went down there, and I don't doubt his word on that one. Just the entry to that hole gives me the shivers. Something isn't right down there. You've seen the rats that run through the tunnels? Well, when I followed him to the mouth of that place last time he was here, it struck me that there weren't any rats to be seen. Not that we had simply scared them off because we were there, mind you. There weren't any droppings. No cave crickets. Nothing living goes near that cave. Nothing except Preston. Whatever he is keeping down there, he can have it. As long as the gold keeps coming in, I'm happy to just do what he tells me." The big man glanced back into the cave mouth and shuddered.

Adams nodded. "Yeah, I have to agree there, but mark my words. I'd wager that silver-tongued devil will have the townsfolk handing him the key to the Carmichael farmhouse before all is said and done."

"Well, take your wager and buy the first pitcher when we get back to town. Let's hurry up and get the last of that lumber hauled in here so we can get going." Landry climbed into the driver seat of the wagon while Hollister mounted a beautiful chestnut mare that stood tied to a hitching post. Together they rode down the trail leading deeper into the woods and out of sight.

Anne-Marie gave the men a few moments before she crept forward towards the mine entrance. A tunnel led down into the ground with support beams spaced about every twenty feet with a lantern mounted on the first one. She called a spark to the wick and adjusted the brightness as she delved deeper into the earth. Most of the stonework was natural, but stretches of the walls showed the chips and scrapes of tool strikes. The air grew chill the deeper she went, but she channeled a shawl of wispy fire around her shoulders to keep away the cold.

The tunnel widened ahead and she exited into a vast chamber that was obviously the main worksite for Preston's men. Crates of raw ore were stacked near the tunnel mouth that she came out of, and the glittering sparkles from the lantern light left no doubt in her mind that she was looking at chunks of gold. She held the lantern higher and saw the far wall of the cavern shimmer with an incalculable fortune in unmined metal.

It all made sense now. If she and Jeremiah hadn't been able to repay their debt to Preston, all of this land, their land, would have been his to mine freely. He had tried to poison their crops to make them default, but Anne-Marie's Ascension to the mantle of Guardian had thwarted his plan. She had to get back to town and show proof that Mathers was every bit as corrupt as people already believed.

She turned back towards the entrance when she felt an eerie sensation from one of the side tunnels hidden at the far end of the cavern. Unlike all the other branches, this entrance was lost in the gloom with no lantern to pierce the darkness. As she stepped closer, a terrible chill radiated from the depths of the dark corridor. A whisper like that of the Elder Guardian found her ear, but it was dark and malevolent. The breeze that blew up from the mineshaft hinted of brimstone and decay.

Anne-Marie realized that this must be the tunnel that Preston's men had discussed above ground. She knew that she shouldn't spend any more time here than necessary, but something down there hammered against her magical senses. She took a deep breath and went into the depths with her lantern held before her.

The tunnel sloped down leading her into the belly of the mountain. The stone walls were dry and bore the marks of ragged claws that had raked gouges in the ancient stone. The wind moaned in her ears, carrying upon it the agonized wail of a thousand tortured souls. Anne-Marie coughed as a cloud of fine dust swirled around her face. She turned her head to the side to keep it out her eyes and locked gazes with a grinning skull housed in one of the barrows along the wall. As she stumbled back in alarm, the scar that Shade had burned into her forearm blazed with an icy fire that dropped her to her knees. It was the voice that purred in her head, however, that sent the true shiver down her spine.

"Hello, sweetling."

She heard a creak of wood and a pale yellow light filled the room. The lid of an ancient chest fell back. Anne-Marie laid eyes upon the sickly pulsating crystal that sat within, realizing that she had discovered the eons-old droplet that had fallen when the Elder Guardian had wounded his Adversary. The gem rose from the velvet cushion it rested upon and began to spin in a slow rotation. As the light from the stone grew more intense, the shadows melted away from the rough walls.

Anne-Marie gasped at the brutal depictions of sacrifice and slaughter that adorned the cavern. Torches flared to life deeper within the chamber, revealing a bloodstained altar dominated from above by the carved maw of a giant wolf's head. She covered her mouth as she took in every last detail of her nemesis' decaying face captured flawlessly by some long-dead sculptor. As she returned her attention to the crystal, a shadow slowly passed across it from within, that took the smoky shape of Shade's wickedly snarling muzzle.

"Convenient of you to find this place on your own. It saves my agents from dragging you here later," came the growling whisper in her thoughts.

"So Mathers serves you in our world." Anne-Marie kept her distance from the spinning gem, but she met the demon's eyes without flinching.

"That fool serves himself. We simply have mutual interests at this point, for which I have seen fit to reward him. The day fast approaches, however, when the blood of your teacher shall drip down my altar and the gateway into your world shall lay open to me."

"You still have no way to find her, wolf."

"I intend to rip that information from you, morsel, just before you take your last gasp. Oh, how I long to hear you scream for mercy and a quick end. I promise that you shall receive neither."

"I do not fear you, Shade, and I damn well am not afraid of Preston or his men. The Guardians of Pioneer Vale still stand against you, so get back to your dreamland," Anne-Marie yelled as lavender flames wrapped around her in a swirling shroud. With a downward motion, she drove the floating crystal back into the chest and slammed the lid closed. The room plunged once more into the flickering shadows of her fires.

Shade's mocking laughter shook the room, sending a shower of gravel from the dark recesses of the cavern. A cloud of dust billowed around her, dampening Anne-Marie's flames as she coughed and choked. Her flames were but a flicker as the last echoes of the demon's glee faded away.

Something skittered in the darkness. A quiet rattling, soft at first, but growing steadier, echoed from the walls around the chamber. The lamenting moans of the dead that rode upon the wind gained intensity, rising from an ominous warning into a war cry from beyond the grave. Anne-Marie threw her hands above her head and lit the room up with her own brilliance.

The shadows fell away from her fires once again, but she gasped as the ancient bones of Shade's past minions wobbled back together, and the dead men rose from their graves on unsteady legs as they turned to face the

Guardian. Cold yellow light danced in the sockets of their eyes as they reached for her.

Anne-Marie backed away, but she bumped into the stone altar. With a glance up at the statue of Shade, she saw the fleeting shadow of a smile cross the stone visage. When the first cold tips of a corpse's fingers brushed her hair from behind, she could take no more.

With a surge of power, Anne-Marie fired a bolt of flame straight ahead, blasting through some of Shade's minions, and scattering several more. Cold bone scraped bloody lines across her arm, and a heavy blow struck her shoulder, spinning her around. Her feet tangled up in the debris that littered the room, and she fell in a heap. The pointed end of a disjointed rib stabbed into her thigh and she felt the hot rush of blood run down her leg. The leers of the dead came closer as icy hands grasped and pulled at her.

Anne-Marie clapped her hands together and a rain of fire fell from the ceiling above her, bowling aside the closest of the shambling corpses like ninepins. She fought her way to her feet, biting back the pain from the bone that stood out from her leg muscle. She lunged forward and hurled two more incinerating blasts towards the tunnel mouth. Skeletal fingers clutched at her as she hobbled by.

A line of dead men blocked the exit ahead, their rictus grins silently sneering at her attempt to escape. Anne-Marie was not one to be mocked, however. She planted her feet and felt the magic swell within her. The Elder's Whisper became a triumphant shout in her ears. With a scream of fury, a tornado of fire erupted around her body, blasting the risen dead in all directions. The walls began to glow from the raging inferno that Anne-Marie had become. When the conflagration finally subsided, nothing surrounded her but blackened remains. She stepped over the ash piles in front of her and went back up the tunnel.

She hurried back to the main cavern, uncertain if she should move against Preston first or get to Henna and warn her of the threat of Shade's altar. The nightmare visions from Shade's realm made more sense to her now. She knew who her enemy was, and where the attacks against her family would come from. It was time to rally her forces to stop Mathers before he could bring his men to bear against her.

She extinguished the globe of fire around her and stumbled as the outpouring of so much magic caught up with her. She went down painfully on her hands and knees, feeling the stone and gravel bite into her skin. Her vision blurred, but she fought to remain conscious. Just as the cobwebs started to clear, a new shadow crossed the floor in front of her. Before she could rise up, the back of her head exploded in pain. She fell face down into the dirt with the taste of blood in her mouth as a pair of scuffed boots stepped in front of her.

"I really wish you hadn't made me do this, Goody Carmichael. You finding us out here is going to make things a wee bit complicated." Hollister Adams' fist pulled back and then shot forward, smashing into the side of her head. Anne-Marie fell into blackness with Shade's laughter echoing again in the back of her mind.

CHAPTER 19
RESPECTING THE ELDERS – PRESENT DAY

They stood in a meadow bordered by ancient oak trees that reached high into the evening sky. The ground showed gouges, scorches, and burns for it was here that Pioneer Vale's Guardians had trained for centuries.

"Your powers are growing quickly," Anne-Marie said. "I can tell that you have been studying."

"I read myself to sleep every night with my spell journal," replied Angelica.

The older woman smiled as her student blasted three flying targets out of the air with precise bolts of lightning. Anne-Marie called forth an elemental in the shape of a large bull of lavender flame that charged at her student. Angelica, her back turned to the approaching threat, didn't miss a step though. She tumbled and rolled out of the summoned creature's path, wrapping herself in a crackling shield as she did so. The glancing blow that creature struck her knocked her a few feet away, but she was on her feet in a heartbeat and threw her fist in a punch aimed in the beast's direction. A blue-white blow like a hammer strike slammed the elemental in the side of its head, sending it back to its own plane in a scattering of purple sparks. She snapped her wrists and extinguished the coruscating power that enveloped her.

"Is that all you've got, old woman?" she said with a grin at Anne-Marie. She braced herself as her 10th great grandmother arched an eyebrow, and slowly reached her arms into the sky. The clouds rolled above them, and thunder rumbled across the nearby hills. The ground beneath her feet bucked and quaked, and Angelica dropped to a crouch to keep from being thrown from her feet. The young Guardian saw Anne-Marie's flames not only surround her teacher but literally roll beneath her skin as she called down power that Angelica could only dare to dream about.

An explosion of violet lava burst from the ground in a volcanic eruption around the elder witch, spraying into the air like a geyser. Fountains of cinders ignited the air while the grass burst into flame before the rolling wave of heat. A cloud of embers blotted out the sun above that left Anne-Marie hovering like a terrible supernova blazing through the dervish-like storm of ash.

The flow spilled towards Angelica, and she fired a blast of her own, carving a deep gouge in the earth between her and the onrushing river of molten rock. The channel she dug routed the danger away from her but she brought her lightning shield to bear just in case it spilled over. She spared a glance at her ancestor, who smiled at her as she floated three feet above the ground with flames dancing where her eyes were, and her long red tresses fanning out behind her in a halo of power.

Anne-Marie brought her hands together in a thunderous clap, and the lava boiled away. She dropped back to the ground, and the living conduit of energy she had become closed.

"Does that answer your question, my dear?" the Guardian asked. She smiled as Angelica stood slack-jawed staring at her.

"How long did it take you to learn that?" Angelica said breathlessly. "And how is that not enough power to throw Shade and Aiden into the darkest pit you can find for them?"

Anne-Marie staggered for a step but waved her granddaughter away as Angelica moved to catch her. "I spend my idle years when I don't have an apprentice with me pushing myself to the limit of what my body can take. After 350 years of practice, I have found that I can withstand quite a bit. To say that an experienced Guardian has earth-shattering power is not far from the truth."

"Then how can Shade stand against you?"

"Because a shattered Earth is precisely what he hopes to bring about. If he and I were able to face off and bring our full powers to bear against one another, the fallout from our battle could be worse than any war in history. He remains barred from our world, but one day we shall be able to take the fight to him. When that happens," Anne-Marie waved her hand around at the battle-scarred meadow, "I'd rather see all of this visited on his home than our own."

"I wonder if his realm is still far enough away. If ripples of power, like our own Ascensions, can be felt across the planes then what are the chances that you two going head to head won't still be felt here? All of this was from practicing our craft, and you can see how damaging that was. We need to stop Aiden here so that he can't help Shade when we fight him."

"Shade holds my son in thrall. Once we find a way to free Aiden's spirit from the demon's influence then I will no longer need to pull any more punches."

Angelica looked around and threw her hands in the air. "The one you need to stop pulling punches against is your son! He's the one threatening us. Today. If we don't hit him first then we are sliding closer to the wasteland from my vision."

"You have no idea the course that leads to that end. We have to combine our efforts against the true threat to us!"

"If Aiden gets strong enough, we won't get a chance to carry the fight to Shade's world and anyone who survives that fallout will live in a world of ashes. Stop protecting him, Anne-Marie. Your son isn't coming back to you. He's out there right now thinking of ways to kill us both so he can open the door for his boss."

Anne-Marie's fires rekindled behind her eyes. "You are so quick to condemn someone to death. I have seen enough lives end because of Shade's war on mankind. So long as one of us breathes, the demon is at an impasse and that buys us time to try to rescue my boy. Aiden is possessed by Shade and the wolf can be driven out. Until that becomes impossible, then I will fight for my son's redemption."

Angelica stood balanced on the balls of her feet, waiting to see if Anne-Marie would lash out in her grief and rage. "I understand your motives, but if I have to stop him alone, then I will."

Anne-Marie took a deep breath and the simmering flames faded. "We make our oaths at the Widow Stone to accept the power granted to us, but we also seal the door between realms. Aiden betrayed that protection, and, instead of a Guardian, he became the original Firstborn. His power comes from his master. If we can drive Shade out, then Aiden becomes just a normal man again. Powerless to stand against the might of two trained Guardians."

"Do you honestly think that he won't still hold a grudge after you kept him locked up for three and a half centuries in an ugly rock? If given the opportunity to strike at you, what choice will he make? You may be his mom, but what if he's too far gone?"

"After he was imprisoned, I spent my years seeking only to bring my wrath to Shade. It became the role of every new Firstborn since then to oppose Aiden specifically. I hope that you will be the one to protect my back as I force the wolf to release my son."

"You're gambling with the fate of the world. I know that I put him one step closer to succeeding in their overall plan, but I won't be a shield against Aiden. I'm going to be a sword. You have my promise that he won't get the chance to stab you in the back with me around. He won't catch you while you're looking the other way."

Anne-Marie took the girl's hand and gave it a gentle squeeze. "He hasn't succeeded yet, but I feel safer knowing that you are here with me. And give me a little credit after the display that I just put on. Aiden is freshly out of his cage. He must remain patient, and that means that we still have time to prepare against him. He bides his time as he grows stronger, but so too are you gaining power. If we can capture him again, then Shade will have no choice but to stand against the two of us by himself." She pulled Angelica to her and held the young woman tightly. "We must move swiftly, but the odds favor us. Let's return to Whisperwind, have a bite to eat, and get some rest. Tomorrow we hunt down my wayward son."

*   *   *

Angelica sat on the edge of her bed. She was so exhausted that she wanted nothing more than to let her head hit the pillow. Every muscle in her body ached, her ears rang, and her head throbbed. That was the toll, however, that so many long hours of training with Anne-Marie took on her body.

The enchanted sideboard had held a golden brown roasted chicken seasoned with garlic butter. Other dishes were piled high with mashed potatoes, warm bread, and a fresh garden salad. The two women ate well, and Angelica realized that the use of their power must also affect their metabolism as she was famished after their training session. Anne-Marie entertained her with stories of the folk of Pioneer Vale, delighting Angelica as she recognized names of neighbors and classmates whose families still thrived here centuries later. After dinner, she and Anne-Marie washed the dishes up the old fashioned way, by hand rather than with magic. A cup of tea near the fireplace ended the long day for the Guardians.

"Don't stay up too late," Anne-Marie told her. "You'll need to be rested when we find Aiden. Everything you have learned so far needs to be yours to command at a moment's notice. I think I have a trick or two up my sleeve that will catch him off guard." Anne-Marie gave her 10th great-granddaughter a gentle kiss on the forehead as they said goodnight and went off to their respective bedrooms.

Angelica closed her door, and let the magic flow through her body. She weaved the mystical threads in and out of the very walls, crafting a barrier around the entire room that would suppress any noise of what she was about to attempt. The images from the news report haunted her still, and she would never forgive herself for that grisly message scrawled upon the brick wall in the poor young woman's blood. Aiden was out there, and she didn't trust that Anne-Marie would fight her son with the same ferocity that she herself felt towards him. He had to be stopped, not just captured. Angelica had no intention of allowing him any more time to wreak havoc.

She flipped open her spell journal and scanned the pages again about healing and rejuvenation. Anne-Marie had shared many stories with her of dire injuries cured with their magic, and she had witnessed firsthand her revitalized ancestor after the night at the waterfall. The power they wielded, while undoubtedly devastating in a fight, was also a life-giving force of nature. Angelica suspected that if she harnessed the magic correctly, she could erase the aches and fatigue from her body and take the fight to Aiden before he could grow any stronger.

Angelica crisscrossed her legs, placed her hands on her knees and closed her eyes. The magical connection was so easy to fall into now that it was almost reflexive. She basked in the warmth of the flow of power as it coursed through her. Her fingers crackled with tiny bolts of lightning that danced across the tips. She pulled the power around herself wrapping her body with the sensations of both a warm blanket and a tender caress.

Immediately, she felt the charge tingling through her, lighting up her very cells. She felt the fatigue of her muscles fade as a storm of power surged through her whole body. She imagined that this was what a full body massage her mother had told her about must feel like, but the hands that kneaded her were stronger and more precise in soothing her discomforts. Her fingers dug into her knees, her back arched, and she found herself biting her lip as she was flooded by the ravages of healing warmth. A low moan escaped her as her aches disappeared one by one. She had a fleeting thought of Anne-Marie's fiery companion that night at the waterfall, and she daydreamed that eyes made of her own blue-white lightning stared at her from somewhere not of this world.

The pounding in her head eased, and the ringing in her ears was now little more than a faint whine in the back of her mind. She opened her eyes just enough to peer through the slits of her eyelids, reluctant to lose the euphoric sensations that rolled over her like ocean waves Her joy vanished, though, and she gasped as the sight of her chamber came into focus.

Angelica hovered a foot above her bed while streaks of lightning roiled and crashed around her room. The bedding directly beneath her was in flames, and the entire room shook with booming thunder that she had been oblivious to while in the throes of her healing trance. The paint on the walls blistered and scorched. She had unleashed the primeval energy of the universe, and it now raged unchecked through her body while leveling her bedroom.

She tried to slam shut her connection to the flow of power, but a backlash of force sent her bouncing off of her bed and crashing to the floor. A wall of lightning washed over her back, pushing her to the ground. She felt arcs like fingers grab at her arms and legs, breaking her concentration as the havoc around her raged on. Sweat poured from Angelica's brow as she fought her way back to her hands and knees against the press of some otherworldly strength. She lifted her chin to face a ball of wild energy that coalesced and hovered before her. Two points of brilliant intensity stared at her like the eyes of a predator watching its next meal. With a growl, Angelica rocked back to sit on her heels, and with pure will, reached into the maelstrom of swirling magic. She screamed as the connection flooded her with an unspeakable agony.

"You are unlike the others. None who have come before could dare summon me," said a booming voice in her head. There was a slight pause. *"You are the one who shattered the fragment."*

Waves of anger washed through Angelica's mind. Flashes of worlds being born and destroyed pummeled her. Strange beings danced and fought as she watched scenes from throughout time race before her eyes. Stars formed, burned, and exploded in the span of seconds as she staggered under the godlike power assaulting her.

"You foolish speck. You have awakened my adversary and weakened the divide between realms. Now the forces of darkness shall rally to lay waste to your world." Another image hammered Angelica, this one of the entire planet engulfed in ash. Continents lay cracked and broken, the entire landscape of Earth was shattered and disfigured.

"I never meant to," she began when a pulse of force threw her back to the floor.

"Such is ever the excuse of those who must face the consequences of their actions." The Elder Guardian's fury rippled around the room, tearing at the walls and flipping her furniture like matchsticks.

"I am not running from my role in this," she shouted back as she once more dragged her way to her hands and knees. "I intend to go tonight and strike the next blow in your war. I came to you for the strength I need to stand against my own enemy!" The pain eased back, allowing the young woman to catch her breath before it slammed into her again.

"You have garnered attention that you may come to regret, Guardian. The battle moves forward once again for us both. Your actions, while unprecedented, will now draw darkness to you. You know only of the fragment your world calls Shade. Far more sinister powers lie in wait for the opportunity that you have now afforded them. You have courage, but have you the wisdom to face the demon that hungers for you? Or will you become another puppet like the charlatan you would now chase after?"

Angelica raised her head and stared into the blazing core that hovered before her. "I am ready to fight. You looked into me and decided I was worthy of becoming Ascended. I have made mistakes along the way, but I will not back down now, and I refuse to live my life looking over my shoulder for monsters. I will take the battle to Shade, and stand against whatever follows after him." A ripple of lightning blossomed around her, adding to the mayhem running through her room. A deep chuckle like a crack of thunder bowled her head over heels once more.

"So shall you be put to the test, then. Go forth and strike the first blow of our renewed struggle. I see dark days and sacrifice before you, Guardian. For the sake of your world, I hope you measure up to the task." The maelstrom of coruscating power lashed out around the room once more, bathing Angelica in a crackling whirlwind of magic.

She threw her head back and screamed as the Elder Guardian's might wracked her entire frame, but she soaked up all the strength that the entity infused her with. At last, the conduit slammed shut within her and the blinding light faded. Her breath came in labored gasps, but she felt strong and refreshed as if she had slept the whole night through.

She fell back against the ruined bed beside her and looked around. Burns covered every surface where uncontrolled lightning strikes had ripped through the chamber. There was certainly no way to cover up the damage she had caused and she knew without a doubt that it was just one more thing that she would end up facing the wrath of Anne-Marie Carmichael for at some point, but that time would have to wait.

It was time to go hunting.

Angelica grabbed her new leather jacket from a hook on the back of the door, noting with a wry grin how it had escaped any sign of damage, and threw it on. The laces across her chest flared with a spark of electricity and tied themselves tight. The young Guardian snapped her fingers to dispel the sound dampening barrier that she had put around the room, amazed that it had held throughout her encounter. She surmised that the Elder Guardian must have held the spell together to keep her out of even deeper trouble than she was already in.

With a grim smile on her lips, Angelica slipped quietly out of her bedroom. She failed to notice, in the fleeting glimpse as she passed by her shattered mirror, the new streak of white that shot through her jet black hair, a telltale scar that marked her own recklessness of the night.

CHAPTER 20
DEALING WITH THE DEVIL - 1671

Patch Erickson led Reynolds into a lavishly decorated library in Preston Mathers' home. Intricately carved furniture of darkly stained oak stood before a similarly crafted desk. An overstuffed chair sat behind the desk and creaked beneath the weight of the lord of the manor. Preston's fingers were steepled under his chin and his grin became both lewd and sinister as he watched the clergyman enter the room.

"Welcome, Corbin," said Mathers as he rose with his hand extended. "Please, do have a seat. I hope you'll forgive me for calling upon you so unexpectedly, but I have a most urgent matter that I felt we need to discuss." Reynolds gave a pointed glare at the proffered hand and sat down without shaking.

"What did you bring me here for, Preston? I hope this isn't simply your way of reminding me that I still owe you a favor. I have far more important things to do with my time than sit across the table from the devil himself." He saw Preston's eyes dart over to his bodyguard. "Please spare me your mock surprise. I have every confidence that your men already know the sordid details of why we even have an arrangement."

"Oh, but you wound me, Parson," said Preston with a sneer. "If I tell you that you have my discretion, then you may count on that very thing." He dropped his prodigious girth back down into his chair and snapped his fingers.

Erickson brought over two snifters of brandy and placed them before Preston. He flashed Corbin a sly grin with his stained teeth, and then let out a low coarse whistle. The big man chuckled as he watched the clergyman bristle.

"Never would have thought you the sort, Parson." The thug returned to his place behind Preston and crossed his arms over his broad chest.

"Is this what you referred to, Preston? Is this counting on your discretion?"

"Mr. Erickson is quite perceptive for a man with his obvious disability. Anything he knows, my friend, he has discovered through his own observations. You haven't been careless yet again, have you?" The moneylender's belly shook with laughter as he heaved his body forward. His meaty fingers scooped up the drinks and he pushed one across the desk to Reynolds. The clergyman turned his head to stare at a blank wall in response. "Come now, Corbin. There's no need to be prudish. Let us toast our future work together. Raise your glass with me to, ...shall we say, indulgences?" He drained his brandy in a gulp and snapped his fingers again for Erickson to refill it from the sideboard.

"Get to the point of this social call, Preston. Am I here for you to collect on your favor or not? Speak plainly or I will show myself to the door." The preacher quivered with barely suppressed rage.

"Parson, I am here to come to your aid, sir. I am nothing more than a concerned member of this community and I have reason to believe that there is a dark stain growing silently in the congregation that you so...amorously protect. I called you here tonight to give you fair warning so that you as a man of the cloth might act against the forces of darkness before they steal into the souls of your flock."

"Are you in search of confession, then?"

"I am speaking of something devilish, Corbin. This is a circumstance so pernicious that the very hearts of the families of Pioneer Vale are at risk of eternal damnation." Preston dramatically placed his hand over his heart. "I seek only to save my neighbors."

"You seek to save your tenants, more likely."

"Very well, Parson. You invited me to speak plainly, and so I will since you continue to rebuke my attempts at friendlier discourse." Preston frowned and all pretense of civility vanished. "My silence regarding your tryst was not without a price, and now the time has come for you to pay your dues. I have need of a man in your particular position and with your influence as the chief clergyman of this settlement. You shall either assist me as I am about to instruct to the letter, or I will expose your dirty little secret. At best, you will be tarred, feathered, and run out of town." Mathers paused as he saw the color drain from Reynolds face at his threat. "At worst," Mathers continued with a cluck of his tongue, "well, let's just hope Goodman Pritchard doesn't get his rather large and bone-crushing hands upon you."

The room spun around Corbin as the details from his nightmare roared back into his head. Was this the moment symbolized in his dream? Was his only chance at salvation to accept the offered assistance of the most hated man in Pioneer Vale? If he refused, how soon would it be until Madeline's husband showed up on his doorstep to avenge his family's honor? He saw again the cold eyes of the beast in the woods after he had fled from Preston in the nightmare. Was his damnation assured if he stepped away from this pretense of friendship?

"I know as surely as I sit here that I am forging a deal with darkness, Mathers. What is it that you need me to do?"

Preston pushed the newly filled snifter across his desk to Reynolds, who took it without hesitation this time and drained it. Corbin wiped his mouth with the back of his hand.

"I have some interest in the Carmichael Farm," Preston began as he leaned back in his chair.

*   *   *

Anne-Marie woke up squinting as the flickering lantern light played havoc on her pounding head. Her cheek throbbed where she had hit the ground, and her jaw protested as she moved it from side to side. Leather cords bit into her wrists that were tied behind her back. As her vision cleared, boxes, barrels, and tools revealed that she was in a small storage cave. Voices drifted down from around the bend past the tunnel mouth that must lead back into the main cavern of the mine. The rough voice of Landry Cross and the whiny sniveling of Hollister Adams made the woman cringe.

"So what exactly are we supposed to do with that bitch?" growled Cross.

"If it were my call alone to make, then I would suggest that we just toss her into an old mine shaft and forget about her," replied Adams. "Except it's not our call to make. You heard Preston's orders. If we were lucky enough to catch her we had to keep her alive. He's got something planned. We caught her, now we wait for the boss to tell us what to do next. Let's finish this load, throw her in the cart, and deliver her to him back in town. Now shut your trap and get back to work so we don't have to end up staying out here all night."

"Why don't we just leave her tied up here? What if we meet someone on the road and she cries out? Leaving her in the mine, won't nobody find her."

"Can't leave Preston's prize alone. What if that knock to her head was worse than we thought? We might come back and find her dead already. Or worse yet, what if she found a way to escape? Imagine what Preston would do if he found out that we had her and she got away? I don't want to see him that kind of mad."

"One of us could stay here and keep a watch over her," offered Landry. "Might get a little boring, but seems like less risk than toting her down Market Road."

"Do you want to camp in this cave all night? Sleep close enough to that damn hole of Preston's over there?" Anne-Marie knew that Hollister referred to the tunnel leading down to Shade's hidden shrine. She could almost imagine the shudder that ran down Cross' spine at the suggestion.

"Well can't we at the very least have a bit of fun with her? She's a damn sight better to look at than your ugly face."

A sharp slap echoed down the tunnel. "Don't lay so much as a finger on that woman unless Mathers himself gives you the nod. His plan to steal back the Carmichael lands will get a bit more complicated if he has to explain why her violated corpse shows up, won't it? Now get your big dumb arse back to work. There's a lot of gold here we still need to crate up."

Anne-Marie sat in shock. She couldn't believe that she and Henna had been so off the mark about Preston's relationship with Shade. Mathers deliberately served the demon here in Pioneer Vale and this treasure trove was the reward for his help. Worse yet, she knew that Preston would not hesitate to torture her to discover the location of Whisperwind. If he found out where she lived, he wouldn't stop until she and Henna were both dead so that Shade could be free at last. She had to get to the town and report his crimes, but report them to who? Mathers owned the Magistrate and had his own private militia. Bringing him to justice would most likely require that she expose her powers, and that could lead to the course that brought about Jeremiah's nightmare.

She could figure all that out later. Right now, she had to escape. She could hear Shade's mocking laughter from within the shard nearby. The demon waited, biding his time until his moment to strike arrived. Anne-Marie strained against her bonds, but they only bit deeper into her skin. She then shook her head when she realized how foolish she was.

With a quick burst of power, lavender fire engulfed her hands and incinerated the leather cords that held her. Anne-Marie stood up and brushed herself off. Her fingers tingled and ached as blood flowed back into her hands. She sent the flow of magic into her own body and sighed as the aches and bruises faded away.

"Did you just see a flash from down there?" asked Cross. "Swear I thought I saw a purple light or something."

"For pity's sake," said Adams. "You can't get that wench out of your brain, can you? Do you think she was toting around a measure of flash powder somewhere?"

"Well, maybe if you'd let me search her over the way I wanted to, then we'd be sure, wouldn't we?" Cross' lewd braying laughter echoed in the cavern.

Anne-Marie stepped out from the shadowy tunnel entrance. "I think that you boys would ultimately have found me far more than either of you could handle. Now, which of you bastards is the coward who hit me from behind?" Her eyes narrowed and her flames leaped around her from head to toe once more.

The two men each jumped back, looking at each other and then back to her with jaws agape.

"What the devil are you?" asked the dimwitted brute. "Hollister, she's a witch!"

Anne-Marie laughed, hoping she sounded far more sinister than she felt. "Oh, no. I am something far more dangerous than that. You have no idea just how much torment that you have brought upon yourselves."

"This must be what Preston wants you brought in for. He knows you aren't natural. Well, you can save your fancy threats," said Landry as he brandished his pickaxe. "We took you down before, and we'll do it again. Only this time, I don't plan to be as friendly about it." A lascivious grin creased his dirty face as he charged forward. He drew his pick back in a wide arc, clearly intent on ending her life.

He never even got close.

A swell of power flowed through Anne-Marie as she grabbed hold of the very air within the room and hurled it towards Cross. From the palm of her hand, a blast of purely concussive force caught him squarely in the chest and knocked him across the cave. He crashed into a stack of crates and casks, bringing them down on his head. Anne-Marie whirled back to face Hollister, who's hesitation and awe had cost him any advantage he might have gained.

"Now hold on there, lady," he said as he dropped the shovel he carried and drew a long thin-bladed knife. His finger fit through a ring in the guard allowing him to spin the blade. "Let's just calm things down a bit. No one needs to get hurt here."

"The knot on the back of my head implies that we are past that point," she retorted. "Stand aside and let me pass."

"Mistress Carmichael, you know that I can't allow that. You'd run straight back to town and bring no end of trouble down on us. I don't understand this witchcraft I see before me, but it makes no difference to me. Landry was right, wasn't he? Preston wants you to work for him, doesn't he? Hell, I know he's in league with some pretty dangerous folks already, but with you by his side, he'd take control of the whole coast. That's his game, I'll bet."

"There is no bargain that Preston could offer that would convince me to partner with he and his fiendish allies. If you knew the truth of the devil behind Mathers, you would run for your life, Hollister. Now, I won't say it again. Stand aside." She leveled her outstretched palm at the man's face.

"I've seen plenty of darkness in my day, Mistress Carmichael. Ran from my own dark deeds too, but here's the thing. Once you outrun your biggest fears, they don't really keep you awake anymore. Now, Preston has done me better than any other employer I've ever had. Hell, treated me better than my own father truth be told, so if your plan is to leave out of here simply to bring him to his knees, then I regret to say it, but one of us will not be walking out of here tonight."

Landry had regained his feet and grabbed up a wooden barrel stave from the pile of debris he lay in. Anne-Marie glanced his way for but a second, and Hollister whipped his knife end over end at her. A hot line stung her cheek as she ducked, and a trickle of blood ran down her face. Hollister snatched up a rusty flintlock pistol from the table beside him, and with a sneer, he leveled the barrel at her.

"Now, let's see how your magic fares against a lead ball to that ample chest."

Anne-Marie's mind flashed back to the vision in Shade's world. Was this the moment he had foretold? She could see Adams' finger tightening on the trigger in slow motion. She heard the click of the spring that released the hammer.

But Anne-Marie was no longer an untrained novice. She felt the elemental forces of the world swirling around her. As the hammer fell, a roaring shield of purple flame sprang up between her and her attacker. The wash of heat startled the scrawny man and his shot went wide. The lead ball ricocheted off the golden wall and creased Landry's forehead. The dull-witted brute fell back, as Anne-Marie unleashed a blast of fire against Hollister's chest. The smaller man was thrown back into a pile of tools. Picks and shovels scattered across the cavern floor.

Anne-Marie rose up to her full height, casting a fearsome and imposing figure to the two men who scrambled on all fours for any kind of weapon to bring against the woman. She let a malevolent grin cross her face although the trembling in her knees would have belied how she truly felt in what she knew was going to be a fight for her life.

Landry found his feet first and scooped up a battered shovel. Hollister grabbed a rusty pickaxe but cowered behind an ore cart. Anne-Marie knew that Cross was the real threat but that she mustn't take her eyes off the cowardly Adams. He had already proven once this night that he would hit when she wasn't looking.

Cross charged forward with a wild swing, but Anne-Marie brought up a fiery purple tornado that caught up stones and debris that pelted the brutish man leaving burning welts peppered across his face and arms. He stumbled back, swinging wildly but never coming close to hitting her.

Hollister tried to circle behind her, but she caught his sudden movement and whirled around on him, her fists aflame. "You wouldn't try to hit a girl from behind twice in the same night would you, dear?" Anne-Marie asked with a snarl on her face. She threw a fireball at his feet causing Adams to fall backward over a barrel.

Landry wiped blood from his brow and gripped his shovel. He raised it over his head and threw it in a mighty two-handed grip at Anne-Marie. She crossed her forearms in front of her and poured an overflow of energy into her shield, making the flames burn hotter than she had ever dared. The resulting heat was so strong that the hurled shovel stopped in mid-flight, floating on the air currents. The wooden handle smoldered, charred, and then burst into flame as the iron shovelhead glowed a dull red and began to drip. As Anne-Marie lowered her guard, the destroyed shovel tumbled to the cave floor.

Anne-Marie staggered, realizing that she hadn't fully recovered from her fight with Shade's hordes in the shrine below. This second battle was taking a toll on her, and she needed to end it quickly. Spots danced before her eyes as she saw Landry and Hollister circling her.

"Seems the witch isn't as strong as Preston might think, eh, Cross?" said Hollister. He drew a second pistol from the waistband of his trousers and aimed once again at Anne-Marie. "Say goodbye, Witch."

"It's Guardian," shouted Anne-Marie as she lashed out with a poorly aimed blast. Her fire went wide, but the shock of the tiny explosion pitched Landry into Hollister, the larger man knocking the smaller one across the dusty floor. Adams' gun flew from his grasp, landed butt first on a chunk of scattered gold ore, and fired.

The lead ball zinged through the air and shattered the handle of one of the hanging lanterns in the room. The lantern smashed on the stone floor sending a runner of flaming oil racing down the sloping room and across a broken cask of black powder that Cross had broken open when he had crashed into it earlier.

A dull thud filled the chamber as the powder ignited. Anne-Marie saw the explosion grow and she reflexively wrapped her lavender shield around her body. She shut her eyes against the blinding light, but she was unable to shut out the screams of Preston's men as the resulting inferno washed over them all. Their cries were audible only for a moment and then they were overcome by the roar of the fire.

The flames from the blast set beams and tools alight, but her cloak of flame made the room feel no warmer than a summer's day to Anne-Marie.

She reached out her open palm, called the heat to her hand, and snapped her fingers shut. As she did, all the fire in the room extinguished.

Landry Cross stared lifelessly at the ceiling, horrible burns running across his face. The head of a broken pickaxe protruded from his chest, having blown through the air with the other debris. Hollister Adams lay face down on the floor, the back of his head crushed by a blood-spattered nugget of gold the size of an apple that lay on the ground beside him.

Anne-Marie shook her head. "You fools," she said softly. "Your lives are Preston's to answer for." She closed Landry's staring eyes, threw a singed piece of sackcloth over Adams' head, and then went into the tunnel that led out of the mine.

CHAPTER 21
AFTER SCHOOL SHOWDOWN – PRESENT DAY

Angelica crept through the shadows as she approached the front doors of Pioneer Vale High School. It made sense to her to start her search for Aiden in the place she had first met him in Shade's nightmare realm. At least the lawn wasn't littered with the bodies of fallen classmates this time, she thought to herself.

The night air was crisp and just cold enough for her to see her breath misting before her. The lights around the school's horseshoe-shaped parking lot lit up the night with a pale yellow glow. The school had been built as a fort during the Revolutionary War, and the stone facade of the building had endured to the present day with the protective battlements still visible along the top of the walls, although access to those areas was off-limits to students.

She sighed and looked around. Although there were several cars in the parking lot belonging to students who were attending the football game, the rest of the schoolyard was empty. No lights brightened the school windows. All was dark and quiet.

So what do I do now, she thought to herself. Where do I begin looking? The thought occurred to her to sneak into the school, but she would probably just end up wasting her time as she wandered aimlessly through the darkened corridors. She needed to make Aiden come to her. As she studied her surroundings, it dawned on that she stood in the same spot here as she had in her vision. Maybe that would be enough to summon the traitor to her.

"I'm here," Angelica called into the night. Her voice echoed off the stone front of the building. "Come and face me, if you dare." It was all she could do to keep the quaking she felt in her gut out of her voice. She wished now that she had told Anne-Marie of her plan, but Angelica was here to stop Aiden. She couldn't afford to risk her mentor going easy in the coming fight. This was her chance to secure the advantage in the Elder's war.

Angelica grappled with the thought that even though she could tap into the incredible power of the Guardians, Anne-Marie's experience could turn the tide if the battle started to go downhill. Her powers had grown, but she was newly trained and had no idea what kind of tricks Aiden may have thought up while trapped in the crystal prison for 300 years. After that horrifying news broadcast, however, she felt that she had to bring whatever power she had to bear against her distant cousin. She had the ability to summon sheets of lightning, but was that enough to stop someone fueled by an ageless demon?

"You are either very brave or very foolish, young one," said the now familiar whispering voice from in front of her. "How very resourceful of you to seek me out here." Aiden stepped through the main doors of the school and into the light of the porch. He stopped at the top of the wide brick steps. His face was once again hidden within the depths of his cowl, but his eyes glimmered with the reflection of the streetlamps' shine. He walked deliberately down the steps, the bounce in each stride screaming of his confidence and arrogance.

"I set you loose, so I guess it's my place to stop this before you cause any more harm. I highly suggest you make this easy on yourself and surrender." She snapped her wrists and lightning coalesced around her hands.

Aiden threw back his head and laughed. The sound, shrill at first, deepened and changed into the barking howl of a wolf. Chills ran down Angelica's spine, but she held her ground comforted by the power coursing through her.

"Surrender to you? You've been a Guardian for what? A matter of hours? I have spent decades with my dark master whispering lessons into my ear as I languished in that damnable prison. Now an untrained witch armed with a few meager spells thinks that she can conquer a student of a supernatural entity that has existed from the dawn of time? Oh, and I know that my mother isn't lurking in the shadows nearby. Our connection would allow me to sense if she were close at hand." Contempt dripped from his every word as he sneered at her and licked his lips.

"You are all alone, little Guardian."

"Your mama thinks you might behave if she turns you over her knee, Aiden. I'm here to do a lot worse."

"The crystal is destroyed, child. You've nothing to shove me back into," he spat at her.

"You are still missing the point. You don't walk away from here tonight, cousin," snarled Angelica. She stepped forward and loosed a double-fisted blast of lightning at him. The roar of thunder filled her ears as she became an open conduit for the intense power.

The blast struck Aiden squarely in the chest, driving him back a step, but he raised a shield of inky black smoke between them that drew the brunt of the strike into it. Angelica's lightning flashed as if it were within a storm cloud until Aiden lunged and fired the energy back at her.

Angelica was thrown back across the damp lawn. Her muscles spasmed and locked as electricity ripped through her body. A wisp of smoke floated up from the front of her jacket where her own strike had hit her. Lightning was her element though, and she reached into herself and channeled the current back under her control, dissipating it into the air around her.

Aiden playfully jumped off the bottom step and strutted towards her. "Oh, this is going to be delightful," he said with a growl. "You've far more spirit in you than any of those we've faced before." Aiden raised his hands above his head, swirling them in ever-widening circles. In front of him, a smoky black whirlwind began to form, gaining speed and size as his hands made their rotations. He suddenly pointed his bony fingers at her and the tornado jumped forward.

Angelica's senses were attuned to the fabric of Aiden's magic, though, and she reached into the swirling weave of power. She crossed her arms before her, taking hold of the maelstrom, and then threw them out wide to her sides ripping apart his attack.

"Splendid," crowed Aiden. "Finally, a natural talent worth the fight. It's just such a shame that you have chosen the wrong side in this conflict." He slammed his hands together in an explosive clap, creating a shockwave of pure concussive force that streaked towards her.

With only a split second to react, Angelica brought her hand down in a chopping motion at the rapidly onrushing cone. Her own elemental signature flashed brilliantly, wrapping around his blast and tearing it down the middle. She watched as Aiden's now lightning enshrouded bolt broke around her. Too late, however, she realized her mistake.

The shockwaves hurtled past her on either side but lost none of their might. Parked cars caught in the twin paths rolled and flipped as though they were playthings swept aside by an angry child. Streetlamps were slapped out of their concrete moorings like matchsticks and crashed down in a hail of sparking power lines. Porch lights from nearby houses flicked to life as the neighborhood reacted to the sudden blare of car alarms.

"Ahh, I guess Mother hasn't preached to you yet about preventing collateral damage," Aiden said with a chuckle. "Don't fret, cousin. It was never a lesson I gave a damn about either." He reached his hand out towards a sparking power cable and drew the electrical current into himself in a blinding arc.

"Electricity is my thing, you bastard," snarled Angelica. She reached her awareness out beyond the power cables and grabbed the fallen lamp post itself, hurling it at her foe like a 30-foot spear. Aiden threw himself to the side, losing his own attack as his concentration was broken. He was struck a glancing blow to his arm, and the crunch of bone tore a scream of agony from him as he fell to the ground.

Angelica looked over her shoulder and focused on the same electrical current that Aiden had tried to use against her. She absorbed the power into her body, rising slowly from the ground. The girl twisted around ready to unleash Aiden's doom, but she heard the doors to the school slam. When she opened her eyes, she saw Aiden's shadow vanish down the front hall of the school. She flicked her fingers, and the overload of power within her wrenched the doors from their hinges and tossed them into the front lawn.

Angelica paused at the entry, standing before the trophy case, giving her eyes a moment to adjust to the surrounding gloom. The lightning that raged through her sent off arcs of light that she fired into the darkest corners, hoping that maybe an errant strike would alert her to Aiden's presence. All she managed to do was leave scorched paint in her wake as she stormed down the hallway.

The doors to the gymnasium ahead boomed in the quiet of the corridor. Angelica charged ahead and hit the doors at a run, blasting them open as the force of her magic led the way. Too late she saw Aiden, step from the shadows behind her, his hands pulsing with dark energy that he hurled at her back as she passed by.

Searing cold bit into Angelica's body, washing over her as if she had fallen into an icy lake. The breath was sucked out of her lungs and she slammed into the hardwood floor, skidding on her knees as the insidious attack sapped her strength and drained away the lightning reserves she carried. Aiden stepped up behind her, his own magic unrelenting as he chuckled.

"And soon there will be but one Guardian left to oppose us," he growled. "Lie down and die, bitch."

But Angelica was far from finished. She had watched her teacher walk through portals of fire numerous times, and instead of trying to direct her own waning magic to counter Aiden's, she ripped open a hole in the fabric of space, between them both. The cold fire that lanced through her body vanished within the blue-white swirl she created. With a wicked smile, the girl opened the exit portal directly behind her opponent.

Aiden saw the flash of lightning as the gateway opened up behind him. His attack hammered him in the back and he stumbled forward under the might of his own assault. He released his attack but dropped to one knee, directly in front of Angelica. He tried to roll away, but the newly Ascended Guardian threw a hard right hook that hammered him in the jaw and sent him sprawling to the floor.

Angelica wobbled as she got back on her feet. She needed to end this fight before the magic weakened her. Aiden, too, was groggy, but she suspected that her punch had more to do with that than his use of whatever his dark magic exacted upon him.

Aiden struggled to stand, shaking his head. His eyes were glassy and unfocused. "That was rather unsportsmanlike, you know?" he said. "I thought we were dueling with magic, my dear?"

"Never hurts to bring a gun to a knife fight," Angelica quipped. "Anne-Marie told me it was okay to fight dirty if I needed to."

"Indeed," Aiden said as he whipped his hand forward, throwing forth a dazzling burst of sparks that blinded and singed Angelica's face. As the girl smacked embers from her skin, she heard the doors slam open again and the slap of Aiden's feet as he ran down the hallway. With a snarl on her lips, she stumbled through the doorway after him again.

She saw his silhouette disappear into the Chemistry lab. Angelica leaned heavily against the wall and felt the drip of blood run over her upper lip. She couldn't drag this out much longer. She didn't dare try to rejuvenate herself again. It was time for that perfect sucker punch.

With a slow smile, she knew what to do.

Angelica raised her hand into the air, her arcane fire racing up and down her arm. In the dark confines of the room that her foe had taken refuge in, she felt the movement of a dozen tiny valves. With a swagger in her step that she truly didn't feel, she made her way to the classroom. She kicked the door open and leaned on the frame, crossing her arms over her chest. Aiden stood in front of the windows cradling his injured shoulder.

"You should have stretched before game time," she quipped. "Now you have to play through the pain." She couldn't allow him the time to fall back and let his dark powers repair the damage of the shattered bone and his other injuries.

"You have proven yourself admirably tonight, cousin. As relentless in your hunt as a starving wolf stalking its prey. Shade would be proud," he said to her. "You could have been a favored general beside my dark master when he comes to level this realm." He watched her closely, but Angelica simply stood against the door.

"You know," Angelica said, "your mother said you were her best student. You might have learned a lot more than me about spellcasting, but you never got to listen to Day One of Mister Albertson's Intro to Chemistry Class."

"And what might I have learned from that?" Aiden asked. He shook his head twice, clearly dizzy, and the young woman knew that he was hurt far worse than he let on. She smiled as the air between them shimmered.

"Always make sure you turn your gas lines off after the lab is finished." Angelica raised her hand and snapped her fingers, shooting a spark of lightning into the room. She rolled around the doorframe, protected by the cinderblock wall, as the cloud from the twelve gas lines that she had opened and let run unchecked ignited into a thunderous fireball. Aiden was blasted through the classroom windows and slammed to the ground on the front lawn of the school.

Sprinklers sprayed water throughout the classroom. Fire alarms blared their klaxon screams into the night. In the distance, the resulting sound of sirens erupted as nearby residents undoubtedly began calling the police and fire departments. Angelica marched through the deluge, the droplets of water bouncing from her skin in a cascade of sparks as electricity coursed around her. She lightly bounded through the hole in the blown-out wall ready to hit her ancestor before he could recover.

She watched Aiden struggle to rise from the grass, but his shoulder failed him. He was covered in glass and choked on the acrid smoke that hung in the air. A look of fear passed over his face and Angelica knew that she must look like some ghastly scintillating apparition with murder in her eyes to him.

Good, she thought as a wicked smile creased her lips.

Aiden scrambled back as Angelica brazenly descended upon him. The Guardian raised her hands to the heavens and a column of lightning engulfed her as she drew in power from the cosmos. She saw Aiden shield his eyes from her brilliant conflagration as a curtain of magic swirled around her. With a snap of her wrists, Angelica loosed the fire of the gods upon her enemy.

Aiden threw his head back and howled into the night. Caught full force without any magical shield at the ready, the lightning wracked his body in excruciating spasms. He jerked about on the lawn as smoke rose from his black robes. Lines of power arced up and down his body while Angelica poured her Guardian's might against him. The Elder wasn't just whispering to her tonight. He was shouting his victory cry.

The deep blare of a horn suddenly split the night. Angelica turned in horror as a school bus pulled into the far end of the horseshoe lot. A banner on the side proudly proclaimed 'Pioneer Vale High - STATE CHAMPS'. The cheers, music, and laughter of her classmates celebrating their victory reached her ears even above the crackling roar of electricity in Angelica's hands.

Yet they had returned home at the worst time possible. To her surprise, her assault on Aiden faltered just enough for him to regain his breath again.

"Collateral damage, bitch," he yelled as he finally managed to raise his own shield. Her lightning deflected away from the smoky black screen and raced across the parking lot, striking the approaching bus head-on. The yellow bus lifted off the ground with the impact, flipped in the air, and crashed on its roof onto one of the previously wrecked cars. The distinctive smell of gasoline filled the air.

Angelica stared at the overturned vehicle and could see the shadowy forms of classmates crawling around inside the bus. She knew that there were injuries from the rough tumble that she had just seen. Someone popped open the emergency exit window and out poked the same dirty blond head of hair that she had known since Kindergarten. At that moment, Clarissa raised her head, a cut in her scalp trickling blood down one side of her face, and locked eyes with her best friend. The young woman suddenly looked beyond Angelica, her eyes widening with fright.

Angelica turned back in time to see Aiden leaping forward like a wolf pouncing on its prey. In the flickering light, Angelica saw his face warp into that of a snarling beast, and then back to human once again. His hand lit up with a pale yellow glow as it swiped down at her. His fingertips transformed into black, razor-sharp claws, and Angelica screamed as four lines of fire exploded across her stomach. Aiden's other hand grabbed her by the throat, choking off her cry of agony. His wicked grin widened as he brought his face closer to hers.

"Time to die, Guardian," he whispered. His teeth flashed between human and canine as his foul breath blew across her face.

"Not today," she croaked as she stomped on his foot, and then brought her knee up into his crotch. Aiden grunted in pain and his grip loosened just enough for Angelica to hit him with another powerful lightning blast. Energy poured through her as her bolt threw him back against the concrete front steps of the school.

Angelica's senses, augmented by the magic that flooded her, saw everything move in slow motion. She whirled around to see the gasoline from the bus' ruptured tank spill out across the parking lot, flowing directly across one of the many sparking power cables that littered the front lawn of the school. With an audible 'whuff', a blue flame ignited and raced back along the volatile stream towards the crowded and overturned bus.

Angelica looked into Clarissa's scared and battered face as her best friend slowly opened her mouth in a silent scream as she too recognized the approaching danger. Other friends that she had known for years now pressed up against the windows. The approaching flames were reflected in the horror-filled gazes of the innocent people who stood in harm's way because of her.

In a horrifying flash, Angelica remembered the destroyed bus full of dead bodies in the wasteland of her trip through the Widow Stone. She had unwittingly walked the road that brought them all to this point. The moment of her nightmare was now, and she had only seconds to keep that terrible vision from taking shape before her.

The young Guardian glanced back to the front steps of the school, but her adversary was gone. With no time to spare she turned and faced the wrecked vehicles. Another damaged car exploded off to her side, but she ignored the wash of heat and prickling bits of metal that hammered against the side of her face. The fiery slashes across her abdomen were forgotten as she focused on the tears running down Clarissa's terror-stricken face.

Angelica dropped to one knee and opened herself to the full inflow of elemental power surrounding her. She felt the flame trail hit the fuel in the bus. Like a wild animal, the gas tank roared as the gasoline ignited. She burned from within as she connected to the blossoming blast. Her mind for one fleeting moment recalled one of Anne-Marie's earliest lessons, and the young woman acted.

As the fireball grew in force, threatening to tear the bus to shrapnel, Angelica funneled the burgeoning eruption through her own body. Her lightning entwined, encircled, and waged war with the conflagration. She became a living pipeline, forcing the heat and shockwave through herself as the relentless energy threatened to rip her apart. She threw back her head and with a scream to the heavens, Angelica turned the blast into the night sky, rather than blowing through the bus and its passengers.

A column of fire launched into the air, the shockwave of the explosion blowing out the windows in the front of the school itself. For several seconds the detonation roared into the night. The waves of heat caused the stone on the school's centuries-old facade to drip, and the face on the bronze Minuteman statue to run. Spent at last, the pillar of flame flickered out of existence as the last of the explosion dispersed.

The overturned school bus remained intact.

Angelica fell over on the grass. Her head felt as though the fireball was still bouncing around inside her. Her vision was so blurred that she couldn't even see her hands before her face. She choked on the blood that ran from her ears and nose, and she couldn't even look at her stomach where Aiden had slashed her. Despite the deafening ringing in her ears, though, the shrieks of the approaching sirens echoed in her head as fire trucks pulled into the horseshoe. The flashing lights from the police cars hammered against her head.

She tried to push herself up, knowing that she had to get away before she was discovered, but didn't have the strength. Gentle hands suddenly cradled her and wrapped her in a soft embrace. Her eyes failed to see anything more distinct than a hazy curtain of coppery tresses pass before her fading vision as she leaned back.

"Rest easy, my dear," said Anne-Marie's gentle voice. "You saved them. It's time to let the local authorities take over. We need to go. Now." Angelica thought she could make out the blonde blur of Clarissa crawling towards her across the lawn, could dimly hear the girl shouting her name, but then a ring of lavender fire burst forth and swept over her. She felt the familiar tingle of an enchanted doorway pass over her body like a warm blanket, and she could barely make out the details of the sitting room at Whisperwind as the sensation faded. She closed her eyes, and let herself fall into blackness.

The last thing she heard before the fiery portal winked shut was the lonesome howl of a wolf in the distance.

CHAPTER 22
ACCUSED! - 1671

Jeremiah loaded the last of his purchases on to the wagon. A barrel of salt pork, a cask of molasses, and several bags of freshly milled flour filled up the cargo bed nicely. He had also met with the town mason and commissioned a beautiful stone lintel that he intended to frame above the barn door. It would make a nice surprise for his wife and would help establish the legacy for the farm that his father had hoped to create. He wiped his brow with a handkerchief and stuffed it back into his pocket. Aiden and Thomas were playing nearby with a few other children from the town. Hairs prickled on the back of his neck, though, as he looked up and down the street of Pioneer Vale.

Something today felt very wrong.

It was as if those who passed by him looked at him with suspicion and an undertone of malice. Jeremiah began to walk down the street towards the town square and frowned as he realized that folks that he had known for years now crossed to the far side of the street at his approach.

Out of the dry goods store walked Abel Harmon, their friend and neighbor who had vouched for Jeremiah before the crowd on Market Day. The two men collided with one another, and Abel's parcels fell to the wooden boards of the store's porch.

"Forgive me, Abel," said Jeremiah as he dropped to his knees and scooped up several paper-wrapped packages from the ground. He stood up and handed them back to his friend. "My mind was further afield than where it should have been. I hope you aren't hurt."

"Ah, there's no harm done to my aging bones, Jeremiah, but thank you for asking all the same. I must say, son, that I am honestly surprised to see you in town tonight."

Jeremiah gave the old farmer a puzzled look. "I just brought the boys with me to make some deliveries and pick up a few things to see us through the next few weeks. Word is a cold spell could be on its way, and I wanted to have a few sundries in the event we can't get into town. Why would you be surprised to see me?"

"You haven't heard the local gossip. Apparently, Parson Reynolds gave a mighty sermon this morning about a great heresy creeping into the town from the outlying reaches of the valley. Although he never called anyone by name, his words did seem to cast a bit of a shadow your way. Tell me, Jeremiah, is everything going well in your household?"

"Of course," said Jeremiah. "We've indulged ourselves a bit recently to celebrate our recent turn of good luck, but if that is the cause of why folks are treating me so oddly tonight, then maybe I need to go have a word with the good Reverend. I think he may need to tell me his concerns face to face."

"Hasten yourself on up the road to the square up ahead, then. Reynolds announced that he intended to address the town folks this evening. The crowd is already gathering. Mind yourself though, Jeremiah. Whole town feels like a powder keg waiting for a spark."

"My thanks, Abel. You've always been a good friend to me and my family. I better get going." Jeremiah turned to go, but Harmon caught him by the arm.

"Just so you know, son, I don't believe a single word the Parson may levy against you, if that's what he is about. I've lived near enough to you and Anne-Marie, and watched you raise those two fine young boys, to know that you are some of the best folk this town could ask for. Just have a care though. This town's got a few folks who don't think as highly of the Carmichaels as I do. Now, go ahead on your way." Abel gave the younger man a gentle shove and got Jeremiah moving again.

A small crowd had gathered before the raised platform that sat in the town square for public announcements. As he got nearer, Jeremiah could hear Parson Reynolds' voice carrying over the crowd as he closed a prayer. He looked around to try to find a good place to observe the proceedings when a sudden shiver ran down his spine. Preston Mathers leaned against a nearby oak tree, his thin clay pipe clenched in his teeth. As he spied Jeremiah, he bared his teeth in a wolfish grin and simply nodded. Patch Erickson stepped up behind Mathers and simply glared at Jeremiah.

"Friends of Pioneer Vale," called Reynolds over the crowd. "I stand before you today not merely as your spiritual advisor, but as a deeply concerned neighbor. Although I strive every day with all of my might to protect my brothers and sisters from the dark temptations that surround us, I fear that despite my efforts I have failed you in this endeavor." Reynolds paused as murmurs ran through the crowd. The clergyman repressed the urge to smile as he looked down on the eager faces hanging on his every word. "I have failed you and in doing so, a pernicious and malevolent force has made its way into the sanctity of our homes, and has come to our peaceful valley unchallenged!"

Gasps and frightened whispers raced through the assembled townsfolk. Jeremiah stood uneasy as familiar faces shot dark looks his way. The blood of the community was rising, and Reynolds knew just how to stir the tempers to a feverish pitch. As if on cue, a blood-curdling howl of a wolf rang from the nearby hills.

"A foul darkness has made its nest right here under our very noses," continued Corbin. "It walks the streets beside you, greeting you with a 'how do ye do', and asking after the wellness of your family! Do not be deceived, my dear friends, for the Dark Enemy deals in honeyed words so that your confidence is gained. This is how the doorway to your own damnation is thrown wide open!" Reynolds emphasized each word by pointing to another startled listener.

"What can we do, Parson?" called out Magistrate Lucas. "How do we root out this villain, and save the good folk of our town?" Jeremiah would have rolled his eyes at the obviously staged placement of Lucas, had the crowd not veritably hummed with fear. Wherever he looked he saw terror and rage on the faces of the townspeople. He took a step back from the edge of the crowd, ready to give himself room to retreat should the night turn hostile. As he moved, he again saw Preston Mathers staring directly at him with what could only be described as predatorial glee. The man's eyes were wide and gleaming, as though madness had overtaken his thoughts.

"Gather your courage up, Goodmen and Goodwomen of Pioneer Vale," called Reynolds over the unsettled throng. "For though the Devil may send his Beast with fury and cloak himself in the fires of the Dark Pit, fear not, for we shall remain pure of heart and determined in our purpose so that the flames of the Betrayer shall not touch us!"

"A name, Parson," yelled someone from the crowd.

"Hide it from us no longer! Who is this servant of Darkness among us?" said another.

The clattering of hooves echoed on the cobblestones, and, as one, the audience turned to see who raced towards the maddening crowd. Jeremiah broke his staredown with Preston, knowing even before he turned that what he was about to see would prove more terrifying than anything Mathers could throw at him.

Anne-Marie's red hair trailed out behind her as she galloped down the dusty street on Hollister Adams' chestnut horse. She reigned in the lathered and panting mount to a skidding halt, smoothly dismounting in a graceful swing from the saddle. Blood ran from a cut along her cheek and bruises adorned her face and arms. Her hair was windblown and wild, with leaves woven into her coppery locks. She stood alone at the end of the street before the staring crowd with her hands on her hips. With her clothes torn and bloodstained, Anne-Marie looked like something from a nightmare standing before her neighbors. With a snarl on her lips and her icy glare, she posed a terrifying vision for the townsfolk to behold.

Jeremiah saw that Reynolds nearly cheered at the timing of Anne-Marie's arrival. He saw Preston nodding anxiously at the preacher. Corbin drew in his breath, pointed an accusing finger at Anne-Marie, and bellowed out to the crowd.

"People of Pioneer Vale, I hereby charge Anne-Marie Carmichael with the heresy of witchcraft! Behold the Witch of Pioneer Vale in all her villainy!"

A stunned silence fell over the throng that had been up in arms just moments ago. Jeremiah watched the crowd turn dozens of piercing stares upon her. He saw Anne-Marie's anger wash away before the sudden hostility born from Reynolds' accusation. She looked back and forth from the crowd to Jeremiah, slowly retreating towards the horse. Jeremiah suddenly felt alone in the calm before an oncoming storm.

"Don't just stand there," called Preston Mathers from his place in the crowd. He met Anne-Marie's eyes with a most wicked, hateful sneer.

"Grab her," he said.

The crowd roared again and surged forward, a veritable wave of fear and anger personified. Jeremiah moved faster though and got to his wife well before the mob. A rock thrown by some unknown assailant glanced off the side of his head, and the world spun circles around him. The burly farmer wobbled, and a second rock hit him in the back as he shielded Anne-Marie from the missiles. He gritted his teeth against the injury, but his pain changed to fear for them all when he saw the fires ignite behind his wife's eyes.

Jeremiah grabbed Anne-Marie's wrists as he stumbled forward, leaning heavily on her. "Do nothing," he whispered harshly, "or you seal your fate." He whirled around, boldly standing between his wife and the oncoming rush. He pulled his hatchet from his belt and swung it in a wide arc to hold the grasping townsfolk at bay. Faces of the people that he had shared laughs and raised toasts with were now full of hatred and murder. He slapped away the first reaching hands, but a punch from his blindside staggered him back against Anne-Marie again.

Blows rained down upon him, but his eyes found his wife and he silently pleaded with her to remain still. A kick to his ribs took his breath away from him, but Jeremiah lashed out with a blind uppercut that caught his attacker in the crotch, taking one of the mob's frenzied members out of the fight at least. Another blow thundered into his jaw, and a thick arm wrapped around his throat from behind him. His mind called forth the nightmare that Shade had brought to him and Jeremiah tried to yell for Anne-Marie to run. Spots danced before his eyes as he reached his hand out to his wife. Tears ran down his face as he saw her brow furrow and her fists clench, afraid that everything Corbin had accused her of was about to be revealed.

A single pistol shot cracked the night like a thunderbolt, stopping everyone in their tracks and allowing Jeremiah to break free from the choking grip. As he crawled over to his wife he saw the hulking form of Marcus Brenner, smoke trailing from the barrel of the gun held high above his head step forward from the porch of the Huntsman. Abel Harmon followed right behind, the musket in his hands sweeping back and forth over the crowd. The mob retreated as the two men pushed their way to stand with the Carmichaels. Abel and Anne-Marie helped Jeremiah back to his feet as Marcus' dark eyes silently dared any man to charge forward again.

"There will be no lynchings here tonight," shouted the burly innkeeper. "You've all known these two for years and they deserve better than this!"

"Beware, Master Brenner," called Reynolds from the platform. "Would you throw your lot in beside this witch?"

Marcus pulled a second pistol from his belt and leveled it at the clergyman. "Beware yourself, Preacher. We have yet to hear a single shred of proof from you to back up your account. Anne-Marie has, by my reckoning, never done anything that wasn't for the good of this town. If you have anything ill-intended to bring against her then you will do so before a proper trial."

"Of course," chimed in Preston. The crowd turned as Mathers stepped forth from his shadowy spot on the sideline. "Our good Magistrate Lucas will honorably preside over any such affair."

"Good Magistrate Lucas is your own man bought and paid for," said Abel. "This will be handled by a council selected by drawn lots. The evidence, should any actually exist," he said with a scowl at the clergyman, "will be presented and heard before any kind of sentence is passed."

"Thank you, Abel," said Jeremiah as he laid a hand on each man's shoulder. "You too, Marcus. Our lives would have been lost if not for you both tonight "

Reynolds wasn't finished yet. "So be it, but she must be taken into custody at the very least. She stands accused of a crime most foul, and she will not be allowed the opportunity to escape the hand of justice and carry her vile craft elsewhere."

Jeremiah's face flushed and he pushed his way back to the foreground. "My wife has done nothing wrong, Reynolds, and you know it!"

"And so I will go to the cell without any more resistance." Anne-Marie's voice rang out over her husband's. Jeremiah spun around, his jaw agape. She walked forward and kissed him lightly on the cheek before advancing through the crowd. As she walked, the townsfolk parted before her, offering no impediment to the platform where the preacher stood.

"I have nothing to hide. No dark secrets for which I am accused of. Corbin, your claims are false and without merit. However, I have reason to believe that another pulls the strings that make you dance to this tune." She looked sadly at Corbin as he glanced towards Preston and fidgeted under her scrutiny.

"Mistress Carmichael," called Marcus, his deep voice booming over the crowd. "If you would be so kind as to follow me? I would feel better about your safety this night if you and Jeremiah would allow me to serve as your escort to the holding cell."

"Thank you, Marcus," said Anne-Marie. "That would suit us just fine." She returned to her protectors and took Jeremiah's arm. Away they went from the town square with Marcus and Abel keeping watch over them. None dared challenge the great hunter.

*   *   *

The crowd buzzed anew with gossip and whispers of shock and awe. Corbin leaned heavily on the railing of the platform as he watched the group leave the square. A meaty hand suddenly grabbed his arm and forcibly spun him around. Sweat beaded on Preston's forehead as he glared at Reynolds.

"That could have gone far better," growled Mathers. "Where was your dauntless rhetoric when I needed it most, Parson? I wanted an angry mob and now we have to wait for a trial. You imbecile!" Preston's sharp backhand slap rocked Corbin's jaw and knocked him back.

"Damn you, Preston," swore the preacher.

"You damn us both, Corbin. Now you force us to produce evidence that we do not have, and deepen our own entanglement. Hear me well, Parson. If you fail to convince the town that she is everything that you claimed, then so help me, you will be the one running from a lynch mob!" Preston stormed away towards his home, pushing his way through the milling crowd that remained. Patch shot Reynolds a grim smile and gave a shake of his head before he followed behind.

Corbin rubbed his stinging face and stared up at the pale moon, wondering once more if he would be better served by just leaving Pioneer Vale behind.

*   *   *

The town stockade reeked with the miasma of human waste and decay. Anne-Marie opened the cage door, wincing at the piercing shriek of the rusty hinges.

"Anne-Marie, I am so sorry to put you through all of this," said Abel. The old farmer wrung his wide-brimmed hat in his hands and looked up at her with his cheeks all aflame. "This just isn't right."

Anne-Marie leaned forward and kissed him on the cheek. "Abel Harmon, you have been a good friend to my family and I swear that your unflinching kindness will never be forgotten. Nor yours, Marcus," she added giving the big innkeeper's hand a gentle squeeze. "I've mucked out stalls, shoveled manure, and changed the smallclothes of two young boys. I can endure this."

"Reynolds is going to pay dearly for this," swore Jeremiah. Her husband paced the length of the room, clenching and unclenching his fists.

"I don't know what he thinks he knows, but I am going to feed him his own Bible before this is all said and done."

"You will not," said Anne-Marie softly. "Corbin is as much a pawn in all of this as we are. This is all Preston's work."

"Mathers," spat Marcus. "How has this town not tarred and feathered that bastard by now?"

"Because he has a private army of mercenaries who will beat down any resident who dares to stand against him," answered Abel.

"Tonight he has two fewer," said Anne-Marie. "I know the reason that he wants Carmichael Farms so badly now. There is a literal gold mine in the caves that run beneath our land. Had we defaulted on our debt to him, then he could have had it all without a fight. Two of his men held me prisoner there tonight, but I...escaped." She gave Jeremiah a meaningful look. "They were caught in a blast from some black powder they were using, and I managed to get out."

"Then I need to get up to that mine and bring back proof of what Preston has been up to. It may be the easiest way to clear your name from these accusations. Where is the entrance to this mine?" Jeremiah grabbed his wife's hands in his own.

"Follow Alistair's Climb. At the third switchback, you will see a side trail. It was concealed but I made a mess of their camouflage efforts on my way back. There is something else, dark and evil, in that place too, though." She squeezed his hands tightly. "Get back to the boys, Jeremiah. You know all about my ...nightmare. With Preston acting so boldly, I fear he may move against them next."

"She's right, son," said Abel. "You've still got your little ones to look after. Take them back home. I can stay here to keep the wolves at bay from your wife, and perhaps Marcus would be willing to check out that mine?" Anne-Marie smiled thankfully even though Abel's unwitting choice of words slapped her in the face.

"I have hunted along the Climb for years," said Marcus. "I can scout it out and bring back whatever I can find to clear things up, my friends."

"Be careful, Marcus. Do not venture too deeply into those tunnels. If you feel anything too unsettling, trust your gut and run," Anne-Marie said as she squeezed the big hunter's arm.

Jeremiah nodded. "Alright then. I'll go off to fetch the boys, but then I will hurry straight back."

"Get some rest first. Come tomorrow," said Anne-Marie. "There is nothing else any of us can do tonight. Just look after Aiden and Thomas. Let them know how much I love them. How badly are you hurt?"

"My ribs are tender but I don't think there is anything broken. Thick skull kept the rocks from doing too much damage." He smiled at her and she laughed despite everything they had faced tonight.

She stepped forward and kissed her husband with such passion that Marcus and Abel each blushed and turned away. With their eyes averted, Anne-Marie sent a wispy purple flame across her husband's muscled frame. Jeremiah started to gasp but she held her lips to his as his bruises and aches faded under her magic.

The couple finally parted and Marcus cleared his throat. "We should probably get moving now. Go on home, Jeremiah. Anne-Marie, you probably ought to get inside the cell in case anyone else insists on checking up on you tonight."

"Of course," she said as she stepped into the filthy cage. The moonlight peeked through a small barred window in the back wall. Marcus closed the cell door and turned the key in the rusty lock with a squeal of metal on metal.

"I will send Dorothea along shortly with something for you to eat and help you get cleaned up. Meanwhile, I will get together what gear I need to check out that mine. Abel will wait just outside in case you need anything else." The three men filed out of the room and shut the outer door with a dull thud.

"Please be careful, all of you," Anne-Marie whispered to the empty room. She sat down on the rickety wooden stool in the prison and felt her brave facade crumble. Did Mathers truly know about her powers? Had Shade already given him insight into what she was?

She played with the amethyst pendant around her neck when suddenly the long low howl of a wolf once more shattered the still of the night. While the echoes of the cry faded into the distance, Anne-Marie Carmichael sat alone in the putrid cell of the town stockade, lowered her face into her hands and wept.

To Be Continued…

www.ingramcontent.com/pod-product-compliance
Lightning Source LLC
Chambersburg PA
CBHW071517110726
47908CB00003B/864